# Purple Hibiscus

# BREAKING GODS

## Palm Sunday

Things started to fall apart at home when my brother, Jaja, did not go to communion and Papa flung his heavy missal across the room and broke the figurines on the étagère. We had just returned from church. Mama placed the fresh palm fronds, which were wet with holy water, on the dining table and then went upstairs to change. Later, she would knot the palm fronds into sagging cross shapes and hang them on the wall beside our gold-framed family photo. They would stay there until next Ash Wednesday, when we would take the fronds to church, to have them burned for ash. Papa, wearing a long, gray robe like the rest of the oblates, helped distribute ash every year. His line moved the slowest because he pressed hard on each forehead to make a perfect cross with his ash-covered thumb and slowly, meaningfully enunciated every word of 'dust and unto dust you shall return.'

Papa always sat in the front pew for Mass, at the end beside the middle aisle, with Mama, Jaja, and me sitting next to him. He was first to receive communion. Most people did not kneel

3

to receive communion at the marble altar, with the blond life-size Virgin Mary mounted nearby, but Papa did. He would hold his eyes shut so hard that his face tightened into a grimace, and then he would stick his tongue out as far as it could go. Afterward, he sat back on his seat and watched the rest of the congregation troop to the altar, palms pressed together and extended, like a saucer held sideways, just as Father Benedict had taught them to do. Even though Father Benedict had been at St Agnes for seven years, people still referred to him as 'our new priest.' Perhaps they would not have if he had not been white. He still looked new. The colors of his face, the colors of condensed milk and a cut-open soursop, had not tanned at all in the fierce heat of seven Nigerian harmattans. And his British nose was still as pinched and as narrow as it always was, the same nose that had had me worried that he did not get enough air when he first came to Enugu. Father Benedict had changed things in the parish, such as insisting that the Credo and kyrie be recited only in Latin; Igbo was not acceptable. Also, hand clapping was to be kept at a minimum, lest the solemnity of Mass be compromised. But he allowed offertory songs in Igbo; he called them native songs, and when he said 'native' his straight-line lips turned down at the corners to form an inverted U. During his sermons, Father Benedict usually referred to the pope, Papa, and Jesus – in that order. He used Papa to illustrate the gospels.

'When we let our light shine before men, we are reflecting Christ's Triumphant Entry,' he said that Palm Sunday. 'Look at Brother Eugene. He could have chosen to be like other Big Men in this country, he could have decided to sit at home and do nothing after the coup, to make sure the government did not threaten his businesses. But no, he used the *Standard* to speak the truth even though it meant the paper lost advertising. Brother Eugene spoke out for freedom. How many of us have stood up for the truth? How many of us have reflected the Triumphant Entry?'

The congregation said 'Yes' or 'God bless him' or 'Amen,' but not too loudly so they would not sound like the mushroom Pentecostal churches; then they listened intently, quietly. Even the babies stopped crying, as if they, too, were listening. On some Sundays, the congregation listened closely even when Father Benedict talked about things everybody already knew, about Papa making the biggest donations to Peter's pence and St Vincent de Paul. Or about Papa paying for the cartons of communion wine, for the new ovens at the convent where the Reverend Sisters baked the host, for the new wing to St Agnes Hospital where Father Benedict gave extreme unction. And I would sit with my knees pressed together, next to Jaja, trying hard to keep my face blank, to keep the pride from showing, because Papa said modesty was very important.

Papa himself would have a blank face when I

looked at him, the kind of expression he had in the photo when they did the big story on him after *Amnesty World* gave him a human rights award. It was the only time he allowed himself to be featured in the paper. His editor, Ade Coker, had insisted on it, saying Papa deserved it, saying Papa was too modest. Mama told me and Jaja; Papa did not tell us such things. That blank look would remain on his face until Father Benedict ended the sermon, until it was time for communion. After Papa took communion, he sat back and watched the congregation walk to the altar and, after Mass, reported to Father Benedict, with concern, when a person missed communion on two successive Sundays. He always encouraged Father Benedict to call and win that person back into the fold; nothing but mortal sin would keep a person away from communion two Sundays in a row.

So when Papa did not see Jaja go to the altar that Palm Sunday when everything changed, he banged his leatherbound missal, with the red and green ribbons peeking out, down on the dining table when we got home. The table was glass, heavy glass. It shook, as did the palm fronds on it.

'Jaja, you did not go to communion,' Papa said quietly, almost a question.

Jaja stared at the missal on the table as though he were addressing it. 'The wafer gives me bad breath.'

I stared at Jaja. Had something come loose in his head? Papa insisted we call it the host because 'host' came close to capturing the essence, the sacredness, of Christ's body. 'Wafer' was too secular, wafer was what one of Papa's factories made – chocolate wafer, banana wafer, what people bought their children to give them a treat better than biscuits.

'And the priest keeps touching my mouth and it nauseates me,' Jaja said. He knew I was looking at him, that my shocked eyes begged him to seal his mouth, but he did not look at me.

'It is the body of our Lord.' Papa's voice was low, very low. His face looked swollen already, with pus-tipped rashes spread across every inch, but it seemed to be swelling even more. 'You cannot stop receiving the body of our Lord. It is death, you know that.'

'Then I will die.' Fear had darkened Jaja's eyes to the color of coal tar, but he looked Papa in the face now. 'Then I will die, Papa.'

Papa looked around the room quickly, as if searching for proof that something had fallen from the high ceiling, something he had never thought would fall. He picked up the missal and flung it across the room, toward Jaja. It missed Jaja completely, but it hit the glass étagerè, which Mama polished often. It cracked the top shelf, swept the beige, finger-size ceramic figurines of ballet dancers in various contorted postures to the hard floor and then landed after them. Or rather it landed on their many pieces. It lay there, a huge leatherbound missal that contained the readings for all three cycles of the church year.

Jaja did not move. Papa swayed from side to side. I stood at the door, watching them. The ceiling fan spun round and round, and the light bulbs attached to it clinked against one another. Then Mama came in, her rubber slippers making *slap-slap* sounds on the marble floor. She had changed from her sequined Sunday wrapper and the blouse with puffy sleeves. Now she had a plain tie-dye wrapper tied loosely around her waist and that white T-shirt she wore every other day. It was a souvenir from a spiritual retreat she and Papa had attended; the words GOD IS LOVE crawled over her sagging breasts. She stared at the figurine pieces on the floor and then knelt and started to pick them up with her bare hands.

The silence was broken only by the whir of the ceiling fan as it sliced through the still air. Although our spacious dining room gave way to an even wider living room, I felt suffocated. The off-white walls with the framed photos of Grandfather were narrowing, bearing down on me. Even the glass dining table was moving toward me.

'*Nne, ngwa.* Go and change,' Mama said to me, startling me although her Igbo words were low and calming. In the same breath, without pausing, she said to Papa, 'Your tea is getting cold,' and to Jaja, 'Come and help me, *biko.*'

Papa sat down at the table and poured his tea from the china tea set with pink flowers on the edges. I waited for him to ask Jaja and me to take a sip, as he always did. A love sip, he called it, because you shared the little things you loved with the people you loved. Have a love sip, he would say, and Jaja would go first. Then I would hold the cup with both hands and raise it to my lips. One sip. The tea was always too hot, always burned my tongue, and if lunch was something peppery, my raw tongue suffered. But it didn't matter, because I knew that when the tea burned my tongue, it burned Papa's love into me. But Papa didn't say, 'Have a love sip'; he didn't say anything as I watched him raise the cup to his lips.

Jaja knelt beside Mama, flattened the church bulletin he held into a dustpan, and placed a jagged ceramic piece on it. 'Careful, Mama, or those pieces will cut your fingers,' he said.

I pulled at one of the cornrows underneath my black church scarf to make sure I was not dreaming. Why were they acting so normal, Jaja and Mama, as if they did not know what had just happened? And why was Papa drinking his tea quietly, as if Jaja had not just talked back to him? Slowly, I turned and headed upstairs to change out of my red Sunday dress.

I sat at my bedroom window after I changed; the cashew tree was so close I could reach out and pluck a leaf if it were not for the silver-colored crisscross of mosquito netting. The bell-shaped yellow fruits hung lazily, drawing buzzing bees that bumped against my window's netting. I heard Papa walk upstairs to his room for his afternoon siesta. I closed my eyes, sat still, waiting to hear him call Jaja, to hear Jaja go into his room. But after long, silent minutes, I opened my eyes and pressed my forehead against the window louvers to look outside. Our yard was wide enough to hold a hundred people dancing atilogu, spacious enough for each dancer to do the usual somersaults and land on the next dancer's shoulders. The compound walls, topped by coiled electric wires, were so high I could not see the cars driving by on our street. It was early rainy season, and the frangipani trees planted next to the walls already filled the yard with the sickly-sweet scent of their flowers. A row of purple bougainvillea, cut smooth and straight as a buffet table, separated the gnarled trees from the driveway. Closer to the house, vibrant bushes of hibiscus reached out and touched one another as if they were exchanging their petals. The purple plants had started to push out sleepy buds, but most of the flowers were still on the red ones. They seemed to bloom so fast, those red hibiscuses, considering how often Mama cut them to decorate the church altar and how often visitors plucked them as they walked past to their parked cars.

It was mostly Mama's prayer group members who plucked flowers; a woman tucked one behind her ear once – I saw her clearly from my window. But even the government agents, two men in black jackets who came some time ago, yanked at the hibiscus as they left. They came in a pickup truck with Federal Government plates and parked close to the hibiscus bushes. They didn't stay long. Later, Jaja said they came to bribe Papa, that he had heard them say that their pickup was full of dollars. I was not sure Jaja had heard correctly. But even now I thought about it sometimes. I imagined the truck full of stacks and stacks of foreign money, wondered if they had put the money in many cartons or in one huge carton, the size our fridge came in.

I was still at the window when Mama came into my room. Every Sunday before lunch, in between telling Sisi to put a little more palm oil in the soup, a little less curry in the coconut rice, and while Papa took his siesta, Mama plaited my hair. She would sit on an armchair near the kitchen door and I on the floor with my head cradled between her thighs. Although the kitchen was airy, with the windows always open, my hair would still manage to absorb the spices, and afterward, when I brought the end of a braid to my nose, I would smell egusi soup, utazi, curry. But Mama did not come into my room with the bag that held combs and hair oils and ask me to come downstairs. Instead, she said, 'Lunch is ready, *nne.*'

I meant to say I am sorry Papa broke your figurines, but the words that came out were, 'I'm sorry your figurines broke, Mama.'

She nodded quickly, then shook her head to show that the figurines did not matter. They did, though. Years ago, before I understood, I used to wonder why she polished them each time I heard the sounds from their room, like something being banged against the door. Her rubber slippers never made a sound on the stairs, but I knew she went downstairs when I heard the dining room door open. I would go down to see her standing by the étagère with a kitchen towel soaked in soapy water. She spent at least a quarter of an hour on each ballet-dancing figurine. There were never tears on her face. The last time, only two weeks ago, when her swollen eye was still the black-purple color of an overripe avocado, she had rearranged them after she polished them.

'I will plait your hair after lunch,' she said, turning to leave.

'Yes, Mama.'

I followed her downstairs. She limped slightly, as though one leg were shorter than the other, a gait that made her seem even smaller than she was. The stairs curved elegantly in an S shape, and I was halfway down when I saw Jaja standing in the hallway. Usually he went to his room to read before lunch, but he had not come upstairs today; he had been in the kitchen the whole time, with Mama and Sisi.

'*Ke kwanu?*' I asked, although I did not need to ask how he was doing. I had only to look at him. His seventeen-year-old face had grown lines; they zigzagged across his forehead, and inside each line a dark tension had crawled in. I reached out and clasped his hand shortly before we went into the dining room. Papa and Mama were already seated, and Papa was washing his hands in the bowl of water Sisi held before him. He waited until Jaja and I sat down opposite him, and started the grace. For twenty minutes he asked God to bless the food. Afterward, he intoned the Blessed Virgin in several different titles while we responded, 'Pray for us.' His favorite title was Our Lady, Shield of the Nigerian People. He had made it up himself. If only people would use it every day, he told us, Nigeria would not totter like a Big Man with the spindly legs of a child.

Lunch was fufu and onugbu soup. The fufu was smooth and fluffy. Sisi made it well; she pounded the yam energetically, adding drops of water into the mortar, her cheeks contracting with the *thump-thump-thump* of the pestle. The soup was thick with chunks of boiled beef and dried fish and dark green onugbu leaves. We ate silently. I molded my fufu into small balls with my fingers, dipped it in the soup, making sure to scoop up fish chunks, and then brought it to my mouth. I was certain the soup was good, but I did not taste it, could not taste it. My tongue felt like paper.

'Pass the salt, please,' Papa said.

We all reached for the salt at the same time. Jaja and I touched the crystal shaker, my finger brushed his gently, then he let go. I passed it to Papa. The silence stretched out even longer.

'They brought the cashew juice this afternoon. It tastes good. I am sure it will sell,' Mama finally said.

'Ask that girl to bring it,' Papa said.

Mama pressed the ringer that dangled above the table on a transparent wire from the ceiling, and Sisi appeared.

'Yes, Madam?'

'Bring two bottles of the drink they brought from the factory.'

'Yes, Madam.'

I wished Sisi had said 'What bottles, Madam?' or 'Where are they, Madam?' Just something to keep her and Mama talking, to veil the nervous movements of Jaja molding his fufu. Sisi was back shortly and placed the bottles next to Papa. They had the same faded-looking labels as every other thing Papa's factories made – the wafers and cream biscuits and bottled juice and banana chips. Papa poured the yellow juice for everyone. I reached out quickly for my glass and took a sip. It tasted watery. I wanted to seem eager; maybe if I talked about how good it tasted, Papa might forget that he had not yet punished Jaja.

'It's very good, Papa,' I said.

Papa swirled it around his bulging cheeks. 'Yes, yes.'

'It tastes like fresh cashew,' Mama said.

Say something, please, I wanted to say to Jaja. He was supposed to say something now, to contribute, to compliment Papa's new product. We always did, each time an employee from one of his factories brought a product sample for us.

'Just like white wine,' Mama added. She was

14

nervous, I could tell – not just because a fresh cashew tasted nothing like white wine but also because her voice was lower than usual. 'White wine,' Mama said again, closing her eyes to better savor the taste. 'Fruity white wine.'

'Yes,' I said. A ball of fufu slipped from my fingers and into the soup.

Papa was staring pointedly at Jaja. 'Jaja, have you not shared a drink with us, *gbo*? Have you no words in your mouth?' he asked, entirely in Igbo. A bad sign. He hardly spoke Igbo, and although Jaja and I spoke it with Mama at home, he did not like us to speak it in public. We had to sound civilized in public, he told us; we had to speak English. Papa's sister, Aunty Ifeoma, said once that Papa was too much of a colonial product. She had said this about Papa in a mild, forgiving way, as if it were not Papa's fault, as one would talk about a person who was shouting gibberish from a severe case of malaria.

'Have you nothing to say, *gbo*, Jaja?' Papa asked again.

'*Mba*, there are no words in my mouth,' Jaja replied.

'What?' There was a shadow clouding Papa's eyes, a shadow that had been in Jaja's eyes. Fear. It had left Jaja's eyes and entered Papa's.

'I have nothing to say,' Jaja said.

'The juice is good—' Mama started to say.

Jaja pushed his chair back. 'Thank you, Lord. Thank you, Papa. Thank you, Mama.'

15

I turned to stare at him. At least he was saying thanks the right way, the way we always did after a meal. But he was also doing what we never did: he was leaving the table before Papa had said the prayer after meals.

'Jaja!' Papa said. The shadow grew, enveloping the whites of Papa's eyes. Jaja was walking out of the dining room with his plate. Papa made to get up and then slumped back on his seat. His cheeks drooped, bulldoglike.

I reached for my glass and stared at the juice, watery yellow, like urine. I poured all of it down my throat, in one gulp. I didn't know what else to do. This had never happened before in my entire life, never. The compound walls would crumble, I was sure, and squash the frangipani trees. The sky would cave in. The Persian rugs on the stretches of gleaming marble floor would shrink. Something would happen. But the only thing that happened was my choking. My body shook from the coughing. Papa and Mama rushed over. Papa thumped my back while Mama rubbed my shoulders and said, '*O zugo*. Stop coughing.'

That evening, I stayed in bed and did not have dinner with the family. I developed a cough, and my cheeks burned the back of my hand. Inside my head, thousands of monsters played a painful game of catch, but instead of a ball, it was a brown leatherbound missal that they threw to each other. Papa came into my room; my mattress sank in

16

when he sat and smoothed my cheeks and asked if I wanted anything else. Mama was already making me ofe nsala. I said no, and we sat silently, our hands clasped for a long time. Papa's breathing was always noisy, but now he panted as if he were out of breath, and I wondered what he was thinking, if perhaps he was running in his mind, running away from something. I did not look at his face because I did not want to see the rashes that spread across every inch of it, so many, so evenly spread that they made his skin look bloated.

Mama brought some ofe nsala up for me a little later, but the aromatic soup only made me nauseated. After I vomited in the bathroom, I asked Mama where Jaja was. He had not come in to see me since after lunch.

'In his room. He did not come down for dinner.' She was caressing my cornrows; she liked to do that, to trace the way strands of hair from different parts of my scalp meshed and held together. She would keep off plaiting it until next week. My hair was too thick; it always tightened back into a dense bunch right after she ran a comb through it. Trying to comb it now would enrage the monsters already in my head.

'Will you replace the figurines?' I asked. I could smell the chalky deodorant under her arms. Her brown face, flawless but for the recent jagged scar on her forehead, was expressionless.

'*Kpa*,' she said. 'I will not replace them.'

Maybe Mama had realized that she would not

need the figurines anymore; that when Papa threw the missal at Jaja, it was not just the figurines that came tumbling down, it was everything. I was only now realizing it, only just letting myself think it.

I lay in bed after Mama left and let my mind rake through the past, through the years when Jaja and Mama and I spoke more with our spirits than with our lips. Until Nsukka. Nsukka started it all; Aunty Ifeoma's little garden next to the verandah of her flat in Nsukka began to lift the silence. Jaja's defiance seemed to me now like Aunty Ifeoma's experimental purple hibiscus: rare, fragrant with the undertones of freedom, a different kind of freedom from the one the crowds waving green leaves chanted at Government Square after the coup. A freedom to be, to do.

But my memories did not start at Nsukka. They started before, when all the hibiscuses in our front yard were a startling red.

# SPEAKING WITH OUR SPIRITS

## Before Palm Sunday

I was at my study desk when Mama came into my room, my school uniforms piled on the crook of her arm. She placed them on my bed. She had brought them in from the lines in the backyard, where I had hung them to dry that morning. Jaja and I washed our school uniforms while Sisi washed the rest of our clothes. We always soaked tiny sections of fabric in the foamy water first to check if the colors would run, although we knew they would not. We wanted to spend every minute of the half hour Papa allocated to uniform washing.

'Thank you, Mama, I was about to bring them in,' I said, getting up to fold the clothes. It was not proper to let an older person do your chores, but Mama did not mind; there was so much that she did not mind.

'A drizzle is coming. I did not want them to get wet.' She ran her hand across my uniform, a gray skirt with a darker-toned waistband, long enough to show no calf when I wore it. '*Nne*, you're going to have a brother or a sister.'

I stared. She was sitting on my bed, knees close together. 'You're going to have a baby?'

'Yes.' She smiled, still running her hand over my skirt.

'When?'

'In October. I went to Park Lane yesterday to see my doctor.'

'Thanks be to God.' It was what Jaja and I said, what Papa expected us to say, when good things happened.

'Yes.' Mama let go of my skirt, almost reluctantly. 'God is faithful. You know after you came and I had the miscarriages, the villagers started to whisper. The members of our umunna even sent people to your father to urge him to have children with someone else. So many people had willing daughters, and many of them were university graduates, too. They might have borne many sons and taken over our home and driven us out, like Mr Ezendu's second wife did. But your father stayed with me, with us.' She did not usually say so much at one time. She spoke the way a bird eats, in small amounts.

'Yes,' I said. Papa deserved praise for not choosing to have more sons with another woman, of course, for not choosing to take a second wife. But then, Papa was different. I wished that Mama would not compare him with Mr Ezendu, with anybody; it lowered him, soiled him.

'They even said somebody had tied up my womb with *ogwu*.' Mama shook her head and smiled, the indulgent smile that stretched across her face when she talked about people who believed in oracles, or when relatives suggested she consult a witch doctor, or when people recounted tales of digging up hair tufts and animal bones wrapped in cloth that had been buried in their front yards to ward off progress. 'They do not know that God works in mysterious ways.'

'Yes,' I said. I held the clothes carefully, making sure the folded edges were even. 'God works in mysterious ways.' I did not know she had been trying to have a baby since the last miscarriage almost six years ago. I could not even think of her and Papa together, on the bed they shared, custom-made and wider than the conventional king-size. When I thought of affection between them, I thought of them exchanging the sign of peace at Mass, the way Papa would hold her tenderly in his arms after they had clasped hands.

'Did school go well?' Mama asked, rising. She had asked me earlier.

'Yes.'

'Sisi and I are cooking *moi-moi* for the sisters; they will be here soon,' Mama said, before going back downstairs. I followed her and placed my folded uniforms on the table in the hallway, where Sisi would get them for ironing.

The sisters, members of Our Lady of the Miraculous Medal prayer group, soon arrived, and their Igbo songs, accompanied by robust hand clapping, echoed upstairs. They would pray and sing for about half an hour, and then Mama would interrupt in her low voice, which barely carried upstairs even with my door open, to tell them she had prepared a 'little something' for them. When Sisi started to bring in the platters of moi-moi and jollof rice and fried chicken, the women would gently chastise Mama. 'Sister Beatrice, what is it? Why have you done this? Are we not content with the *anara* we are offered in other sisters' homes? You shouldn't have, really.' Then a piping voice would say, 'Praise the Lord!' dragging out the first word as long as she could. The 'Alleluia' response would push against the walls of my room, against the glass furnishings of the living room. Then they would pray, asking God to reward Sister Beatrice's generosity, and add more blessings to the many she already had. Then the *clink-clink-clink* of forks and spoons scraping against plates would echo over the house. Mama never used plastic cutlery, no matter how big the group was.

They had just started to pray over the food when I heard Jaja bound up the stairs. I knew he would come into my room first because Papa was not home. If Papa was home, Jaja would go into his own room first to change.

'*Ke kwanu?*' I asked when he came in. His school uniform, blue shorts, and white shirt with the St Nicholas badge blazing from his left breast still had the ironed lines running down the front and back. He was voted neatest junior boy last year, and Papa had hugged him so tight that Jaja thought his back had snapped.

'Fine.' He stood by my desk, flipped idly through the *Introductory Technology* textbook open before me. 'What did you eat?'

'*Garri.*'

*I wish we still had lunch together*, Jaja said with his eyes.

'Me, too,' I said, aloud.

Before, our driver, Kevin, would pick me up first at Daughters of the Immaculate Heart, and then we would drive over to get Jaja at St Nicholas. Jaja and I would have lunch together when we got home. Now, because Jaja was in the new gifted student program at St Nicholas, he attended after-school lessons. Papa had revised his schedule but not mine, and I could not wait to have lunch with him. I was to have had lunch, taken my siesta, and started studying by the time Jaja came home.

Still, Jaja knew what I ate for lunch every day. We had a menu on the kitchen wall that Mama changed twice a month. But he always asked me, anyway. We did that often, asking each other questions whose answers we already knew. Perhaps it was so that we would not ask the other questions, the ones whose answers we did not want to know.

'I have three assignments to do,' Jaja said, turning to leave.

'Mama is pregnant,' I said.

Jaja came back and sat down at the edge of my bed. 'She told you?'

'Yes. She's due in October.'

Jaja closed his eyes for a while and then opened

25

them. 'We will take care of the baby; we will protect him.'

I knew that Jaja meant from Papa, but I did not say anything about protecting the baby. Instead, I asked, 'How do you know it will be a he?'

'I feel it. What do you think?'

'I don't know.'

Jaja sat on my bed for a while longer before he went downstairs to have lunch; I pushed my textbook aside, looked up, and stared at my daily schedule, pasted on the wall above me. *Kambili* was written in bold letters on top of the white sheet of paper, just as *Jaja* was written on the schedule above Jaja's desk in his room. I wondered when Papa would draw up a schedule for the baby, my new brother, if he would do it right after the baby was born or wait until he was a toddler. Papa liked order. It showed even in the schedules themselves, the way his meticulously drawn lines, in black ink, cut across each day, separating study from siesta, siesta from family time, family time from eating, eating from prayer, prayer from sleep. He revised them often. When we were in school, we had less siesta time and more study time, even on weekends. When we were on vacation, we had a little more family time, a little more time to read newspapers, play chess or monopoly, and listen to the radio.

It was during family time the next day, a Saturday, that the coup happened. Papa had just checkmated Jaja when we heard the martial music on the radio, the solemn strains making us stop to listen. A general with a strong Hausa accent came on and announced that there had been a coup and that we had a new government. We would be told shortly who our new head of state was.

Papa pushed the chessboard aside and excused himself to use the phone in his study. Jaja and Mama and I waited for him, silently. I knew he was calling his editor, Ade Coker, perhaps to tell him something about covering the coup. When he came back, we drank the mango juice, which Sisi served in tall glasses, while he talked about the coup. He looked sad; his rectangular lips seemed to sag. Coups begat coups, he said, telling us about the bloody coups of the sixties, which ended up in civil war just after he left Nigeria to study in England. A coup always began a vicious cycle. Military men would always overthrow one another, because they could, because they were all power drunk.

Of course, Papa told us, the politicians were corrupt, and the *Standard* had written many stories about the cabinet ministers who stashed money in foreign bank accounts, money meant for paying teachers' salaries and building roads. But what we Nigerians needed was not soldiers ruling us, what we needed was a renewed democracy. *Renewed Democracy.* It sounded important, the way he said it, but then most of what Papa said sounded important. He liked to lean back and look upwards when he talked, as though he were searching for something in the air. I would focus on his lips, the movement, and sometimes I forgot myself, sometimes I wanted to stay like that forever, listening to his voice, to the important things he said. It was the same way I felt when he smiled, his face breaking open like a coconut with the brilliant white meat inside.

The day after the coup, before we left for evening benediction at St Agnes, we sat in the living room and read the newspapers; our vendor delivered the major papers every morning, four copies each, on Papa's orders. We read the *Standard* first. Only the *Standard* had a critical editorial, calling on the new military government to quickly implement a return to democracy plan. Papa read one of the articles in *Nigeria Today* out aloud, an opinion column by a writer who insisted that it was indeed time for a military president, since the politicians had gone out of control and our economy was in a mess.

'The *Standard* would never write this nonsense,' Papa said, putting the paper down. 'Not to talk of calling the man a "president."'

'"President" assumes he was elected,' Jaja said. '"Head of state" is the right term.'

Papa smiled, and I wished I had said that before Jaja had.

'The *Standard* editorial is well done,' Mama said.

'Ade is easily the best out there,' Papa said, with an offhand pride, while scanning another paper.

' "Change of Guard." What a headline. They are all afraid. Writing about how corrupt the civilian government was, as if they think the military will not be corrupt. This country is going down, way down.'

'God will deliver us,' I said, knowing Papa would like my saying that.

'Yes, yes,' Papa said, nodding. Then he reached out and held my hand, and I felt as though my mouth were full of melting sugar.

In the following weeks, the newspapers we read during family time sounded different, more subdued. The *Standard*, too, was different; it was more critical, more questioning than it used to be. Even the drive to school was different. The first week after the coup, Kevin plucked green tree branches every morning and stuck them to the car, lodged above the number plate, so that the demonstrators at Government Square would let us drive past. The green branches meant Solidarity. Our branches never looked as bright as the demonstrators', though, and sometimes as we drove past, I wondered what it would be like to join them, chanting 'Freedom,' standing in the way of cars.

In later weeks, when Kevin drove past Ogui Road, there were soldiers at the roadblock near the market, walking around, caressing their long guns. They stopped some cars and searched them. Once, I saw a man kneeling on the road beside his Peugeot 504, with his hands raised high in the air.

But nothing changed at home. Jaja and I still followed our schedules, still asked each other questions whose answers we already knew. The only change was Mama's belly: it started to bulge, softly and subtly. At first it looked like a deflated football, but by Pentecost Sunday, it had elevated her red and gold-embroidered church wrapper just enough to hint that it was not just the layer of cloth underneath or the knotted end of the wrapper. The altar was decorated in the same shade of red as Mama's wrapper. Red was the color of Pentecost. The visiting priest said Mass in a red robe that seemed too short for him. He was young, and he looked up often as he read the gospel, his brown eyes piercing the congregation. He kissed the Bible slowly when he was done. It could have seemed dramatic if someone else had done it, but with him it was not. It seemed real. He was newly ordained, waiting to be assigned a parish, he told us. He and Father Benedict had a close mutual friend, and he was pleased when Father Benedict asked him to visit and say Mass. He did not say how beautiful our St Agnes altar was, though, with its steps that glowed like polished ice blocks. Or that it was one of the best altars in Enugu, perhaps even in the whole of Nigeria. He did not suggest, as all the other visiting priests had, that God's presence dwelled more in St Agnes, that the iridescent saints on the floor-to-ceiling stained-glass windows stopped God from leaving. And halfway through his sermon, he broke into an Igbo song: *'Bunie ya enu . . .'*

31

The congregation drew in a collective breath, some sighed, some had their mouths in a big O. They were used to Father Benedict's sparse sermons, to Father Benedict's pinch-your-nose monotone. Slowly they joined in. I watched Papa purse his lips. He looked sideways to see if Jaja and I were singing and nodded approvingly when he saw our sealed lips.

After Mass, we stood outside the church entrance, waiting while Papa greeted the people crowded around him.

'Good morning, praise God,' he said, before shaking hands with the men, hugging the women, patting the toddlers, and tugging at the babies' cheeks. Some of the men whispered to him, Papa whispered back, and then the men thanked him, shaking his hand with both of theirs before leaving. Papa finally finished the greetings, and, with the wide churchyard now mostly emptied of the cars that had cluttered it like teeth in a mouth, we headed to our car.

'That young priest, singing in the sermon like a Godless leader of one of these Pentecostal churches that spring up everywhere like mushrooms. People like him bring trouble to the church. We must remember to pray for him,' Papa said, as he unlocked the Mercedes door and placed the missal and bulletin on the seat before turning toward the parish residence. We always dropped in to visit Father Benedict after Mass.

'Let me stay in the car and wait, *biko*,' Mama

said, leaning against the Mercedes. 'I feel vomit in my throat.'

Papa turned to stare at her. I held my breath. It seemed a long moment, but it might have been only seconds.

'Are you sure you want to stay in the car?' Papa asked.

Mama was looking down; her hands were placed on her belly, to hold the wrapper from untying itself or to keep her bread and tea breakfast down. 'My body does not feel right,' she mumbled.

'I asked if you were sure you wanted to stay in the car.'

Mama looked up. 'I'll come with you. It's really not that bad.'

Papa's face did not change. He waited for her to walk toward him, and then he turned and they started to walk to the priest's house. Jaja and I followed. I watched Mama as we walked. Till then I had not noticed how drawn she looked. Her skin, usually the smooth brown of groundnut paste, looked like the liquid had been sucked out of it, ashen, like the color of cracked harmattan soil. Jaja spoke to me with his eyes: *What if she vomits?* I would hold up my dress hems so Mama could throw up into it, so we wouldn't make a big mess in Father Benedict's house.

The house looked as though the architect had realized too late that he was designing residential quarters, not a church. The arch that led to the dining area looked like an altar entrance; the alcove

33

with the cream telephone looked ready to receive the Blessed Sacrament; the tiny study room off the living room could have been a sacristy crammed with holy books and Mass vestments and extra chalices.

'Brother Eugene!' Father Benedict said. His pale face broke into a smile when he saw Papa. He was at the dining table, eating. There were slices of boiled yam, like lunch, but then a plate of fried eggs, too, more like breakfast. He asked us to join him. Papa refused on our behalf and then went up to the table to talk in muted tones.

'How are you, Beatrice?' Father Benedict asked, raising his voice so Mama would hear from the living room. 'You don't look well.'

'I'm fine, Father. It's only my allergies because of the weather, you know, the clash of harmattan and rainy season.'

'Kambili and Jaja, did you enjoy Mass, then?'

'Yes, Father.' Jaja and I spoke at the same time.

We left shortly afterward, a little sooner than on the usual visit to Father Benedict. Papa said nothing in the car, his jaw moving as if he were gritting his teeth. We all stayed silent and listened to the 'Ave Maria' on the cassette player. When we got home, Sisi had Papa's tea set out, in the china teapot with a tiny, ornate handle. Papa placed his missal and bulletin on the dining table and sat down. Mama hovered by him.

'Let me pour your tea,' she offered, although she never served Papa's tea.

Papa ignored her and poured his tea, and then he told Jaja and me to take sips. Jaja took a sip, placed the cup back on the saucer. Papa picked it up and gave it to me. I held it with both hands, took a sip of the Lipton tea with sugar and milk, and placed it back on the saucer.

'Thank you, Papa,' I said, feeling the love burn my tongue.

We went upstairs to change, Jaja and Mama and I. Our steps on the stairs were as measured and as silent as our Sundays: the silence of waiting until Papa was done with his siesta so we could have lunch; the silence of reflection time, when Papa gave us a scripture passage or a book by one of the early church fathers to read and meditate on; the silence of evening rosary; the silence of driving to the church for benediction afterward. Even our family time on Sundays was quiet, without chess games or newspaper discussions, more in tune with the Day of Rest.

'Maybe Sisi can cook lunch by herself today,' Jaja said, when we got to the top of the curved staircase. 'You should rest before lunch, Mama.'

Mama was going to say something, but then she stopped, her hand flew to her mouth, and she hurried into her room. I stayed to hear the sharp groans of vomiting from deep in her throat before I went into my room.

Lunch was jollof rice, fist-size chunks of azu fried until the bones were crisp, and ngwo-ngwo. Papa ate most of the ngwo-ngwo, his spoon

35

swooping through the spicy broth in the glass bowl. Silence hung over the table like the blue-black clouds in the middle of rainy season. Only the chirping of the ochiri birds outside interrupted it. Every year, they arrived before the first rains came and nested on the avocado tree right outside the dining room. Jaja and I sometimes found fallen nests on the ground, nests made of entwined twigs and dried grass and bits of thread that Mama had used to plait my hair, which the ochiri picked out of the backyard dustbin.

I finished lunch first. 'Thank you, Lord. Thank you, Papa. Thank you, Mama.' I folded my arms and waited until everybody was done so we could pray. I did not look at anybody's face; I focused instead on the picture of Grandfather that hung on the opposite wall.

When Papa started the prayer, his voice quavered more than usual. He prayed for the food first, then he asked God to forgive those who had tried to thwart His will, who had put selfish desires first and had not wanted to visit His servant after Mass. Mama's 'Amen!' resounded throughout the room.

I was in my room after lunch, reading James chapter five because I would talk about the biblical roots of the anointing of the sick during family time, when I heard the sounds. Swift, heavy thuds on my parents' hand-carved bedroom door. I imagined the door had gotten stuck and Papa was trying to open it. If I imagined it hard enough, then it would be true. I sat down, closed my eyes, and started to count. Counting made it seem not that long, made it seem not that bad. Sometimes it was over before I even got to twenty. I was at nineteen when the sounds stopped. I heard the door open. Papa's gait on the stairs sounded heavier, more awkward, than usual.

I stepped out of my room just as Jaja came out of his. We stood at the landing and watched Papa descend. Mama was slung over his shoulder like the jute sacks of rice his factory workers bought in bulk at the Seme Border. He opened the dining room door. Then we heard the front door open, heard him say something to the gate man, Adamu.

'There's blood on the floor,' Jaja said. 'I'll get the brush from the bathroom.'

We cleaned up the trickle of blood, which trailed away as if someone had carried a leaking jar of red watercolor all the way downstairs. Jaja scrubbed while I wiped.

Mama did not come home that night, and Jaja and I had dinner alone. We did not talk about Mama. Instead, we talked about the three men who were publicly executed two days before, for drug trafficking. Jaja had heard some boys talking about it in school. It had been on television. The men were tied to poles, and their bodies kept shuddering even after the bullets were no longer being pumped into them. I told Jaja what a girl in my class had said: that her mother turned their TV off, asking why she should watch fellow human beings die, asking what was wrong with all those people who had gathered at the execution ground.

After dinner, Jaja said grace, and at the end he added a short prayer for Mama. Papa came home when we were in our rooms studying, according to our schedules. I was drawing pregnant stick images on the inner flap of my *Introductory Agriculture for Junior Secondary Schools* when he came into my room. His eyes were swollen and red, and somehow that made him look younger, more vulnerable.

'Your mother will be back tomorrow, about the time you get back from school. She will be fine,' he said.

'Yes, Papa.' I looked away from his face, back at my books.

He held my shoulders, rubbing them in gentle circular motions.

'Stand up,' he said. I stood up and he hugged me, pressed me close so that I felt the beat of his heart under his soft chest.

Mama came home the next afternoon. Kevin brought her in the Peugeot 505 with the factory name emblazoned on the passenger door, the one that often took us to and from school. Jaja and I stood waiting by the front door, close enough for our shoulders to touch, and we opened the door before she got to it.

'*Umu m*,' she said, hugging us. 'My children.'

She wore the same white T-shirt with GOD IS LOVE written on the front. Her green wrapper hung lower than usual on her waist; it had been knotted with a lazy effort at the side. Her eyes were vacant, like the eyes of those mad people who wandered around the roadside garbage dumps in town, pulling grimy, torn canvas bags with their life fragments inside.

'There was an accident, the baby is gone,' she said.

I moved back a little, stared at her belly. It still looked big, still pushed at her wrapper in a gentle arc. Was Mama sure the baby was gone? I was still staring at her belly when Sisi came in. Sisi's cheekbones were so high they gave her an angular, eerily amused expression, as if she were mocking you, laughing at you, and you would never know why. 'Good afternoon, Madam, *nno*,' she said. 'Will you eat now or after you bathe?'

'Eh?' For a moment Mama looked as though she did not know what Sisi had said. 'Not now, Sisi, not now. Get me water and a towel.'

Mama stood hugging herself in the center of the living room, near the glass table, until Sisi brought a plastic bowl of water and a kitchen towel. The étagère had three shelves of delicate glass, and each one held beige ballet-dancing figurines. Mama started at the lowest layer, polishing both the shelf and the figurines. I sat down on the leather sofa closest to her, close enough to reach out and straighten her wrapper.

'*Nne*, this is your study time. Go upstairs,' she said.

'I want to stay here.'

She slowly ran the cloth over a figurine, one of its match-stick-size legs raised high in the air, before she spoke. '*Nne*, go.'

I went upstairs then and sat staring at my text-book. The black type blurred, the letters swimming into one another, and then changed to a bright red, the red of fresh blood. The blood was watery, flowing from Mama, flowing from my eyes.

Later, at dinner, Papa said we would recite sixteen different novenas. For Mama's forgiveness. And on Sunday, the first Sunday of Trinity, we stayed back after Mass and started the novenas. Father Benedict sprinkled us with holy water. Some of the holy water landed on my lips, and I tasted the stale saltiness of it as we prayed. If Papa felt Jaja or me beginning to drift off at the thirteenth recitation of the Plea to St Jude, he suggested we start all over. We had to get it right. I did not think, I did not even think to think, what Mama needed to be forgiven for.

The words in my textbooks kept turning into blood each time I read them. Even as my first-term exams approached, even when we started to do class reviews, the words still made no sense.

A few days before my first exam, I was in my room studying, trying to focus on one word at a time, when the doorbell rang. It was Yewande Coker, the wife of Papa's editor. She was crying. I could hear her because my room was directly above the living room and because I had never heard crying that loud before.

'They have taken him! They have taken him!' she said, between throaty sobs.

'Yewande, Yewande,' Papa said, his voice much lower than hers.

'What will I do, sir? I have three children! One is still sucking my breast! How will I raise them alone?' I could hardly hear her words; instead, what I heard clearly was the sound of something catching in her throat. Then Papa said, 'Yewande, don't talk that way. Ade will be fine, I promise you. Ade will be fine.'

I heard Jaja leave his room. He would walk downstairs and pretend that he was going to the kitchen to drink water and stand close to the living room door for a while, listening. When he came back up, he told me soldiers had arrested Ade Coker as he drove out of the editorial offices of the *Standard*. His car was abandoned on the road-side, the front door left open. I imagined Ade Coker being pulled out of his car, being squashed into another car, perhaps a black station wagon filled with soldiers, their guns hanging out of the windows. I imagined his hands quivering with fear, a wet patch spreading on his trousers.

I knew his arrest was because of the big cover story in the last *Standard*, a story about how the Head of State and his wife had paid people to transport heroin abroad, a story that questioned the recent execution of three men and who the real drug barons were.

Jaja said that when he looked through the keyhole, Papa was holding Yewande's hand and praying, telling her to repeat 'none of those who trust in Him shall be left desolate.'

Those were the words I said to myself as I took my exams the following week. And I repeated them, too, as Kevin drove me home on the last day of school, my report card tightly pressed to my chest. The Reverend Sisters gave us our cards unsealed. I came second in my class. It was written in figures: '2/25.' My form mistress, Sister Clara, had written, 'Kambili is intelligent beyond her years, quiet and responsible.' The principal, Mother Lucy, wrote, 'A brilliant, obedient student and a daughter to be proud of.' But I knew Papa would not be proud. He had often told Jaja and me that he did not spend so much money on Daughters of the Immaculate Heart and St Nicholas to have us let other children come first. Nobody had spent money on his own schooling, especially not his Godless father, our Papa-Nnukwu, yet he had always come first. I wanted to make Papa proud, to do as well as he had done. I needed him to touch the back of my neck and tell me that I was fulfilling God's purpose. I needed him to hug me close and say that to whom much is given, much is also expected. I needed him to smile at me, in that way that lit up his face, that warmed something inside me. But I had come second. I was stained by failure.

Mama opened the door even before Kevin stopped the car in the driveway. She always waited by the front door on the last day of school, to sing praise songs in Igbo and hug Jaja and me and caress our report cards in her hands. It was the only time she sang aloud at home.

'*O me mma, Chineke, o me mma . . .*' Mama started her song and then stopped when I greeted her.

'Good afternoon, Mama.'

'*Nne*, did it go well? Your face is not bright.' She stood aside to let me pass.

'I came second.'

43

Mama paused. 'Come and eat. Sisi cooked coconut rice.'

I was sitting at my study desk when Papa came home. He lumbered upstairs, each heavy step creating turbulence in my head, and went into Jaja's room. He had come first, as usual, so Papa would be proud, would hug Jaja, leave his arm resting around Jaja's shoulders. He took a while in Jaja's room, though; I knew he was looking through each individual subject score, checking to see if any had decreased by one or two marks since last term. Something pushed fluids into my bladder, and I rushed to the toilet. Papa was in my room when I came out.

'Good evening, Papa, *nno.*'

'Did school go well?'

I wanted to say I came second so that he would know immediately, so that I would acknowledge my failure, but instead I said, 'Yes,' and handed him the report card. He seemed to take forever to open it and even longer to read it. I tried to pace my breathing as I waited, knowing all the while that I could not.

'Who came first?' Papa asked, finally.

'Chinwe Jideze.'

'Jideze? The girl who came second last term?'

'Yes,' I said. My stomach was making sounds, hollow rumbling sounds that seemed too loud, that would not stop even when I sucked in my belly.

Papa looked at my report card for a while longer; then he said, 'Come down for dinner.'

I walked downstairs, my legs feeling joint-free, like long strips of wood. Papa had come home with samples of a new biscuit, and he passed the green packet around before we started dinner. I bit into the biscuit. 'Very good, Papa.'

Papa took a bite and chewed, then looked at Jaja.

'It has a fresh taste,' Jaja said.

'Very tasty,' Mama said.

'It should sell by God's grace,' Papa said. 'Our wafers lead the market now and this should join them.'

I did not, could not, look at Papa's face when he spoke. The boiled yam and peppery greens refused to go down my throat; they clung to my mouth like children clinging to their mothers' hand at a nursery school entrance. I downed glass after glass of water to push them down, and by the time Papa started the grace, my stomach was swollen with water. When he was done, Papa said, 'Kambili, come upstairs.'

I followed him. As he climbed the stairs in his red silk pajamas, his buttocks quivered and shook like akamu, properly made akamu, jellylike. The cream décor in Papa's bedroom was changed every year but always to a slightly different shade of cream. The plush rug that sank in when you stepped on it was plain cream; the curtains had only a little brown embroidery at the edges; the cream leather armchairs were placed close together as if two people were sitting in an intimate conversation. All that cream blended and made the room seem wider, as if it never ended, as if you could not run even if you wanted to, because there was nowhere to run to. When I had thought of heaven as a child, I visualized Papa's room, the softness, the creaminess, the endlessness. I would snuggle into Papa's arms when harmattan thunderstorms raged outside, flinging mangoes against the window netting and making the electric wires hit each other and spark bright orange flames. Papa would lodge me between his knees or wrap me in the cream blanket that smelled of safety.

I sat on a similar blanket now, on the edge of the bed. I slipped off my slippers and sank my feet into the rug and decided to keep them sunk in so that my toes would feel cushioned. So that a part of me would feel safe.

'Kambili,' Papa said, breathing deeply. 'You didn't put in your best this term. You came second because you chose to.' His eyes were sad. Deep and sad. I wanted to touch his face, to run my hand over his rubbery cheeks. There were stories in his eyes that I would never know.

The phone rang then; it had been ringing more often since Ade Coker was arrested. Papa answered it and spoke in low tones. I sat waiting for him until he looked up and waved me away. He did not call me the next day, or the day after, to talk about my report card, to decide how I would be punished. I wondered if he was too preoccupied with Ade Coker's case, but even after he got him out of jail a week later, he did not talk about my report card. He did not talk about getting Ade Coker out of jail, either; we simply saw his editorial back in the *Standard*, where he wrote about the value of freedom, about how his pen would not, could not, stop writing the truth. But he did not mention where he had been detained or who had arrested him or what had been done to him. There was a postscript in italics where he thanked his publisher: '*a man of integrity, the bravest man I know.*' I was sitting next to Mama on the couch, during family time, and I read that line over and over and then closed my eyes, felt a surge run through me, the same feeling I got when Father Benedict talked about Papa at Mass, the same feeling I got after I sneezed: a clear, tingling sensation.

'Thank God Ade is safe,' Mama said, running her hands over the newspaper.

'They put out cigarettes on his back,' Papa said, shaking his head. 'They put out so many cigarettes on his back.'

'They will receive their due, but not on this earth, *mba*,' Mama said. Although Papa did not smile at her – he looked too sad to smile – I wished I had thought to say that, before Mama did. I knew Papa liked her having said that.

'We are going to publish underground now,' Papa said. 'It is no longer safe for my staff.'

I knew that publishing underground meant that the newspaper would be published from a secret location. Yet I imagined Ade Coker and the rest of the staff in an office beneath the ground, a fluorescent lamp flooding the dark damp room, the men bent over their desks, writing the truth.

That night, when Papa prayed, he added longer passages urging God to bring about the downfall of the Godless men ruling our country, and he intoned over and over, 'Our Lady Shield of the Nigerian People, pray for us.'

The school break was short, only two weeks, and the Saturday before school resumed, Mama took Jaja and me to the market to get new sandals and bags. We didn't need them; our bags and brown leather sandals were still new, only a term old. But it was the only ritual that was ours alone, going to the market before the start of each new term, rolling the car window down as Kevin drove us there without having to ask permission from Papa. In the outskirts of the market, we let our eyes dwell on the half-naked mad people near the rubbish dumps, on the men who casually stopped to unzip their trousers and urinate at corners, on the women who seemed to be haggling loudly with mounds of green vegetables until the head of the trader peeked out from behind.

Inside the market, we shrugged off traders who pulled us along the dark passages, saying, 'I have what you want,' or 'Come with me, it's here,' even though they had no idea what we wanted. We scrunched up our noses at the smells of bloody fresh meat and musty dried fish, and lowered our heads from the bees that buzzed in thick clouds over the sheds of the honey sellers.

As we left the markets with our sandals and some fabric Mama had bought, we saw a small crowd gathered around the vegetable stalls we had passed earlier, the ones lining the road. Soldiers were milling around. Market women were shouting, and many had both hands placed on their heads, in the way that people do to show despair or shock. A woman lay in the dirt, wailing, tearing at her short afro. Her wrapper had come undone and her white underwear showed.

'Hurry up,' Mama said, moving closer to Jaja and me, and I felt that she wanted to shield us from seeing the soldiers and the women. As we hurried past, I saw a woman spit at a soldier, I saw the soldier raise a whip in the air. The whip was long. It curled in the air before it landed on the woman's shoulder. Another soldier was kicking down trays of fruits, squashing papayas with his boots and laughing. When we got into the car, Kevin told Mama that the soldiers had been ordered to demolish the vegetable stalls because they were illegal structures. Mama said nothing; she was looking out of the window, as though she wanted to catch the last sight of those women.

I thought about the woman lying in the dirt as we drove home. I had not seen her face, but I felt that I knew her, that I had always known her. I wished I could have gone over and helped her up, cleaned the red mud from her wrapper.

I thought about her, too, on Monday, as Papa drove me to school. He slowed down on Ogui Road to fling some crisp naira notes at a beggar sprawled by the roadside, near some children hawking peeled oranges. The beggar stared at the note, then stood up and waved after us, clapping and jumping. I had assumed he was lame. I watched him in the rearview mirror, my eyes steadily on him, until he disappeared from sight. He reminded me of the market woman in the dirt. There was a helplessness to his joy, the same kind of helplessness as in that woman's despair.

The walls that surrounded Daughters of the Immaculate Heart Secondary School were very high, similar to our compound walls, but instead of coiled electrified wires, they were topped by jagged pieces of green glass with sharp edges jutting out. Papa said the walls had swayed his decision when I finished elementary school. Discipline was important, he said. You could not have youngsters scaling walls to go into town and go wild, the way they did at the federal government colleges.

'These people cannot drive,' Papa muttered when we got to the school gates, where cars nosed up to each other, horning. 'There is no prize for being first to get into the school compound.'

Hawkers, girls much younger than I, defied the school gate men, edging closer and closer to the cars to offer peeled oranges and bananas and groundnuts, their moth-eaten blouses slipping off their shoulders. Papa finally eased the car into the wide school compound and parked near the volleyball court, beyond the stretch of manicured lawn.

'Where is your class?' he asked.

I pointed to the building by the group of mango trees. Papa came out of the car with me and I wondered what he was doing, why he was here, why he had driven me to school and asked Kevin to take Jaja.

Sister Margaret saw him as we walked to my class. She waved gaily, from the midst of students and a few parents, then quickly waddled over to us. Her words flew generously out of her mouth: how was Papa doing, was he happy with my progress at Daughters of the Immaculate Heart, would he be at the reception for the bishop next week?

Papa changed his accent when he spoke, sounding British, just as he did when he spoke to Father Benedict. He was gracious, in the eager-to-please way that he always assumed with the religious, especially with the white religious. As gracious as when he presented the check for refurbishing the Daughters of the Immaculate Heart library. He said he had just come to see my class, and Sister Margaret told him to let her know if he needed anything.

'Where is Chinwe Jideze?' Papa asked, when we got to the front of my class. A group of girls stood at the door, talking. I looked around, feeling a weight around my temples. What would Papa do?

Chinwe's light-skinned face was at the center of the group, as usual.

'She is the girl in the middle,' I said. Was Papa going to talk to her? Yank at her ears for coming first? I wanted the ground to open up and swallow the whole compound.

'Look at her,' Papa said. 'How many heads does she have?'

'One.' I did not need to look at her to know that, but I looked at her, anyway.

Papa pulled a small mirror, the size of a powder compact, from his pocket. 'Look in the mirror.'

I stared at him.

'Look in the mirror.'

I took the mirror, peered at it.

'How many heads do you have, *gbo*?' Papa asked, speaking Igbo for the first time.

'One.'

'The girl has one head, too, she does not have two. So why did you let her come first?'

'It will not happen again, Papa.' A light dust lkuku was blowing, in brown spirals like uncoiling springs, and I could taste the sand that settled on my lips.

'Why do you think I work so hard to give you and Jaja the best? You have to do something with all these privileges. Because God has given you much, he expects much from you. He expects perfection. I didn't have a father who sent me to the best schools. My father spent his time worshiping gods of wood and stone. I would be nothing today but for the priests and sisters at the mission. I was a houseboy for the parish priest for two years. Yes, a houseboy. Nobody dropped me off at school. I walked eight miles every day to Nimo until I finished elementary school. I was a gardener for the priests while I attended St Gregory's Secondary School.'

I had heard this all before, how hard he had worked, how much the missionary Reverend Sisters and priests had taught him, things he would never have learned from his idol-worshiping father, my Papa-Nnukwu. But I nodded and looked alert. I hoped my class girls were not wondering why my father and I had chosen to come to school to have a long conversation in front of the classroom building. Finally, Papa stopped talking and took the mirror back.

'Kevin will be here to pick you up,' he said.

'Yes, Papa.'

'Bye. Read well.' He hugged me, a brief side hug.

'Bye, Papa.' I was watching him walk down the path bordered by flowerless green bushes when the assembly bell rang.

Assembly was raucous, and Mother Lucy had to say, 'Now, girls, may we have silence!' a few times. I stood in the front of the line as always, because the back was for the girls who belonged to cliques, girls who giggled and whispered to one another, shielded from the teachers. The teachers stood on an elevated podium, tall statues in their white-and-blue habits. After we sang a welcoming song from the Catholic Hymnal, Mother Lucy read Matthew chapter five up to verse eleven, and then we sang the national anthem. Singing the national anthem was relatively new at Daughters of the Immaculate Heart. It had started last year, because some parents were concerned that their children did not know the national anthem or the pledge. I watched the sisters as we sang. Only the Nigerian Reverend Sisters sang, teeth flashing against their dark skins. The white Reverend Sisters stood with arms folded, or lightly touching the glass rosary beads that dangled at their waists, carefully watching to see that every student's lips moved. Afterward, Mother Lucy narrowed her eyes behind her thick lenses and scanned the lines. She always picked one student to start the pledge before the others joined in.

'Kambili Achike, please start the pledge,' she said.

Mother Lucy had never chosen me before. I opened my mouth, but the words would not come out.

'Kambili Achike?' Mother Lucy and the rest of the school had turned to stare at me.

I cleared my throat, willed the words to come. I knew them, thought them. But they would not come. The sweat was warm and wet under my arms.

'Kambili?'

Finally, stuttering, I said, 'I pledge to Nigeria, my country / To be faithful, loyal, and honest . . .'

The rest of the school joined in, and while I mouthed along, I tried to slow my breathing. After assembly, we filed to our classrooms. My class went through the routine of settling down, scraping chairs, dusting desks, copying the new term timetable written on the board.

'How was your holiday, Kambili?' Ezinne leaned over and asked.

'Fine.'

'Did you travel abroad?'

'No,' I said. I didn't know what else to say, but I wanted Ezinne to know that I appreciated that she was always nice to me even though I was awkward and tongue-tied. I wanted to say thank you for not laughing at me and calling me a 'back-yard snob' the way the rest of the girls did, but the words that came out were, 'Did you travel?'

Ezinne laughed. 'Me? *O di egwu.* It's people like you and Gabriella and Chinwe who travel, people with rich parents. I just went to the village to visit my grandmother.'

'Oh,' I said.

'Why did your father come this morning?'

'I . . . I . . .' I stopped to take a breath because I knew I would stutter even more if I didn't. 'He wanted to see my class.'

'You look a lot like him. I mean, you're not big, but the features and the complexion are the same,' Ezinne said.

'Yes.'

'I heard Chinwe took the first position from you last term. *Abi?*'

'Yes.'

'I'm sure your parents didn't mind. Ah! Ah! You have been coming first since we started class one. Chinwe said her father took her to London.'

'Oh.'

'I came fifth and it was an improvement for me because I came eighth the term before. You know, our class is very competitive. I used to always come first in my primary school.'

Chinwe Jideze came over to Ezinne's table then. She had a high, birdlike voice. 'I want to remain class prefect this term, Ezi-Butterfly, so make sure you vote for me,' Chinwe said. Her school skirt was tight at the waist, dividing her body into two rounded halves like the number 8.

'Of course,' Ezinne said.

I was not surprised when Chinwe walked past me to the girl at the next desk and repeated herself, only with a different nickname that she had thought up. Chinwe had never spoken to me, not even when we were placed in the same agricultural science group to collect weeds for an album. The girls flocked around her desk during short break, their laughter ringing out often. Their hairstyles were usually exact copies of hers – black, thread-covered sticks if Chinwe wore isi owu that week, or zigzagging cornrows that ended in a pony tail atop their heads if Chinwe wore shuku that week. Chinwe walked as if there were a hot object underfoot, raising each leg almost as soon as her other foot touched the floor. During long break, she bounced in front of a group of girls as they went to the tuck shop to buy biscuits and coke. According to Ezinne, Chinwe paid for everyone's soft drinks. I usually spent long break reading in the library.

'Chinwe just wants you to talk to her first,' Ezinne whispered. 'You know, she started calling you backyard snob because you don't talk to anybody. She said just because your father owns a newspaper and all those factories does not mean you have to feel too big, because her father is rich, too.'

'I don't feel too big.'

'Like today, at assembly, she said you were feeling too big, that was why you didn't start the pledge the first time Mother Lucy called you.'

'I didn't hear the first time Mother Lucy called me.'

'I'm not saying you feel too big, I am saying that is what Chinwe and most of the girls think. Maybe you should try and talk to her. Maybe after school you should stop running off like that and walk with us to the gate. Why do you always run, anyway?'

'I just like running,' I said, and wondered if I would count that as a lie when I made confession next Saturday, if I would add it to the lie about not having heard Mother Lucy the first time. Kevin always had the Peugeot 505 parked at the school gates right after the bells rang. Kevin had many other chores to do for Papa and I was not allowed to keep him waiting, so I always dashed out of my last class. Dashed, as though I were running the 200-meters race at the interhouse sports competition. Once, Kevin told Papa I took a few minutes longer, and Papa slapped my left and right cheeks at the same time, so his huge palms left parallel marks on my face and ringing in my ears for days.

'Why?' Ezinne asked. 'If you stay and talk to people, maybe it will make them know that you are really not a snob.'

'I just like running,' I said again.

I remained a backyard snob to most of my class girls until the end of term. But I did not worry too much about that because I carried a bigger load – the worry of making sure I came first this term. It was like balancing a sack of gravel on my head every day at school and not being allowed to steady it with my hand. I still saw the print in my textbooks as a red blur, still saw my baby brother's spirit strung together by narrow lines of blood. I memorized what the teachers said because I knew my textbooks would not make sense if I tried to study later. After every test, a tough lump like poorly made fufu formed in my throat and stayed there until our exercise books came back.

School closed for Christmas break in early December. I peered into my report card while Kevin was driving me home and saw 1/25, written in a hand so slanted I had to study it to make sure it was not 7/25. That night, I fell asleep hugging close the image of Papa's face lit up, the sound of Papa's voice telling me how proud of me he was, how I had fulfilled God's purpose for me.

★ ★ ★

Dust-laden winds of harmattan came with December. They brought the scent of the Sahara and Christmas, and yanked the slender, ovate leaves down from the frangipani and the needle-like leaves from the whistling pines, covering everything in a film of brown. We spent every Christmas in our hometown. Sister Veronica called it the yearly migration of the Igbo. She did not understand, she said in that Irish accent that rolled her words across her tongue, why many Igbo people built huge houses in their hometowns, where they spent only a week or two in December, yet were content to live in cramped quarters in the city the rest of the year. I often wondered why Sister Veronica needed to understand it, when it was simply the way things were done.

The morning winds were swift on the day we left, pulling and pushing the whistling pine trees so that they bent and twisted, as if bowing to a dusty god, their leaves and branches making the same sound as a football referee's whistle. The cars were parked in the driveway, doors and boots open, waiting to be loaded. Papa would drive the Mercedes, with Mama in the front seat and Jaja and me in the back. Kevin would drive the factory car with Sisi, and the factory driver, Sunday, who usually stood in when Kevin took his yearly one-week leave, would drive the Volvo.

Papa stood by the hibiscuses, giving directions, one hand sunk in the pocket of his white tunic while the other pointed from item to car. 'The suitcases go in the Mercedes, and those vegetables also. The yams will go in the Peugeot 505, with the cases of Remy Martin and cartons of juice. See if the stacks of *okporoko* will fit in, too. The bags of rice and *garri* and beans and the plantains go in the Volvo.'

There was a lot to pack, and Adamu came over from the gate to help Sunday and Kevin. The yams alone, wide tubers the size of young puppies, filled the boot of the Peugeot 505, and even the front seat of the Volvo had a bag of beans slanting across it, like a passenger who had fallen asleep. Kevin and Sunday drove off first, and we followed, so that if the soldiers at the roadblocks stopped them, he would see and stop, too.

Papa started the rosary before we drove out of our gated street. He stopped at the end of the first decade so Mama could continue with the next set of ten Hail Marys. Jaja led the next decade; then it was my turn. Papa took his time driving. The expressway was a single lane, and when we got behind a lorry he stayed put, muttering that the roads were unsafe, that the people in Abuja had stolen all the money meant for making the expressways dual-carriage. Many cars horned and overtook us; some were so full of Christmas yams and bags of rice and crates of soft drinks that their boots almost grazed the road.

At Ninth Mile, Papa stopped to buy bread and okpa. Hawkers descended on our car, pushing boiled eggs, roasted cashew nuts, bottled water, bread, okpa, agidi into every window of the car, chanting: 'Buy from me, oh, I will sell well to you.' Or 'Look at me, I am the one you are looking for.'

Although Papa bought only bread and okpa wrapped in hot banana leaves, he gave a twenty-naira note to each of the other hawkers, and their 'Thank sir, God bless you' chants echoed in my ear as we drove off and approached Abba.

The green WELCOME TO ABBA TOWN sign that led off the expressway would have been easy to miss because it was so small. Papa turned onto the dirt road, and soon I heard the *screech-screech-screech* of the low underbelly of the Mercedes scraping the bumpy, sun-baked dirt road. As we drove past, people waved and called out Papa's title: *'Omelora!'* Mud-and-thatch huts stood close to three-story houses that nestled behind ornate metal gates. Naked and semi-naked children played with limp footballs. Men sat on benches beneath trees, drinking palm wine from cow horns and cloudy glass mugs. The car was coated in dust by the time we got to the wide black gates of our country home. Three elderly men standing under the lone ukwa tree near our gates waved and shouted, *'Nno nu! Nno nu!* Have you come back? We will come in soon to say welcome!' Our gateman threw the gates open.

'Thank you, Lord, for journey mercies,' Papa said as he drove into the compound, crossing himself.

'Amen,' we said.

Our house still took my breath away, the four-story white majesty of it, with the spurting fountain in front and the coconut trees flanking it on both sides and the orange trees dotting the front yard. Three little boys rushed into the compound to greet Papa. They had been chasing our cars down the dirt road.

'*Omelora!* Good afun, sah!' they chorused. They wore only shorts, and each one's belly button was the size of a small balloon.

'*Kedu nu?*' Papa gave them each ten naira from a wad of notes he pulled out of his hold-all. 'Greet your parents, make sure you show them this money.'

'Yes sah! Tank sah!' They dashed out of the compound, laughing loudly.

Kevin and Sunday unpacked the foodstuffs while Jaja and I unpacked the suitcases from the Mercedes. Mama went to the backyard with Sisi to put away the cast iron cooking tripods. Our food would be cooked on the gas cooker inside the kitchen, but the metal tripods would balance the big pots that would cook rice and stews and soups for visitors. Some of the pots were big enough to fit a whole goat. Mama and Sisi hardly did any of that cooking; they simply stayed around and provided more salt, more Maggi cubes, more utensils, because the wives of the members of our umunna came over to do the cooking. They wanted Mama to rest, they said, after the stress of the city. And every year they took the leftovers – the fat

63

pieces of meat, the rice and beans, the bottles of soft drink and maltina and beer – home with them afterward. We were always prepared to feed the whole village at Christmas, always prepared so that none of the people who came in would leave without eating and drinking to what Papa called a reasonable level of satisfaction. Papa's title was omelora, after all, The One Who Does for the Community. But it was not only Papa who received visitors; the villagers trooped to every big house with a big gate, and sometimes they took plastic bowls with firm covers. It was Christmas.

Jaja and I were upstairs unpacking when Mama came in and said, 'Ade Coker came by with his family to wish us a merry Christmas. They are on their way to Lagos. Come downstairs and greet them.'

Ade Coker was a small, round, laughing man. Every time I saw him, I tried to imagine him writing those editorials in the *Standard*; I tried to imagine him defying the soldiers. And I could not. He looked like a stuffed doll, and because he was always smiling, the deep dimples in his pillowy cheeks looked like permanent fixtures, as though someone had sunk a stick into his cheeks. Even his glasses looked dollish: they were thicker than window louvers, tinted a strange bluish shade, and framed in white plastic. He was throwing his baby, a perfectly round copy of himself, in the air when we came in. His little daughter was standing close to him, asking him to throw her in the air, too.

'Jaja, Kambili, how are you?' he said, and before we could reply, he laughed his tinkling laugh and, gesturing to the baby, said, 'You know they say the higher you throw them when they're young, the more likely they are to learn how to fly!' The baby gurgled, showing pink gums, and reached out for his father's glasses. Ade Coker tilted his head back, threw the baby up again.

His wife, Yewande, hugged us, asked how we were, then slapped Ade Coker's shoulder playfully and took the baby from him. I watched her and remembered her loud, choking cries to Papa.

'Do you like coming to the village?' Ade Coker asked us.

We looked at Papa at the same time; he was on the sofa, reading a Christmas card and smiling. 'Yes,' we said.

'Eh? You like coming to this bush place?' His eyes widened theatrically. 'Do you have friends here?'

'No,' we said.

'So what do you do in this back of beyond, then?' he teased.

Jaja and I smiled and said nothing.

'They are always so quiet,' he said, turning to Papa. 'So quiet.'

'They are not like those loud children people are raising these days, with no home training and no fear of God,' Papa said, and I was certain that it was pride that stretched Papa's lips and lightened his eyes.

65

'Imagine what the *Standard* would be if we were all quiet.'

It was a joke. Ade Coker was laughing; so was his wife, Yewanda. But Papa did not laugh. Jaja and I turned and went back upstairs, silently.

The rustling of the coconut fronds woke me up. Outside our high gates, I could hear goats bleating and cocks crowing and people yelling greetings across mud compound walls.

'Gudu morni. Have you woken up, eh? Did you rise well?'

'Gudu morni. Did the people of your house rise well, oh?'

I reached out to slide open my bedroom window, to hear the sounds better and to let in the clean air tinged with goat droppings and ripening oranges. Jaja tapped on my door before he came into my room. Our rooms adjoined; back in Enugu, they were far apart.

'Are you up?' he asked. 'Let's go down for prayers before Papa calls us.'

I tied my wrapper, which I had used as a light cover in the warm night, over my night-dress, knotted it under my arm, and followed Jaja downstairs.

The wide passages made our house feel like a hotel, as did the impersonal smell of doors kept locked most of the year, of unused bathrooms and kitchens and toilets, of uninhabited rooms. We used only the ground floor and first floor;

the other two were last used years ago, when Papa was made a chief and took his omelora title. The members of our umunna had urged him for so long, even when he was still a manager at Leventis and had not bought the first factory, to take a title. He was wealthy enough, they insisted; besides, nobody among our umunna had ever taken a title. So when Papa finally decided to, after extensive talks with the parish priest and insisting that all pagan undertones be removed from his title-taking ceremony, it was like a mini New Yam festival. Cars had taken up every inch of the dirt road running through Abba. The third and fourth floors had swarmed with people. Now I went up there only when I wanted to see farther than the road just outside our compound walls.

'Papa is hosting a church council meeting today,' Jaja said. 'I heard him telling Mama.'

'What time is the meeting?'

'Before noon.' And with his eyes he said, We *can spend time together then.*

In Abba, Jaja and I had no schedules. We talked more and sat alone in our rooms less, because Papa was too busy entertaining the endless stream of visitors and attending church council meetings at five in the morning and town council meetings until midnight. Or maybe it was because Abba was different, because people strolled into our compound at will, because the very air we breathed moved more slowly.

Papa and Mama were in one of the small living rooms that led off the main living room downstairs.

'Good morning, Papa. Good morning, Mama,' Jaja and I said.

'How are you both?' Papa asked.

'Fine,' we said.

Papa looked bright-eyed; he must have been awake for hours. He was flipping through his Bible, the Catholic version with the deutero-canonical books, bound in shiny black leather. Mama looked sleepy. She rubbed her crusty eyes as she asked if we had slept well. I could hear voices from the main living room. Guests arrived with dawn here. When we had made the sign of the cross and gotten down on our knees, around the table, someone knocked on the door. A middle-aged man in a threadbare T-shirt peeked in.

'*Omelora!*' the man said in the forceful tone people used when they called others by their titles. 'I am leaving now. I want to see if I can buy a few Christmas things for my children at Oye Abagana.' He spoke English with an Igbo accent so strong it decorated even the shortest words with extra vowels. Papa liked it when the villagers made an effort to speak English around him. He said it showed they had good sense.

'*Ogbunambala!*' Papa said. 'Wait for me, I am praying with my family. I want to give you a little something for the children. You will also share my tea and bread with me.'

'Hei! *Omelora!* Thank sir. I have not drank milk this year.' The man still hovered at the door. Perhaps he imagined that leaving would make Papa's promise of tea with milk disappear.

'*Ogbunambala!* Go and sit down and wait for me.'

The man retreated. Papa read from the psalms before saying the Our Father, the Hail Mary, the Glory Be, and the Apostles Creed. Although we spoke aloud after Papa said the first few words alone, an outer silence enveloped us all, shrouding us. But when he said, 'We will now pray to the spirit in our own words, for the spirit intercedes for us in accordance with His will,' the silence was broken. Our voices sounded loud, discordant. Mama started with a prayer for peace and for the rulers of our country. Jaja prayed for priests and for the religious. I prayed for the Pope. Finally, for twenty minutes, Papa prayed for our protection from ungodly people and forces, for Nigeria and the Godless men ruling it, and for us to continue to grow in righteousness. Finally, he prayed for the conversion of our Papa-Nnukwu, so that Papa-Nnukwu would be saved from hell. Papa spent some time describing hell, as if God did not know that the flames were eternal and raging and fierce. At the end we raised our voices and said, 'Amen!'

Papa closed the Bible. 'Kambili and Jaja, you will go this afternoon to your grandfather's house and greet him. Kevin will take you. Remember, don't touch any food, don't drink anything. And, as usual, you will stay not longer than fifteen minutes. Fifteen minutes.'

'Yes, Papa.' We had heard this every Christmas for the past few years, ever since we had started to visit Papa-Nnukwu. Papa-Nnukwu had called an umunna meeting to complain to the extended family that he did not know his grandchildren and that we did not know him. Papa-Nnukwu had told Jaja and me this, as Papa did not tell us such things. Papa-Nnukwu had told the umunna how Papa had offered to build him a house, buy him a car, and hire him a driver, as long as he converted and threw away the chi in the thatch shrine in his yard. Papa-Nnukwu laughed and said he simply wanted to see his grandchildren when he could. He would not throw away his chi; he had already told Papa this many times. The members of our umunna sided with Papa, they always did, but they urged him to let us visit Papa-Nnukwu, to greet him, because every man who was old enough to be called grandfather deserved to be greeted by his grandchildren. Papa himself never greeted Papa-Nnukwu, never visited him, but he sent slim wads of naira through Kevin or through one of our umunna members, slimmer wads than he gave Kevin as a Christmas bonus.

'I don't like to send you to the home of a heathen, but God will protect you,' Papa said. He put the Bible in a drawer and then pulled Jaja and me to his side, gently rubbed the sides of our arms.

'Yes, Papa.'

He went into the large living room. I could hear more voices, more people coming in to say '*Nno nu*' and complain about how hard life was, how they could not buy new clothes for their children this Christmas.

'You and Jaja can have breakfast upstairs. I will bring the things up. Your father will eat with the guests,' Mama said.

'Let me help you,' I offered.

'No, *nne*, go upstairs. Stay with your brother.'

I watched Mama walk toward the kitchen, in her limping gait. Her braided hair was piled into a net that tapered to a golf-ball-like lump at the end, like a Father Christmas hat. She looked tired.

'Papa-Nnukwu lives close by, we can walk there in five minutes, we don't need Kevin to take us,' Jaja said, as we went back upstairs. He said that every year, but we always climbed into the car so that Kevin could take us, so that he could watch us.

As Kevin drove us out of the compound later that morning, I turned to allow my eyes to stroke, once again, the gleaming white walls and pillars of our house, the perfect silver-colored water arch the fountain made. Papa-Nnukwu had never set foot in it, because when Papa had decreed that heathens were not allowed in his compound, he had not made an exception for his father.

'Your father said you are to stay fifteen minutes,' Kevin said, as he parked on the roadside, near Papa-Nnukwu's thatch-enclosed compound. I stared at the scar on Kevin's neck before I got out of the car. He had fallen from a palm tree in his hometown in the Niger Delta area, a few years ago while on vacation. The scar ran from the center of his head to the nape of his neck. It was shaped like a dagger.

'We know,' Jaja said.

Jaja swung open Papa-Nnukwu's creaking wooden gate, which was so narrow that Papa might have to enter sideways if he ever were to visit. The compound was barely a quarter of the size of our backyard in Enugu. Two goats and a few chickens sauntered around, nibbling and pecking at drying stems of grass. The house that stood in the middle of the compound was small, compact like dice, and it was hard to imagine Papa and Aunty Ifeoma growing up here. It looked just like the pictures of houses I used to draw in kindergarten: a square house with a square door at the center and two square windows on each side. The only difference was that Papa-Nnukwu's house had a verandah, which was bounded by rusty metal bars. The first time Jaja and I visited, I had walked in looking for the bathroom, and Papa-Nnukwu had laughed and pointed at the outhouse, a closet-size building of unpainted cement blocks with a mat of entwined palm fronds pulled across the gaping entrance. I had examined him that day, too, looking away when his eyes met mine, for signs of difference, of Godlessness. I didn't see any, but I was sure they were there somewhere. They had to be.

Papa-Nnukwu was sitting on a low stool on the verandah, bowls of food on a raffia mat before him. He rose as we came in. A wrapper was slung across his body and tied behind his neck, over a once white singlet now browned by age and yellowed at the armpits.

'*Neke! Neke! Neke!* Kambili and Jaja have come to greet their old father!' he said. Although he was stooped with age, it was easy to see how tall he once had been. He shook Jaja's hand and hugged me. I pressed myself to him just a moment longer, gently, holding my breath because of the strong, unpleasant smell of cassava that clung to him.

'Come and eat,' he said, gesturing to the raffia mat. The enamel bowls contained flaky fufu and watery soup bereft of chunks of fish or meat. It was custom to ask, but Papa-Nnukwu expected us to say no – his eyes twinkled with mischief.

'No, thank sir,' we said. We sat on the wood bench next to him. I leaned back and rested my head on the wooden window shutters, which had parallel openings running across them.

'I hear that you came in yesterday,' he said. His lower lip quivered, as did his voice, and sometimes I understood him a moment or two after he spoke

73

because his dialect was ancient; his speech had none of the anglicized inflections that ours had.

'Yes,' Jaja said.

'Kambili, you are so grown up now, a ripe *agbogho*. Soon the suitors will start to come,' he said, teasing. His left eye was going blind and was covered by a film the color and consistency of diluted milk. I smiled as he stretched out to pat my shoulder; the age spots that dotted his hand stood out because they were so much lighter than his soil-colored complexion.

'Papa-Nnukwu, are you well? How is your body?' Jaja asked.

Papa-Nnukwu shrugged as if to say there was a lot that was wrong but he had no choice. 'I am well, my son. What can an old man do but be well until he joins his ancestors?' He paused to mold a lump of fufu with his fingers. I watched him, the smile on his face, the easy way he threw the molded morsel out toward the garden, where parched herbs swayed in the light breeze, asking Ani, the god of the land, to eat with him. 'My legs ache often. Your Aunty Ifeoma brings me medicine when she can put the money together. But I am an old man; if it is not my legs that ache, it will be my hands.'

'Will Aunty Ifeoma and her children come back this year?' I asked.

Papa-Nnukwu scratched at the stubborn white tufts that clung to his bald head. '*Ehye*, I expect them tomorrow.'

'They did not come last year,' Jaja said.

'Ifeoma could not afford it.' Papa-Nnukwu shook his head. 'Since the father of her children died, she has seen hard times. But she will bring them this year. You will see them. It is not right that you don't know them well, your cousins. It is not right.'

Jaja and I said nothing. We did not know Aunty Ifeoma or her children very well because she and Papa had quarreled about Papa-Nnukwu. Mama had told us. Aunty Ifeoma stopped speaking to Papa after he barred Papa-Nnukwu from coming to his house, and a few years passed before they finally started speaking to each other.

'If I had meat in my soup,' Papa Nnukwu said, 'I would offer it to you.'

'It's all right, Papa-Nnukwu,' Jaja said.

Papa-Nnukwu took his time swallowing his food. I watched the food slide down his throat, struggling to get past his sagging Adam's apple, which pushed out of his neck like a wrinkled nut. There was no drink beside him, not even water. 'That child that helps me, Chinyelu, will come in soon. I will send her to go and buy soft drinks for you two, from Ichie's shop,' he said.

'No, Papa-Nnukwu. Thank sir,' Jaja said.

'*Ezi okwu?* I know your father will not let you eat here because I offer my food to our ancestors, but soft drinks also? Do I not buy that from the store as everyone else does?'

'Papa-Nnukwu, we just ate before we came here,'

75

Jaja said. 'If we're thirsty, we will drink in your house.'

Papa-Nnukwu smiled. His teeth were yellowed and widely spaced because of the many he had lost. 'You have spoken well, my son. You are my father, Ogbuefi Olioke, come back. He spoke with wisdom.'

I stared at the fufu on the enamel plate, which was chipped of its leaf-green color at the edges. I imagined the fufu, dried to crusts by the harmattan winds, scratching the inside of Papa-Nnukwu's throat as he swallowed. Jaja nudged me. But I did not want to leave; I wanted to stay so that if the fufu clung to Papa-Nnukwu's throat and choked him, I could run and get him water. I did not know where the water was, though. Jaja nudged me again and I still could not get up. The bench held me back, sucked me in. I watched a gray rooster walk into the shrine at the corner of the yard, where Papa-Nnukwu's god was, where Papa said Jaja and I were never to go near. The shrine was a low, open shed, its mud roof and walls covered with dried palm fronds. It looked like the grotto behind St Agnes, the one dedicated to Our Lady of Lourdes.

'Let us go, Papa-Nnukwu,' Jaja said, finally, rising.

'All right, my son,' Papa-Nnukwu said. He did not say 'What, so soon?' or 'Does my house chase you away?' He was used to our leaving moments after we arrived. When he walked us to the car, balancing on his crooked walking stick made from a tree branch, Kevin came out of the car and greeted him, then handed him a slim wad of cash.

'Oh? Thank Eugene for me,' Papa-Nnukwu said, smiling. 'Thank him.'

He waved as we drove off. I waved back and kept my eyes on him while he shuffled back into his compound. If Papa-Nnukwu minded that his son sent him impersonal, paltry amounts of money through a driver, he didn't show it. He hadn't shown it last Christmas, or the Christmas before. He had never shown it. It was so different from the way Papa had treated my maternal grandfather until he died five years ago. When we arrived at Abba every Christmas, Papa would stop by Grandfather's house at our ikwu nne, Mother's maiden home, before we even drove to our own compound. Grandfather was very light-skinned, almost albino, and it was said to be one of the reasons the missionaries had liked him. He determinedly spoke English, always, in a heavy Igbo accent. He knew Latin, too, often quoted the articles of Vatican I, and spent most of his time at St Paul's, where he had been the first catechist. He had insisted that we call him Grandfather, in English, rather than Papa-Nnukwu or Nna-Ochie. Papa still talked about him often, his eyes proud, as if Grandfather were his own father. He opened his eyes before many of our people did, Papa would say; he was one of the few who welcomed the missionaries. Do you know how quickly he learned English? When he became an interpreter, do you know how many converts he helped win? Why, he converted most of Abba himself! He did things the right way, the way the white people did, not what our people do now! Papa had a photo of Grandfather, in the full regalia of the Knights of St John, framed in deep mahogany and hung on our wall back in Enugu. I did not need that photo to remember Grandfather, though. I was only ten when he died, but I remembered his almost-green albino eyes, the way he seemed to use the word *sinner* in every sentence.

'Papa-Nnukwu does not look as healthy as last year,' I whispered close to Jaja's ear as we drove off. I did not want Kevin to hear.

'He is an old man,' Jaja said.

When we got home, Sisi brought up our lunch, rice and fried beef, on fawn-colored elegant plates, and Jaja and I ate alone. The church council meeting had started, and we heard the male voices rise sometimes in argument, just as we heard the up-down cadence of the female voices in the backyard, the wives of our umunna who were oiling pots to make them easier to wash later and grinding spices in wooden mortars and starting fires underneath the tripods.

'Will you confess it?' I asked Jaja, as we ate.

'What?'

'What you said today, that if we were thirsty,

we would drink in Papa-Nnukwu's house. You know we can't drink in Papa-Nnukwu's house,' I said.

'I just wanted to say something to make him feel better.'

'He takes it well.'

'He hides it well,' Jaja said.

Papa opened the door then and came in. I had not heard him come up the stairs, and besides, I did not think he would come up because the church council meeting was still going on downstairs.

'Good afternoon, Papa,' Jaja and I said.

'Kevin said you stayed up to twenty-five minutes with your grandfather. Is that what I told you?' Papa's voice was low.

'I wasted time, it was my fault,' Jaja said.

'What did you do there? Did you eat food sacrificed to idols? Did you desecrate your Christian tongue?'

I sat frozen; I did not know that tongues could be Christian, too.

'No,' Jaja said.

Papa was walking toward Jaja. He spoke entirely in Igbo now. I thought he would pull at Jaja's ears, that he would tug and yank at the same pace as he spoke, that he would slap Jaja's face and his palm would make that sound, like a heavy book falling from a library shelf in school. And then he would reach across and slap me on the face with the casualness of reaching for the pepper shaker. But he said, 'I want you to finish that food and go to your rooms and pray for forgiveness,' before turning to go back downstairs. The silence he left was heavy but comfortable, like a well-worn, prickly cardigan on a bitter morning.

'You still have rice on your plate,' Jaja said, finally.

I nodded and picked up my fork. Then I heard Papa's raised voice just outside the window and put the fork down.

'What is he doing in my house? What is Anikwenwa doing in my house?' The enraged timbre in Papa's voice made my fingers cold at the tips. Jaja and I dashed to the window, and because we could see nothing, we dashed out to the verandah and stood by the pillars.

Papa was standing in the front yard, near an orange tree, screaming at a wrinkled old man in a torn white singlet and a wrapper wound round his waist. A few other men stood around Papa.

'What is Anikwenwa doing in my house? What is a worshiper of idols doing in my house? Leave my house!'

'Do you know that I am in your father's age group, *gho*?' the old man asked. The finger he waved in the air was meant for Papa's face, but it only hovered around his chest. 'Do you know that I sucked my mother's breast when your father sucked his mother's?'

'Leave my house!' Papa pointed at the gate.

Two men slowly ushered Anikwenwa out of the compound. He did not resist; he was too old to, anyway. But he kept looking back and throwing words at Papa. '*Ifukwa gi!* You are like a fly blindly following a corpse into the grave!'

I followed the old man's unsteady gait until he walked out through the gates.

Aunty Ifeoma came the next day, in the evening, when the orange trees started to cast long, wavy shadows across the water fountain in the front yard. Her laughter floated upstairs into the living room, where I sat reading. I had not heard it in two years, but I would know that cackling, hearty sound anywhere. Aunty Ifeoma was as tall as Papa, with a well-proportioned body. She walked fast, like one who knew just where she was going and what she was going to do there. And she spoke the way she walked, as if to get as many words out of her mouth as she could in the shortest time.

'Welcome, Aunty, *nno*,' I said, rising to hug her.

She did not give me the usual brief side hug. She clasped me in her arms and held me tightly against the softness of her body. The wide lapels of her blue, A-line dress smelled of lavender.

'Kambili, *kedu*?' A wide smile stretched her dark-complected face, revealing a gap between her front teeth.

'I'm fine, Aunty.'

'You have grown so much. Look at you, look at

you.' She reached out and pulled my left breast. 'Look how fast these are growing!'

I looked away and inhaled deeply so that I would not start to stutter. I did not know how to handle that kind of playfulness.

'Where is Jaja?' she asked.

'He's asleep. He has a headache.'

'A headache three days to Christmas? No way. I will wake him up and cure that headache.' Aunty Ifeoma laughed. 'We got here before noon; we left Nsukka really early and would have gotten here sooner if the car didn't break down on the road, but it was near Ninth Mile, thank God, so it was easy finding a mechanic.'

'Thanks be to God,' I said. Then, after a pause I asked, 'How are my cousins?' It was the polite thing to say; still, I felt strange asking about the cousins I hardly knew.

'They're coming soon. They're with your Papa-Nnukwu, and he had just started one of his stories. You know how he likes to go on and on.'

'Oh,' I said. I did not know that Papa-Nnukwu liked to go on and on. I did not even know that he told stories.

Mama came in holding a tray piled high with bottles of soft and malt drinks lying on their sides. A plate of chin-chin was balanced on top of the drinks.

'*Nwunye m*, who are those for?' Aunty Ifeoma asked.

'You and the children,' Mama said. 'Did you not

say the children were coming soon, *okwia?*'

'You should not have bothered, really. We bought *okpa* on our way and just ate it.'

'Then I will put the chin-chin in a bag for you,' Mama said. She turned to leave the room. Her wrapper was dressy, with yellow print designs, and her matching blouse had yellow lace sewn onto the puffy, short sleeves.

'*Nwunye m,*' Aunty Ifeoma called, and Mama turned back.

The first time I heard Aunty Ifeoma call Mama '*nwunye m,*' years ago, I was aghast that a woman called another woman 'my wife.' When I asked, Papa said it was the remnants of ungodly traditions, the idea that it was the family and not the man alone that married a wife, and later Mama whispered, although we were alone in my room, 'I am her wife, too, because I am your father's wife. It shows that she accepts me.'

'*Nwunye m,* come and sit down. You look tired. Are you well?' Aunty Ifeoma asked.

A tight smile appeared on Mama's face. 'I am well, very well. I have been helping the wives of our *umunna* with the cooking.'

'Come and sit down,' Aunty Ifeoma said again. 'Come and sit down and rest. The wives of our *umunna* can look for the salt themselves and find it. After all, they are all here to take from you, to wrap meat in banana leaves when nobody is looking and then sneak it home.' Aunty Ifeoma laughed.

Mama sat down next to me. 'Eugene is arranging for extra chairs to be put outside, especially on Christmas day. So many people have come already.'

'You know our people have no other work at Christmas than to go from house to house,' Aunty Ifeoma said. 'But you can't stay here serving them all day. We should take the children to Abagana for the Aro festival tomorrow, to look at the *mmuo*.'

'Eugene will not let the children go to a heathen festival,' Mama said.

'Heathen festival, *kwa*? Everybody goes to Aro to look at the *mmuo*.'

'I know, but you know Eugene.'

Aunty Ifeoma shook her head slowly. 'I will tell him we are going for a drive, so we can all spend time together, especially the children.'

Mama fiddled with her fingers and said nothing for a while. Then she asked, 'When will you take the children to their father's hometown?'

'Perhaps today, although I don't have the strength for Ifediora's family right now. They eat more and more shit every year. The people in his *umunna* said he left money somewhere and I have been hiding it. Last Christmas, one of the women from their compound even told me I had killed him. I wanted to stuff sand in her mouth. Then I thought that I should sit her down, eh, and explain that you do not kill a husband you love, that you do not orchestrate a car accident in which a trailer rams into your husband's car, but again, why waste my time?

85

They all have the brains of guinea fowls.' Aunty Ifeoma made a loud hissing sound. 'I don't know how much longer I will take my children there.'

Mama clucked in sympathy. 'People do not always talk with sense. But it is good that the children go, especially the boys. They need to know their father's homestead and the members of their father's *umunna.*'

'I honestly do not know how Ifediora came from an *umunna* like that.'

I watched their lips move as they spoke; Mama's bare lips were pale compared to Aunty Ifeoma's, covered in a shiny bronze lipstick.

'*Umunna* will always say hurtful things,' Mama said. 'Did our own *umunna* not tell Eugene to take another wife because a man of his stature cannot have just two children? If people like you had not been on my side then . . .'

'Stop it, stop being grateful. If Eugene had done that, he would have been the loser, not you.'

'So you say. A woman with children and no husband, what is that?'

'Me.'

Mama shook her head. 'You have come again, Ifeoma. You know what I mean. How can a woman live like that?' Mama's eyes had grown round, taking up more space on her face.

'*Nwunye m*, sometimes life begins when marriage ends.'

'You and your university talk. Is this what you tell your students?' Mama was smiling.

'Seriously, yes. But they marry earlier and earlier these days. What is the use of a degree, they ask me, when we cannot find a job after graduation?'

'At least somebody will take care of them when they marry.'

'I don't know who will take care of whom. Six girls in my first-year seminar class are married, their husbands visit in Mercedes and Lexus cars every weekend, their husbands buy them stereos and textbooks and refrigerators, and when they graduate, the husbands own them and their degrees. Don't you see?'

Mama shook her head. 'University talk again. A husband crowns a woman's life, Ifeoma. It is what they want.'

'It is what they think they want. But how can I blame them? Look what this military tyrant is doing to our country.' Aunty Ifeoma closed her eyes, in the way that people do when they want to remember something unpleasant. 'We have not had fuel for three months in Nsukka. I spent the night in the petrol station last week, waiting for fuel. And at the end, the fuel did not come. Some people left their cars in the station because they did not have enough fuel to drive back home. If you could see the mosquitoes that bit me that night, eh, the bumps on my skin were as big as cashew nuts.'

'Oh.' Mama shook her head sympathetically. 'How are things generally at the university, though?'

'We just called off yet another strike, even though no lecturer has been paid for the last two months. They tell us the Federal Government has no money.' Aunty Ifeoma chuckled with little humor. '*Ifukwa*, people are leaving the country. Phillipa left two months ago. You remember my friend Phillipa?'

'She came back with you for Christmas a few years ago. Dark and plump?'

'Yes. She is now teaching in America. She shares a cramped office with another adjunct professor, but she says at least teachers are paid there.' Aunty Ifeoma stopped and reached out to brush something off Mama's blouse. I watched every movement she made; I could not tear my ears away. It was the fearlessness about her, about the way she gestured as she spoke, the way she smiled to show that wide gap.

'I have brought out my old kerosene stove,' she continued. 'It is what we use now; we don't even smell the kerosene in the kitchen anymore. Do you know how much a cooking-gas cylinder costs? It is outrageous!'

Mama shifted on the sofa. 'Why don't you tell Eugene? There are gas cylinders in the factory . . .'

Aunty Ifeoma laughed, patted Mama's shoulder fondly. '*Nwunye m*, things are tough, but we are not dying yet. I tell you all these things because it is you. With someone else, I would rub Vaseline on my hungry face until it shone.'

Papa came in then, on his way to his bedroom.

I was sure it was to get more stacks of naira notes that he would give to visitors for igba krismas, and then tell them 'It is from God, not me' when they started to sing their thanks.

'Eugene,' Aunty Ifeoma called out. 'I was saying that Jaja and Kambili should spend some time with me and the children tomorrow.'

Papa grunted and kept walking to the door.

'Eugene!'

Every time Aunty Ifeoma spoke to Papa, my heart stopped, then started again in a hurry. It was the flippant tone; she did not seem to recognize that it was Papa, that he was different, special. I wanted to reach out and press her lips shut and get some of that shiny bronze lipstick on my fingers.

'Where do you want to take them?' Papa asked, standing by the door.

'Just to look around.'

'Sightseeing?' Papa asked. He spoke English, while Aunty Ifeoma spoke Igbo.

'Eugene, let the children come out with us!' Aunty Ifeoma sounded irritated; her voice was slightly raised. 'Is it not Christmas that we are celebrating, eh? The children have never really spent time with one another. *Imakwa*, my little one, Chima, does not even know Kambili's name.'

Papa looked at me and then at Mama, searched our faces as if looking for letters beneath our noses, above our foreheads, on our lips, that would spell something he would not like. 'Okay. They can go with you, but you know I do not want my children near anything ungodly. If you drive past *mmuo*, keep your windows up.'

'I have heard you, Eugene,' Aunty Ifeoma said, with an exaggerated formality.

'Why don't we all have lunch on Christmas day?' Papa asked. 'The children can spend time together then.'

'You know that the children and I spend Christmas day with their Papa-Nnukwu.'

'What do idol worshipers know about Christmas?'

'Eugene . . .' Aunty Ifeoma took a deep breath. 'Okay, the children and I will come on Christmas day.'

Papa had gone back downstairs, and I was still sitting on the sofa, watching Aunty Ifeoma talk to Mama, when my cousins arrived. Amaka was a thinner, teenage copy of her mother. She walked and talked even faster and with more purpose than Aunty Ifeoma did. Only her eyes were different; they did not have the unconditional warmth of Aunty Ifeoma's. They were quizzical eyes, eyes that asked many questions and did not accept many answers. Obiora was a year younger, very light-skinned, with honey-colored eyes behind thick glasses, and his mouth turned up at the sides in a perpetual smile. Chima had skin as dark as the bottom of a burnt pot of rice, and was tall for a boy of seven. They all laughed alike: throaty, cackling sounds pushed out with enthusiasm.

They greeted Papa, and when he gave them money for igba krismas, Amaka and Obiora thanked him, holding out the two thick wads of naira notes. Their eyes were politely surprised, to show that they were not presumptuous, that they had not expected money.

'You have satellite here, don't you?' Amaka asked me. It was the first thing she said after we greeted each other. Her hair was cut short, higher at the front and gradually reducing in an arch until it got to the back of her head, where there was little hair.

'Yes.'

'Can we watch CNN?'

I forced a cough out of my throat; I hoped I would not stutter.

'Maybe tomorrow,' Amaka continued, 'because right now I think we're going to visit my dad's family in Ukpo.'

'We don't watch a lot of TV,' I said.

'Why?' Amaka asked. It was so unlikely that we were the same age, fifteen. She seemed so much older, or maybe it was her striking resemblance to Aunty Ifeoma or the way she stared me right in the eyes. 'Because you're bored with it? If only we all had satellite so everybody could be bored with it.'

I wanted to say I was sorry, that I did not want her to dislike us for not watching satellite. I wanted to tell her that although huge satellite dishes lounged on top of the houses in Enugu and here, we did not watch TV. Papa did not pencil in TV time on our schedules.

But Amaka had turned to her mother, who was sitting hunched with Mama. 'Mom, if we are going to Ukpo, we should leave soon so we can get back before Papa-Nnukwu falls asleep.'

Aunty Ifeoma rose. 'Yes, *nne*, we should leave.'

She held Chima's hand as they all walked downstairs. Amaka said something, pointing at our banister, with its heavy hand-carved detail, and Obiora laughed. She did not turn to say good-bye to me, although the boys did and Aunty Ifeoma waved and said, 'I'll see you and Jaja tomorrow.'

Aunty Ifeoma drove into the compound just as we finished breakfast. When she barged into the dining room upstairs, I imagined a proud ancient forebear, walking miles to fetch water in homemade clay pots, nursing babies until they walked and talked, fighting wars with machetes sharpened on sun-warmed stone. She filled a room. 'Are you ready, Jaja and Kambili?' she asked. '*Nwunye m*, will you not come with us?'

Mama shook her head. 'You know Eugene likes me to stay around.'

'Kambili, I think you will be more comfortable in trousers,' Aunty Ifeoma said as we walked to the car.

'I'm fine, Aunty,' I said. I wondered why I did not tell her that all my skirts stopped well past my knees, that I did not own any trousers because it was sinful for a woman to wear trousers.

Her Peugeot 504 station wagon was white and rusted to an unpleasant brown at the fenders. Amaka was seated in the front; Obiora and Chima were in the back seat. Jaja and I climbed into the middle seats. Mama stood watching until the car disappeared from her sight. I knew because I felt her eyes, felt her presence. The car made rattling sounds as if some bolts had come loose and were shaking with every rise and fall of the bumpy road. There were gaping rectangular spaces on the dashboard instead of air-conditioner vents, so the windows were kept down. Dust sailed across my mouth, into my eyes and nose.

'We're going to pick up Papa-Nnukwu, he will come with us,' Aunty Ifeoma said.

I felt a lurch in my stomach and I glanced at Jaja. His eyes met mine. What would we tell Papa? Jaja looked away; he did not have an answer.

Before Aunty Ifeoma stopped the engine in front of the mud-and-thatch-enclosed compound, Amaka had opened the front door and bounded out. 'I'll fetch Papa-Nnukwu!'

The boys climbed out of the car and followed Amaka past the small wooden gate.

'Don't you want to come out?' Aunty Ifeoma asked, turning to Jaja and me.

I looked away. Jaja was sitting as still as I was.

'You don't want to come into your Papa-Nnukwu's compound? But didn't you come to

93

greet him two days ago?' Aunty Ifeoma widened her eyes to stare at us.

'We are not allowed to come here after we've greeted him,' Jaja said.

'What kind of nonsense is that, eh?' Aunty Ifeoma stopped then, perhaps remembering that the rules were not ours. 'Tell me, why do you think your father doesn't want you here?'

'I don't know,' Jaja said.

I sucked my tongue to unfreeze it, tasting the gritty dust. 'Because Papa-Nnukwu is a pagan.' Papa would be proud that I had said that.

'Your Papa-Nnukwu is not a pagan, Kambili, he is a traditionalist,' Aunty Ifeoma said.

I stared at her. Pagan, traditionalist, what did it matter? He was not Catholic, that was all; he was not of the faith. He was one of the people whose conversion we prayed for so that they did not end in the everlasting torment of hellfire.

We sat silently until the gate swung open and Amaka came out, walking close enough to Papa-Nnukwu to support him if he needed it. The boys walked behind them. Papa-Nnukwu wore a loose print shirt and a pair of knee-length khaki shorts. I had never seen him in anything but the threadbare wrappers that were wound around his body when we visited him.

'I got him those shorts,' Aunty Ifeoma said, with a laugh. 'See how he looks so youthful, who would believe he is eighty?'

Amaka helped Papa-Nnukwu get into the front seat, and then she got in the middle with us.

'Papa-Nnukwu, good afternoon sir,' Jaja and I greeted.

'Kambili, Jaja, I see you again before you go back to the city? *Ehye*, it is a sign that I am going soon to meet the ancestors.'

'*Nna anyi*, are you not tired of predicting your death?' Aunty Ifeoma said, starting the engine. 'Let us hear something new!' She called him nna anyi, our father. I wondered if Papa used to call him that and what Papa would call him now if they spoke to each other.

'He likes to talk about dying soon,' Amaka said, in amused English. 'He thinks that will get us to do things for him,'

'Dying soon indeed. He'll be here when we are as old as he is now,' Obiora said, in equally amused English.

'What are those children saying, *gbo*, Ifeoma?' Papa-Nnukwu asked. 'Are they conspiring to share my gold and many lands? Will they not wait for me to go first?'

'If you had gold and lands, we would have killed you ourselves years ago,' Aunty Ifeoma said.

My cousins laughed, and Amaka glanced at Jaja and me, perhaps wondering why we did not laugh, too. I wanted to smile, but we were driving past our house just then, and the sight of the looming black gates and white walls stiffened my lips.

'This is what our people say to the High God, the *Chukwu*,' Papa-Nnukwu said. 'Give me both wealth and a child, but if I must choose one, give me a child because when my child grows, so will my wealth.' Papa-Nnukwu stopped, turned to look back toward our house. '*Nekenem*, look at me. My son owns that house that can fit in every man in Abba, and yet many times I have nothing to put on my plate. I should not have let him follow those missionaries.'

'*Nna anyi*,' Aunty Ifeoma said. 'It was not the missionaries. Did I not go to the missionary school, too?'

'But you are a woman. You do not count.'

'Eh? So I don't count? Has Eugene ever asked about your aching leg? If I do not count, then I will stop asking if you rose well in the morning.'

Papa-Nnukwu chuckled. 'Then my spirit will haunt you when I join the ancestors.'

'It will haunt Eugene first.'

'I joke with you, *nwa m*. Where would I be today if my *chi* had not given me a daughter?' Papa Nnukwu paused. 'My spirit will intercede for you, so that *Chukwu* will send a good man to take care of you and the children.'

'Let your spirit ask *Chukwu* to hasten my promotion to senior lecturer, that is all I ask,' Aunty Ifeoma said.

Papa-Nnukwu did not reply for a while, and I wondered if the mix of high life music from the car radio and the rattling of the loose screws and the harmattan haze had eased him into sleep.

'Still, I say it was the missionaries that misled my son,' he said, startling me.

'We have heard this many times. Tell us something else,' Aunty Ifeoma said. But Papa-Nnukwu kept talking as though he had not heard her.

'I remember the first one that came to Abba, the one they called Fada John. His face was red like palm oil; they say our type of sun does not shine in the white man's land. He had a helper, a man from Nimo called Jude. In the afternoon they gathered the children under the ukwa tree in the mission and taught them their religion. I did not join them, *kpa*, but I went sometimes to see what they were doing. One day I said to them, Where is this god you worship? They said he was like *Chukwu*, that he was in the sky. I asked then, Who is the person that was killed, the person that hangs on the wood outside the mission? They said he was the son, but that the son and the father are equal. It was then that I knew that the white man was mad. The father and the son are equal? *Tufia!* Do you not see? That is why Eugene can disregard me, because he thinks we are equal.'

My cousins chuckled. So did Aunty Ifeoma, who soon stopped and said to Papa-Nnukwu, 'It is enough, close your mouth and rest. We are almost there and you will need your energy to tell the children about the *mmuo*.'

97

'Papa-Nnukwu, are you comfortable?' Amaka asked, leaning across toward the front seat. 'Do you want me to adjust your seat, to make more room for you?'

'No, I am fine. I am an old man now and my height is gone. I would not have fit in this car in my prime. In those days, I plucked *icheku* from the trees by just reaching out high; I did not need to climb.'

'Of course,' Aunty Ifeoma said, laughing again. 'And could you not reach out and touch the sky, too?'

She laughed so easily, so often. They all did, even little Chima.

When we got to Ezi Icheke, cars lined the road almost bumper to bumper. The crowds that pressed around the cars were so dense there was no space between people and they blended into one another, wrappers blended into T-shirts, trousers into skirts, dresses into shirts. Aunty Ifeoma finally found a spot and eased the station wagon in. The mmuo had started to walk past, and often a long line of cars waited for an mmuo to walk past so they could drive on. Hawkers were at every corner, with glass-enclosed cases of akara and suya and browned chicken drumsticks, with trays of peeled oranges, with coolers the size of bathtubs full of Walls banana ice cream. It was like a vibrant painting that had come alive. I had never been to see mmuo, to sit in a stationary car alongside thousands of people who had all come to watch. Papa had driven us past the crowds at Ezi Icheke once, some years ago, and he muttered about ignorant people participating in the ritual of pagan masquerades. He said that the stories about mmuo, that they were spirits who had climbed out of ant holes, that they could make chairs run and baskets hold water, were all devilish folklore. *Devilish Folklore*. It sounded dangerous the way Papa said it.

'Look at this,' Papa-Nnukwu said. 'This is a woman spirit, and the women *mmuo* are harmless. They do not even go near the big ones at the festival.' The mmuo he pointed to was small; its carved wooden face had angular, pretty features and rouged lips. It stopped often to dance, wiggling this way and that, so that the string of beads around its waist swayed and rippled. The crowds nearby cheered, and some people threw money toward it. Little boys – the followers of the mmuo who were playing music with metal ogenes and wooden ichakas – picked up the crumpled naira notes. They had hardly passed us when Papa Nnukwu shouted, 'Look away! Women cannot look at this one!'

The mmuo making its way down the road was surrounded by a few elderly men who rang a shrill bell as the mmuo walked. Its mask was a real, grimacing human skull with sunken eye sockets. A squirming tortoise was tied to its forehead. A snake and three dead chickens hung from its grass-covered body, swinging as the mmuo walked. The crowds near the road moved back quickly, fearfully.

A few women turned and dashed into nearby compounds.

Aunty Ifeoma looked amused, but she turned her head away. 'Don't look, girls. Let's humor your grandfather,' she said in English. Amaka had already looked away. I looked away, too, toward the crowd of people that pressed around the car. It was sinful, deferring to a heathen masquerade. But at least I had looked at it very briefly, so maybe it would technically not be deferring to a heathen masquerade.

'That is our *agwonatumbe*,' Papa-Nnukwu said, proudly, after the mmuo had walked past. 'It is the most powerful *mmuo* in our parts, and all the neighboring villages fear Abba because of it. At last year's Aro festival, *agwonatumbe* raised a staff and all the other *mmuo* turned and ran! They didn't even wait to see what would happen!'

'Look!' Obiora pointed at another mmuo moving down the road. It was like a floating white cloth, flat, taller than the huge avocado tree in our yard in Enugu. Papa-Nnukwu grunted as the mmuo went by. It was eerie, watching it, and I thought then of chairs running, their four legs knocking together, of water being held in a basket, of human forms climbing out of ant holes.

'How do they do that, Papa-Nnukwu? How do people get inside that one?' Jaja asked.

'Shh! These are *mmuo*, spirits! Don't speak like a woman!' Papa-Nnukwu snapped, turning to glare at Jaja.

Aunty Ifeoma laughed and spoke in English. 'Jaja, you're not supposed to say there are people in there. Didn't you know that?'

'No,' Jaja said.

She was watching Jaja. 'You didn't do the *ima mmuo*, did you? Obiora did it two years ago in his father's hometown.'

'No, I didn't,' Jaja mumbled.

I looked at Jaja and wondered if the dimness in his eyes was shame. I suddenly wished, for him, that he had done the ima mmuo, the initiation into the spirit world. I knew very little about it; women were not supposed to know anything at all, since it was the first step toward the initiation to manhood. But Jaja once told me that he heard that boys were flogged and made to bathe in the presence of a taunting crowd. The only time Papa had talked about ima mmuo was to say that the Christians who let their sons do it were confused, that they would end up in hellfire.

We left Ezi Icheke soon afterward. Aunty Ifeoma dropped off a sleepy Papa-Nnukwu first; his good eye was half closed while his going-blind eye stayed open, the film covering it looked thicker now, like concentrated milk. When Aunty Ifeoma stopped inside our compound, she asked her children if they wanted to come into the house, and Amaka said no, in a loud voice that seemed to prompt her brothers to say the same. Aunty Ifeoma took us in, waved to Papa, who was in the middle of a meeting, and hugged Jaja and me in her tight way before leaving.

That night, I dreamed that I was laughing, but it did not sound like my laughter, although I was not sure what my laughter sounded like. It was cackling and throaty and enthusiastic, like Aunty Ifeoma's.

P apa drove us to Christmas Mass at St Paul's. Aunty Ifeoma and her children were climbing into their station wagon as we drove into the sprawling church compound. They waited for Papa to stop the Mercedes and then came over to greet us. Aunty Ifeoma said they had gone to the early Mass and they would see us at lunchtime. She looked taller, even more fearless, in a red wrapper and high heels. Amaka wore the same bright red lipstick as her mother; it made her teeth seem whiter when she smiled and said, 'Merry Christmas.'

Although I tried to concentrate on Mass, I kept thinking of Amaka's lipstick, wondering what it felt like to run color over your lips. It was even harder to keep my mind on Mass because the priest, who spoke Igbo throughout, did not talk about the gospel during the sermon. Instead he talked about zinc and cement. 'You people think I ate the money for the zinc, *okwia*?' he shouted, gesticulating, pointing accusingly at the congregation. 'After all, how many of you give to this church, *gbo*? How can we build the house if you don't give? Do you think zinc and cement cost a mere ten *kobo*?'

Papa wished the priest would talk about something else, something about the birth in the manger, about the shepherds and the guiding star; I knew from the way Papa held his missal too tight, the way he shifted often on the pew. We were sitting in the first pew. An usher wearing a Blessed Virgin Mary medal on her white cotton dress had rushed forward to seat us, telling Papa in loud, urgent whispers that the front pews were reserved for the important people; Chief Umeadi, the only man in Abba whose house was bigger than ours, sat on our left, and His Royal Highness, the Igwe, was on our right. The Igwe came over to shake Papa's hand during Peace and Love, and he said, '*Nno nu*, I will stop by later, so we can greet properly.'

After Mass, we accompanied Papa to a fund-raising in the multipurpose hall next to the church building. It was for the priest's new house. An usher with a scarf tied tight across her forehead passed out pamphlets with pictures of the priest's old house, uncertain arrows pointing at where the roof leaked, where termites had eaten up the door frames. Papa wrote a check and handed it to the usher, telling her he did not want to make a speech. When the M.C. announced the amount, the priest got up and started to dance, jerking his behind this way and that, and the crowd rose up and cheered so loudly it was like the rumblings of thunder at the end of rainy season.

'Let's go,' Papa said, when the M.C. finally moved on to announce a new donation. He led the way out of the hall, smiling and waving at the many hands that reached out to grasp his white tunic as if touching him would heal them of an illness.

When we got home, all the couches and sofas in the living room were full; some people were perched on the side tables. The men and women all rose when Papa came in, and chants of *'Omelora!'* filled the air. Papa went about shaking hands and hugging and saying 'Merry Christmas' and 'God bless you.' Somebody had left the door that led to the backyard open, and the blue-gray firewood smoke that hung heavy in the living room blurred the facial features of the guests. I could hear the wives of the umunna, chattering in the backyard, scooping soup and stew from the huge pots on the fire into bowls that would be taken to serve the people.

'Come and greet the wives of our *umunna*,' Mama said to Jaja and me.

We followed her out to the backyard. The women clapped and hooted when Jaja and I said, *'Nno nu.'* Welcome.

They all looked alike, in ill-fitting blouses, threadbare wrappers, and scarves tied around their heads. They all had the same wide smile, the same chalk-colored teeth, the same sundried skin the color and texture of groundnut husks.

*'Nekene,* see the boy that will inherit his father's

riches!' one woman said, hooting even more loudly, her mouth shaped like a narrow tunnel.

'If we did not have the same blood in our veins, I would sell you my daughter,' another said to Jaja. She was squatting near the fire, arranging the firewood underneath the tripod. The others laughed.

'The girl is a ripe *agbogho*! Very soon a strong young man will bring us palm wine!' another said. Her dirty wrapper was not knotted properly, and one end trailed in the dirt as she walked, carrying a tray mounded with bits of fried beef.

'Go up and change,' Mama said, holding Jaja and me around the shoulders. 'Your aunty and cousins will be here soon.'

Upstairs, Sisi had set eight places at the dining table, with wide plates the color of caramel and matching napkins ironed into crisp triangles. Aunty Ifeoma and her children arrived while I was still changing out of my church clothes. I heard her loud laughter, and it echoed and went on for a while. I did not realize it was my cousins' laughter, the sound reflecting their mother's, until I went out to the living room. Mama, who was still in the pink, heavily sequined wrapper she had worn to church, sat next to Aunty Ifeoma on a couch. Jaja was talking to Amaka and Obiora near the étagère. I went over to join them, starting to pace my breathing so that I would not stutter.

'That's a stereo, isn't it? Why don't you play some music? Or are you bored with the stereo, too?' Amaka asked, her placid eyes darting from Jaja to me.

'Yes, it's a stereo,' Jaja said. He did not say that we never played it, that we never even thought to, that all we listened to was the news on Papa's radio during family time. Amaka went over and pulled out the LP drawer. Obiora joined her.

'No wonder you don't play the stereo, everything in here is so dull!' she said.

'They're not that dull,' Obiora said, looking through the LPs. He had a habit of pushing his thick glasses up the bridge of his nose. Finally he put one on, an Irish church choir singing 'O Come All Ye Faithful.' He seemed fascinated by the stereo player and, as the song played, stood watching it as if he would learn the secrets of its chrome entrails by staring hard at it.

Chima came into the room. 'The toilet here is so nice, Mommy. It has big mirrors and creams in glass bottles.'

'I hope you didn't break anything,' Aunty Ifeoma said.

'I didn't,' Chima said. 'Can we put the TV on?'

'No,' Aunty Ifeoma said. 'Your Uncle Eugene is coming up soon so we can have lunch.'

Sisi came into the room, smelling of food and spices, to tell Mama that the Igwe had arrived, that Papa wanted us all to come down and greet him. Mama rose, tightened her wrapper, and then waited for Aunty Ifeoma to lead the way.

'I thought the Igwe was supposed to stay at

his palace and receive guests. I didn't know he visits people's homes,' Amaka said, as we went downstairs. 'I guess that's because your father is a Big Man.'

I wished she had said 'Uncle Eugene' instead of 'your father.' She did not even look at me as she spoke. I felt, looking at her, that I was helplessly watching precious flaxen sand slip away between my fingers.

The Igwe's palace was a few minutes from our house. We had visited him once, some years back. We never visited him again, though, because Papa said that although the Igwe had converted, he still let his pagan relatives carry out sacrifices in his palace. Mama had greeted him the traditional way that women were supposed to, bending low and offering him her back so that he would pat it with his fan made of the soft, straw-colored tail of an animal. Back home that night, Papa told Mama that it was sinful. You did not bow to another human being. It was an ungodly tradition, bowing to an Igwe. So, a few days later, when we went to see the bishop at Awka, I did not kneel to kiss his ring. I wanted to make Papa proud. But Papa yanked my ear in the car and said I did not have the spirit of discernment: the bishop was a man of God; the Igwe was merely a traditional ruler.

'Good afternoon, sir, *nno*,' I said to the Igwe when I got downstairs. The hairs that peeked out of his wide nose quivered as he smiled at me and said, 'Our daughter, *kedu*?'

One of the smaller sitting rooms had been cleared for him and his wife and four assistants, one of whom was fanning him with a gilded fan although the air conditioner was on. Another was fanning his wife, a woman with yellow skin and rows and rows of jewelry hanging round her neck, gold pendants and beads and corals. The scarf wound around her head flared out in front, wide like a banana leaf and so high that I imagined the person sitting behind her in church having to stand up to see the altar.

I watched Aunty Ifeoma sink to one knee and say, *'Igwe!'* in the raised voice of a respectful salute, watched him pat her back. The gold sequins that covered his tunic glittered in the afternoon sunlight. Amaka bowed deeply before him. Mama, Jaja, and Obiora shook hands with him, respectfully enclosing his hand in both of theirs. I stood at the door a little longer, to make sure that Papa saw that I did not go close enough to the Igwe to bow to him.

Back upstairs, Mama and Aunty Ifeoma went into Mama's room. Chima and Obiora stretched out on the rug, playing with the whot cards that Obiora had discovered in his pockets. Amaka wanted to see a book Jaja told her he had brought, and they went into Jaja's room. I sat on the sofa, watching my cousins play with the cards. I did not understand the game, nor why at intervals one of them yelled 'Donkey!' amid laughter. The stereo had stopped. I got up and went into the hallway, standing by Mama's bedroom door. I wanted to go in and sit with Mama and Aunty Ifeoma, but instead I just stood still, listening. Mama was whispering; I could barely make out the words 'there are many full gas cylinders lying around in the factory.' She was trying to persuade Aunty Ifeoma to ask Papa for them.

Aunty Ifeoma was whispering, too, but I heard her well. Her whisper was like her – tall, exuberant, fearless, loud, larger than life. 'Have you forgotten that Eugene offered to buy me a car, even before Ifediora died? But first he wanted us to join the Knights of St John. He wanted us to send Amaka to convent school. He even wanted me to stop wearing makeup! I want a new car, *nwunye m*, and I want to use my gas cooker again and I want a new freezer and I want money so that I will not have to unravel the seams of Chima's trousers when he outgrows them. But I will not ask my brother to bend over so that I can lick his buttocks to get these things.'

'Ifeoma, if you . . .' Mama's soft voice trailed off again.

'You know why Eugene did not get along with Ifediora?' Aunty Ifeoma's whisper was back, fiercer, louder. 'Because Ifediora told him to his face what he felt. Ifediora was not afraid to tell the truth. But you know Eugene quarrels with the truths that he does not like. Our father is dying, do you hear me? Dying. He is an old man, how much longer does he have, *gbo*? Yet Eugene will not let him into

110

this house, will not even greet him. *O joka!* Eugene has to stop doing God's job. God is big enough to do his own job. If God will judge our father for choosing to follow the way of our ancestors, then let God do the judging, not Eugene.'

I heard the word *umunna*. Aunty Ifeoma laughed her throaty laugh before she replied. 'You know that the members of our *umunna*, in fact everybody in Abba, will tell Eugene only what he wants to hear. Do our people not have sense? Will you pinch the finger of the hand that feeds you?'

I did not hear Amaka come out of Jaja's room and walk toward me, perhaps because the hallway was so wide, until she said, so close that her breath fanned my neck, 'What are you doing?'

I jumped. 'Nothing.'

She was looking at me oddly, right in the eye. 'Your father has come upstairs for lunch,' she finally said.

Papa watched as we all sat down at the table, and then started grace. It was a little longer than usual, more than twenty minutes, and when he finally said, 'Through Christ our Lord,' Aunty Ifeoma raised her voice so that her 'Amen' stood out from the rest of ours.

'Did you want the rice to get cold, Eugene?' she muttered. Papa continued to unfold his napkin, as though he had not heard her.

The sounds of forks meeting plates, of serving spoons meeting platters, filled the dining room. Sisi had drawn the curtains and turned the chandelier on, even though it was afternoon. The yellow light made Obiora's eyes seem a deeper golden, like extra-sweet honey. The air conditioner was on, but I was hot.

Amaka piled almost everything on her dish – jollof rice, fufu and two different soups, fried chicken and beef, salad and cream – like someone who would not have an opportunity to eat again soon. Strips of lettuce reached across from the edge of her plate to touch the dining table.

'Do you always eat rice with a fork and a knife and napkins?' she asked, turning to watch me.

I nodded, keeping my eyes on my jollof rice. I wished Amaka would keep her voice low. I was not used to this kind of conversation at table.

'Eugene, you must let the children come and visit us in Nsukka,' Aunty Ifeoma said. 'We don't have a mansion, but at least they can get to know their cousins.'

'The children don't like to be away from home,' Papa said.

'That's because they have never been away from home. I'm sure they will like to see Nsukka. Jaja and Kambili, won't you?'

I mumbled to my plate, then started to cough as if real, sensible words would have come out of my mouth but for the coughing.

'If Papa says it is all right,' Jaja said. Papa smiled at Jaja, and I wished I had said that.

'Maybe the next time they are on holiday,' Papa said, firmly. He expected Aunty Ifeoma to let it go.

'Eugene, *biko*, let the children come and spend one week with us. They do not resume school until late January. Let your driver bring them to Nsukka.'

'*Ngwanu*, we will see,' Papa said. He spoke Igbo for the first time, his brows almost meeting in a quick frown.

'Ifeoma was saying that they just called off a strike,' Mama said.

'Are things getting any better in Nsukka?' Papa asked, reverting to English. 'The university is living on past glory nowadays.'

Aunty Ifeoma narrowed her eyes. 'Have you ever picked up the phone and called me to ask me that question, eh, Eugene? Will your hands wither away if you pick up the phone one day and call your sister, *gbo*?' Her Igbo words had a teasing lilt, but the steeliness in her tone created a knot in my throat.

'I did call you, Ifeoma.'

'How long ago was that? I ask you – how long ago was that?' Aunty Ifeoma put her fork down. She sat still for a long, tense moment, as still as Papa was, as still as we all were. Finally Mama cleared her throat and asked Papa if the bottle of juice was empty.

'Yes,' Papa said. 'Ask that girl to bring more bottled juice.'

Mama got up to call Sisi. The long bottles Sisi brought looked as though they contained an elegant liquid, the way they tapered like a slender,

113

shapely woman. Papa poured for everyone and proposed a toast. 'To the spirit of Christmas and to the glory of God.'

We repeated him in a chorus. Obiora's sentence had a lift at the end, and it came out sounding like a question: 'to the glory of God?'

'And to us, and to the spirit of family,' Aunty Ifeoma added, before she drank.

'Does your factory make this, Uncle Eugene?' Amaka asked, squinting to see what was written on the bottles.

'Yes,' Papa answered.

'It's a little too sweet. It would be nicer if you reduced the sugar in it.' Amaka's tone was as polite and normal as everyday conversation with an older person. I was not sure if Papa nodded or if his head simply moved as he chewed. Another knot formed in my throat, and I could not get a mouthful of rice down. I knocked my glass over as I reached for it, and the blood-colored juice crept over the white lace tablecloth. Mama hastily placed a napkin on the spot, and when she raised the reddened napkin, I remembered her blood on the stairs.

'Did you hear about Aokpe, Uncle Eugene?' Amaka asked. 'It's a tiny village in Benue. The Blessed Virgin is appearing there.'

I wondered how Amaka did it, how she opened her mouth and had words flow easily out.

Papa spent some time chewing and swallowing before he said, 'Yes, I heard about it.'

114

'I plan to go on pilgrimage there with the children,' Aunty Ifeoma said. 'Maybe Kambili and Jaja can go with us.'

Amaka looked up quickly, surprised. She started to say something and then stopped.

'Well, the church has not verified the authenticity of the apparitions,' Papa said, staring thoughtfully at his plate.

'You know we will all be dead before the church officially speaks about Aokpe,' Aunty Ifeoma said. 'Even if the church says it is not authentic, what matters is why we go, and it is from faith.'

Papa looked unexpectedly pleased with what Aunty Ifeoma had said. He nodded slowly. 'When do you plan to go?'

'Sometime in January, before the children resume school.'

'Okay. I will call you when we get back to Enugu to arrange for Jaja and Kambili to go for a day or two.'

'A week, Eugene, they will stay a week. I do not have monsters that eat human heads in my house!' Aunty Ifeoma laughed, and her children reproduced the throaty sounds, their teeth flashing like the insides of a cracked palm kernel. Only Amaka did not laugh.

The next day was a Sunday. It did not seem like a Sunday, maybe because we had just gone to church on Christmas day. Mama came into my room and shook me gently, hugged me, and I smelled her mint-scented deodorant.

'Did you sleep well? We are going to the earlier Mass today because your father has a meeting right afterward. *Kunie*, get into the bathroom, it's past seven.'

I yawned and sat up. There was a red stain on my bed, wide as an open notebook.

'Your period,' Mama said. 'Did you bring pads?'

'Yes.'

I barely let the water run over my body before I came out of the shower, so that I would not delay. I picked out a blue-and-white dress and tied a blue scarf around my head. I knotted it twice at the back of my neck and then tucked the ends of my cornrows underneath. Once, Papa had hugged me proudly, kissed my forehead, because Father Benedict told him that my hair was always properly covered for Mass, that I was not like the other young girls in church who let some of their hair show, as if they did not know that exposing your hair in church was ungodly.

Jaja and Mama were dressed and waiting in the living room upstairs when I came out. Cramps racked my belly. I imagined someone with buck-teeth rhythmically biting deep into my stomach walls and letting go. 'Do you have Panadol, Mama?'

'Cramps *abia*?'

'Yes. My stomach is so empty, too.'

Mama looked at the wall clock, a gift from a charity Papa donated to, oval shaped and embossed

116

with his name in gold lettering. It was 7:37. The Eucharist fast mandated that the faithful not eat solid food an hour before Mass. We never broke the Eucharistic fast; the table was set for breakfast with teacups and cereal bowls side by side, but we would not eat until we came home.

'Eat a little corn flakes, quickly,' Mama said, almost in a whisper. 'You need something in your stomach to hold the Panadol.'

Jaja poured the cereal from the carton on the table, scooped in powdered milk and sugar with a teaspoon, and added water. The glass bowl was transparent, and I could see the chalky clumps the milk made with the water at the bottom of the bowl.

'Papa is with visitors, we will hear him as he comes up,' he said.

I started to wolf the cereal down, standing. Mama gave me the Panadol tablets, still in the silver-colored foil, which crinkled as I opened it. Jaja had not put much cereal in the bowl, and I was almost done eating it when the door opened and Papa came in.

Papa's white shirt, with its perfectly tailored lines, did little to minimize the mound of flesh that was his stomach. While he stared at the glass bowl of corn flakes in my hand, I looked down at the few flaccid flakes floating among the clumps of milk and wondered how he had climbed the stairs so soundlessly.

'What are you doing, Kambili?'

I swallowed hard. 'I . . . I . . .'

'You are eating ten minutes before Mass? Ten minutes before Mass?'

'Her period started and she has cramps—' Mama said.

Jaja cut her short. 'I told her to eat corn flakes before she took Panadol, Papa. I made it for her.'

'Has the devil asked you all to go on errands for him?' The Igbo words burst out of Papa's mouth. 'Has the devil built a tent in my house?' He turned to Mama. 'You sit there and watch her desecrate the Eucharistic fast, *maka nnidi*?'

He unbuckled his belt slowly. It was a heavy belt made of layers of brown leather with a sedate leather-covered buckle. It landed on Jaja first, across his shoulder. Then Mama raised her hands as it landed on her upper arm, which was covered by the puffy sequined sleeve of her church blouse. I put the bowl down just as the belt landed on my back. Sometimes I watched the Fulani nomads, white jellabas flapping against their legs in the wind, making clucking sounds as they herded their cows across the roads in Enugu with a switch, each smack of the switch swift and precise. Papa was like a Fulani nomad – although he did not have their spare, tall body – as he swung his belt at Mama, Jaja, and me, muttering that the devil would not win. We did not move more than two steps away from the leather belt that swished through the air.

Then the belt stopped, and Papa stared at the leather in his hand. His face crumpled; his eyelids

118

sagged. 'Why do you walk into sin?' he asked. 'Why do you like sin?'

Mama took the belt from him and laid it on the table.

Papa crushed Jaja and me to his body. 'Did the belt hurt you? Did it break your skin?' he asked, examining our faces. I felt a throbbing on my back, but I said no, that I was not hurt. It was the way Papa shook his head when he talked about liking sin, as if something weighed him down, something he could not throw off.

We went to the later Mass. But first we changed our clothes, even Papa, and washed our faces.

We left Abba right after New Year's. The wives of the umunna took the leftover food, even the cooked rice and beans that Mama said were spoiled, and they knelt in the backyard dirt to thank Papa and Mama. The gate man waved with both hands over his head as we drove off. His name was Haruna, he had told Jaja and me a few days before, and in his Hausa-accented English that reversed $P$ and $F$, he told us that our pather was the best Big Man he had ever seen, the best emfloyer he had ever had. Did we know our pather faid his children's school pees? Did we know our pather had helfed his wipe get the messenger job at the Local Government oppice? We were lucky to have such a pather.

Papa started the rosary as we drove onto the expressway. We had driven for less than half an hour when we came to a checkpoint; there was a traffic jam, and policemen, many more than was usual, were waving their guns and diverting traffic. We didn't see the cars involved in the accident until we were in the thick of the jam. One car had stopped at the checkpoint, and another had rammed into it from behind. The second car was crushed to half of its size. A bloodied corpse, a man in blue jeans, lay on the roadside.

'May his soul rest in peace,' Papa said, crossing himself.

'Look away,' Mama said, turning back to us.

But Jaja and I were already looking at the corpse. Papa was talking about the policemen, about how they set up the roadblocks in wooded parts, even if it was dangerous for motorists, just so that they could use the bushes to hide the money they extorted from travelers. But I was not really listening to Papa; I was thinking of the man in the blue jeans, the dead man. I was wondering where he was going and what he had planned to do there.

Papa called Aunty Ifeoma two days later. Perhaps he would not have called her if we had not gone to confession that day. And perhaps then we would never have gone to Nsukka and everything would have remained the same.

It was the feast of the Epiphany, a holy day of obligation, so Papa did not go to work. We went to morning Mass, and although we did not usually visit Father Benedict on holy days of obligation, we went to his house afterward. Papa wanted Father Benedict to hear our confession. We had not gone in Abba because Papa did not like to make his confession in Igbo, and besides, Papa said that the parish priest in Abba was not spiritual enough. That was the problem with our people, Papa told us, our priorities were wrong; we cared too much about huge church buildings and mighty statues. You would never see white people doing that.

In Father Benedict's house, Mama and Jaja and I sat in the living room, reading the newspapers and magazines that were spread on the low, coffinlike table as if they were for sale while Papa talked with Father Benedict in the adjoining study room. Papa emerged and asked us to prepare for confession; he would go first. Even though Papa shut the door firmly, I heard his voice, words flowing into each other in an endless rumble like a revving car engine. Mama went next, and the door remained open a crack, but I could not hear her. Jaja took the shortest time. When he came out, still crossing himself as if he had been in too much of a hurry to leave the room, I asked him with my eyes if he had remembered the lie to Papa-Nnukwu, and he nodded. I went into the room, barely big enough to hold a desk and two chairs, and pushed the door to make sure it shut properly.

'Bless me, Father, for I have sinned,' I said,

sitting on the very edge of the chair. I longed for a confessional, for the safety of the wood cubicle and the green curtain that separated priest and penitent. I wished I could kneel, and then I wished I could shield my face with a file from Father Benedict's desk. Face-to-face confessions made me think of Judgment Day come early, made me feel unprepared.

'Yes, Kambili,' Father Benedict said. He sat upright on his chair, fingering the purple stole across his shoulders.

'It has been three weeks since my last confession,' I said. I was staring fixedly at the wall, right below the framed photo of the Pope, which had a signature scrawled underneath. 'Here are my sins. I lied two times. I broke the Eucharistic fast once. I lost concentration during the rosary three times. For all I have said and for all I have forgotten to say, I beg pardon from your hands and the hands of God.'

Father Benedict shifted on his chair. 'Go on, then. You know it's a sin against the Holy Spirit to willfully keep something back at confession.'

'Yes, Father.'

'Go on, then.'

I looked away from the wall to glance at him. His eyes were the same green shade of a snake I had seen once, slithering across the yard near the hibiscus bushes. The gardener had said it was a harmless garden snake.

'Kambili, you must confess all your sins.'

'Yes, Father. I have.'

'It is wrong to hide from the Lord. I will give you a moment to think.'

I nodded and stared back at the wall. Was there something I had done that Father Benedict knew about that I did not know? Had Papa told him something?

'I spent more than fifteen minutes at my grandfather's house,' I said finally. 'My grandfather is a pagan.'

'Did you eat any of the native foods sacrificed to idols?'

'No, Father.'

'Did you participate in any pagan rituals?'

'No, Father.' I paused. 'But we looked at *mmuo*. Masquerades.'

'Did you enjoy that?'

I looked up at the photo on the wall and wondered if the Pope himself had actually signed it. 'Yes, Father.'

'You understand that it is wrong to take joy in pagan rituals, because it breaks the first commandment. Pagan rituals are misinformed superstition, and they are the gateway to Hell. Do you understand that, then?'

'Yes, Father.'

'For your penance say the Our Father ten times, Hail Mary six times, and the Apostles' Creed once. And you must make a conscious effort to convert everyone who enjoys the ways of heathens.'

'Yes, Father.'

'All right, then, make the Act of Contrition.'

While I recited the Act of Contrition, Father Benedict murmured blessings and made the sign of the cross.

Papa and Mama were still sitting on the sofa, heads bent, when I came out. I sat next to Jaja, bent my head, and made my penance.

As we drove home, Papa talked loudly, above the 'Ave Maria.' 'I am spotless now, we are all spotless. If God calls us right now, we are going straight to Heaven. Straight to Heaven. We will not require the cleansing of Purgatory.' He was smiling, his eyes bright, his hand gently drumming the steering wheel. And he was still smiling when he called Aunty Ifeoma soon after we got back home, before he had his tea.

'I discussed it with Father Benedict, and he says the children can go on pilgrimage to Aokpe but you must make it clear that what is happening there has not been verified by the church.' A pause. 'My driver, Kevin, will take them.' A pause. 'Tomorrow is too soon. The day after.' A long pause. 'Oh, all right. God bless you and the children. Bye.'

Papa put the phone down and turned to us. 'You will leave tomorrow, so go up and pack your things. Pack for five days.'

'Yes, Papa,' Jaja and I said together.

'Maybe, *anam asi*,' Mama said, 'they should not visit Ifeoma's house empty-handed.'

Papa stared at her as if surprised that she had

124

spoken. 'We will put some food in the car, of course, yams and rice,' he said.

'Ifeoma mentioned that gas cylinders were scarce in Nsukka.'

'Gas cylinders?'

'Yes, cooking gas. She said she uses her old kerosene stove now. You remember the story of adulterated kerosene that was blowing up stoves and killing people? I thought maybe you might send one or two gas cylinders to her from the factory.'

'Is that what you and Ifeoma planned?'

'*Kpa*, I am just making a suggestion. It is up to you to decide.'

Papa examined Mama's face for a while. 'Okay,' he said. He turned back to Jaja and me. 'Go up and pack your things. You can take twenty minutes from your study time.'

We climbed the curving stairs slowly. I wondered if Jaja's stomach rumbled at the lower part like mine did. It was the first time in our lives that we would be sleeping outside home without Papa.

'Do you want to go to Nsukka?' I asked when we got to the landing,.

'Yes,' he said, and his eyes said that he knew I did, too. And I could not find the words in our eye language to tell him how my throat tightened at the thought of five days without Papa's voice, without his footsteps on the stairs.

★   ★   ★

125

The next morning, Kevin brought two full gas cylinders from Papa's factory and put them into the boot of the Volvo alongside bags of rice and beans, a few yams, bunches of green plantains, and pineapples. Jaja and I stood by the hibiscus bushes, waiting. The gardener was clipping away at the bougainvillea, taming the flowers that defiantly stuck out of the leveled top. He had raked underneath the frangipani trees, and dead leaves and pink flowers lay in piles, ready for the wheelbarrow.

'Here are your schedules for the week you will stay in Nsukka,' Papa said. The sheet of paper he thrust into my hand was similar to the schedule pasted above my study desk upstairs, except he had penciled in two hours of 'time with your cousins' each day.

'The only day you are excused from that schedule is when you go to Aokpe with your aunt,' Papa said. When he hugged Jaja and then me, his hands were shaking. 'I have never been without you two for more than a day.'

I did not know what to say, but Jaja nodded and said, 'We will see you in a week.'

'Kevin, drive carefully. Do you understand?' Papa asked, as we got in the car.

'Yes, sir.'

'Get petrol on your way back, at Ninth Mile, and don't forget to bring me the receipt.'

'Yes, sir.'

Papa asked us to get out of the car. He hugged us both again, smoothed the back of our necks, and asked us not to forget to say the full fifteen decades of the rosary during the drive. Mama hugged us one more time before we got back in the car.

'Papa is still waving,' Jaja said, as Kevin nosed the car up the driveway. He was looking in the mirror above his head.

'He's crying,' I said.

'The gardener is waving, too,' Jaja said, and I wondered if he had really not heard me. I pulled my rosary from my pocket, kissed the crucifix, and started the prayer.

I looked out the window as we drove, counting the blackened hulks of cars on the roadside, some left for so long they were covered with reddish rust. I wondered about the people who had been inside, how they had felt just before the accident, before the smashing glass and crunched metal and leaping flames. I did not concentrate on any of the glorious Mysteries, and knew that Jaja did not, either, because he kept forgetting when it was his turn to start a decade of the rosary. About forty minutes into the drive, I saw a sign on the roadside that read UNIVERSITY OF NIGERIA, NSUKKA, and I asked Kevin if we were almost there.

'No,' he said. 'A little while longer.'

Near the town of Opi – the dust-covered church and school signs read OPI – we came to a police checkpoint. Old tires and nail-studded logs were strewn across most of the road, leaving only a narrow space. A policeman flagged us down as we approached. Kevin groaned. Then as he slowed, he reached into the glove compartment and pulled out a ten-naira note and flung it out of the window,

128

toward the policeman. The policeman gave a mock salute, smiled, and waved us through. Kevin would not have done that if Papa had been in the car. When policemen or soldiers stopped Papa, he spent so long showing them all his car papers, letting them search his car, anything but bribe them to let him pass. We cannot be part of what we fight, he often told us.

'We're entering the town of Nsukka,' Kevin said, a few minutes later. We were driving past the market. The crowded roadside stores with their sparse shelves of goods threatened to spill over onto a thin strip of road already full of double-parked cars, hawkers with trays balanced on their heads, motorcyclists, boys pushing wheelbarrows full of yams, women holding baskets, beggars looking up from their mats and waving. Kevin drove slowly now; potholes suddenly materialized in the middle of the road, and he followed the swerving motion of the car ahead of us. When we came to a point just past the market where the road had narrowed, eaten away by erosion at the sides, he stopped for a while to let other cars go by.

'We're at the university,' he said, finally.

A wide arch towered over us, bearing the words *University of Nigeria Nsukka* in black, cut-out metal. The gates underneath the arch were flung wide open and manned by security men in dark brown uniforms and matching berets. Kevin stopped and rolled down the windows.

'Good afternoon. Please, how can we get to Marguerite Cartwright Avenue?' he asked.

The security man closest to us, his facial skin creased like a rumpled dress, asked, 'How are you?' before he told Kevin that Marguerite Cartwright Avenue was very close; we had only to keep straight and then make a right at the first junction and an almost immediate left. Kevin thanked him and we drove off. A lawn the color of spinach splashed across the side of the road. I turned to stare at the statue in the middle of the lawn, a black lion standing on its hind legs, tail curved upward, chest puffed out. I didn't realize Jaja was looking, too, until he read aloud the words inscribed on the pedestal: ' "To restore the dignity of man." ' Then, as though I could not tell, he added, 'It's the university's motto.'

Marguerite Cartwright Avenue was bordered by tall gmelina trees. I imagined the trees bending during a rainy-season thunderstorm, reaching across to touch each other and turning the avenue into a dark tunnel. The duplexes with gravel-covered driveways and BEWARE OF DOGS signs in the front yard soon gave way to bungalows with driveways the length of two cars and then blocks of flats with wide stretches of space in front of them instead of driveways. Kevin drove slowly, muttering Aunty Ifeoma's house number as if that would make us find it sooner. It was in the fourth block we came to, a tall, bland building with peeling blue paint and with television aerials sticking out from the verandahs. It had three flats on each side, and Aunty Ifeoma's was on the ground floor on the left. In front was a circular burst of bright colors – a garden – fenced around with barbed wire. Roses and hibiscuses and lilies and ixora and croton grew side by side like a hand-painted wreath. Aunty Ifeoma emerged from the flat in a pair of shorts, rubbing her hands over the front of her T-shirt. The skin at her knees was very dark.

'Jaja! Kambili!' She barely waited for us to climb out of the car before hugging us, squeezing us close together so we both fit in the stretch of her arms.

'Good afternoon, Mah,' Kevin greeted before he went around to open the boot.

'Ah! Ah!' Aunty Ifeoma said. 'Does Eugene think we are starving? Even a bag of rice?'

Kevin smiled. '*Oga* said it is to greet you, Mah.'

'Hei!' Aunty yelped, looking into the boot. 'Gas cylinders? Oh, *nwunye m* should not have bothered herself so much.' Then Aunty Ifeoma did a little dance, moving her arms in rowing motions, throwing each leg in front of her and stamping down hard.

Kevin stood by and rubbed his hands together in pleasure, as if he had orchestrated the big surprise. He hoisted a gas cylinder out of the boot, and Jaja helped him carry it into the flat.

'Your cousins will be back soon, they went out to say happy birthday to Father Amadi, he's our friend and he works at our chaplaincy. I have been cooking, I even killed a chicken for you two!' Aunty Ifeoma laughed and pulled me to her. She smelled of nutmeg.

'Where do we place these, Mah?' Kevin asked.

'Just leave the things on the verandah. Amaka and Obiora will put them away later.'

Aunty Ifeoma still held on to me as we entered the living room. I noticed the ceiling first, how low it was. I felt I could reach out and touch it; it was so unlike home, where the high ceilings gave our rooms an airy stillness. The pungent fumes of kerosene smoke mixed with the aroma of curry and nutmeg from the kitchen.

'Let me see if my jollof rice is burning!' Aunty Ifeoma dashed into the kitchen.

I sat down on the brown sofa. The seams of the cushions were frayed and slipping apart. It was the only sofa in the living room; next to it were cane chairs, softened with brown cushions. The center table was cane, too, supporting an oriental vase with pictures of kimono-clad dancing women. Three long-stemmed roses, so piercingly red I wondered if they were plastic, were in the vase.

'*Nne*, don't behave like a guest. Come in, come in,' Aunty Ifeoma said, coming out from the kitchen.

I followed her down a short hallway lined with crammed bookshelves. The gray wood looked as though it would collapse if just one more book were added. Each book looked clean; they were all either read often or dusted often.

'This is my room. I sleep here with Chima,' Aunty Ifeoma said, opening the first door. Cartons and bags of rice were stacked against the wall near the door. A tray held giant tins of dried milk and Bournvita, near a study table with a reading lamp, bottles of medicine, books. At another corner, suitcases were piled on top of one another. Aunty Ifeoma led the way to another room, with two beds along one wall. They were pushed together to create space for more than two people. Two dressers, a mirror, and a study desk and chair managed to fit in also. I wondered where Jaja and I would be sleeping, and as if Aunty Ifeoma had read my thoughts, she said, 'You and Amaka will sleep here, *nne*. Obiora sleeps in the living room, so Jaja will stay with him.'

I heard Kevin and Jaja come into the flat.

'We have finished bringing the things in, Mah. I'm leaving now,' Kevin said. He spoke from the living room, but the flat was so small he did not have to raise his voice.

'Tell Eugene I said thank you. Tell him we are well. Drive carefully.'

'Yes, Mah.'

I watched Kevin leave, and suddenly my chest felt tight. I wanted to run after him, to tell him to wait while I got my bag and got back in the car.

'*Nne*, Jaja, come and join me in the kitchen until your cousins come back.' Aunty Ifeoma sounded so casual, as if it were completely normal to have us visit, as if we had visited so many times in the past. Jaja led the way into the kitchen and sat down on a low wooden stool. I stood by the door because there was hardly enough room in the kitchen not to get in her way, as she drained rice at the sink, checked on the cooking meat, blended tomatoes in a mortar. The light blue kitchen tiles were worn and chipped at the corners, but they looked scrubbed clean, as did the pots, whose lids did not fit, one side slipping crookedly into the pot. The kerosene stove was on a wooden table by the window. The walls near the window and the threadbare curtains had turned black-gray from the kerosene smoke. Aunty Ifeoma chattered as she put the rice back on the stove and chopped two purple onions, her stream of sentences punctuated by her cackling laughter. She seemed to be laughing and crying at the same time because she reached up often to brush away the onion tears with the back of her hand.

Her children came in a few minutes later. They looked different, maybe because I was seeing them for the first time in their own home rather than in Abba, where they were visitors in Papa-Nnukwu's house. Obiora took off a dark pair of sunglasses and slipped them in the pockets of his shorts as they came in. He laughed when he saw me.

'Jaja and Kambili are here!' Chima piped.

We all hugged in greeting, brief clasps of our bodies. Amaka barely let her sides meet mine before she backed away. She was wearing lipstick, a different shade that was more red than brown, and her dress was molded to her lean body.

'How was the drive down here?' she asked, looking at Jaja.

'Fine,' Jaja said. 'I thought it would be longer than it was.'

'Oh, Enugu really isn't that far from here,' Amaka said.

'We still haven't bought the soft drinks, Mom,' Obiora said.

'Did I not tell you to buy them before you left, *gbo*?' Aunty Ifeoma slid the onion slices into hot oil and stepped back.

'I'll go now. Jaja, do you want to come with me? We're just going to a kiosk in the next compound.'

'Don't forget to take empty bottles,' Aunty Ifeoma said.

I watched Jaja leave with Obiora. I could not see his face, could not tell if he felt as bewildered as I did.

'Let me go and change, Mom, and I'll fry the plantains,' Amaka said, turning to leave.

'*Nne*, go with your cousin,' Aunty Ifeoma said to me.

I followed Amaka to her room, placing one frightened foot after the next. The cement floors were rough, did not let my feet glide over them the way the smooth marble floors back home did. Amaka took her earrings off, placed them on top of the dresser, and looked at herself in the full-length mirror. I sat on the edge of the bed, watching her, wondering if she knew that I had followed her into the room.

'I'm sure you think Nsukka is uncivilized compared to Enugu,' she said, still looking in the mirror. 'I told Mom to stop forcing you both to come.'

'I . . . we . . . wanted to come.'

Amaka smiled into the mirror, a thin, patronizing smile that seemed to say I should not have bothered lying to her. 'There's no happening place in Nsukka, in case you haven't realized that already. Nsukka has no Genesis or Nike Lake.'

'What?'

'Genesis and Nike Lake, the happening places in Enugu. You go there all the time, don't you?'

'No.'

Amaka gave me an odd look. 'But you go once in a while?'

'I . . . yes.' I had never been to the restaurant Genesis and had only been to the hotel Nike Lake when Papa's business partner had a wedding reception there. We had stayed only long enough for Papa to take pictures with the couple and give them a present.

Amaka picked up a comb and ran it through the ends of her short hair. Then she turned to me and asked, 'Why do you lower your voice?'

'What?'

'You lower your voice when you speak. You talk in whispers.'

'Oh.' I said, my eyes focused on the desk, which

136

was full of things – books, a cracked mirror, felt-tipped pens.

Amaka put the comb down and pulled her dress over her head. In her white lacy bra and light blue underwear, she looked like a Hausa goat: brown, long and lean. I quickly averted my gaze. I had never seen anyone undress; it was sinful to look upon another person's nakedness.

'I'm sure this is nothing close to the sound system in your room in Enugu,' Amaka said. She pointed at the small cassette player at the foot of the dresser. I wanted to tell her that I did not have any kind of music system in my room back home, but I was not sure she would be pleased to hear that, just as she would not be pleased to hear it if I did have one.

She turned the cassette player on, nodding to the polyphonic beat of drums. 'I listen mostly to indigenous musicians. They're culturally conscious; they have something real to say. Fela and Osadebe and Onyeka are my favorites. Oh, I'm sure you probably don't know who they are, I'm sure you're into American pop like other teenagers.' She said 'teenagers' as if she were not one, as if teenagers were a brand of people who, by not listening to culturally conscious music, were a step beneath her. And she said 'culturally conscious' in the proud way that people say a word they never knew they would learn until they do.

I sat still on the edge of the bed, hands clasped, wanting to tell Amaka that I did not own a cassette player, that I could hardly tell any kinds of pop music apart.

'Did you paint this?' I asked, instead. The water-color painting of a woman with a child was much like a copy of the Virgin and Child oil painting that hung in Papa's bedroom, except the woman and child in Amaka's painting were dark-skinned.

'Yes, I paint sometimes.'

'It's nice.' I wished that I had known that my cousin painted realistic watercolors. I wished that she would not keep looking at me as if I were a strange laboratory animal to be explained and catalogued.

'Did something hold you girls in there?' Aunty Ifeoma called from the kitchen.

I followed Amaka back to the kitchen and watched her slice and fry the plantains. Jaja soon came back with the boys, the bottles of soft drinks in a black plastic bag. Aunty Ifeoma asked Obiora to set the table. 'Today we'll treat Kambili and Jaja as guests, but from tomorrow they will be family and join in the work,' she said.

The dining table was made of wood that cracked in dry weather. The outermost layer was shedding, like a molting cricket, brown slices curling up from the surface. The dining chairs were mismatched. Four were made of plain wood, the kind of chairs in my classroom, and the other two were black and padded. Jaja and I sat side by side. Aunty Ifeoma said the grace, and after my cousins said 'Amen,' I still had my eyes closed.

'*Nne*, we have finished praying. We do not say Mass in the name of grace like your father does,' Aunty Ifeoma said with a chuckle.

I opened my eyes, just in time to catch Amaka watching me.

'I hope Kambili and Jaja come every day so we can eat like this. Chicken and soft drinks!' Obiora pushed at his glasses as he spoke.

'Mommy! I want the chicken leg,' Chima said.

'I think these people have started to put less Coke in the bottles,' Amaka said, holding her Coke bottle back to examine it.

I looked down at the jollof rice, fried plantains, and half of a drumstick on my plate and tried to concentrate, tried to get the food down. The plates, too, were mismatched. Chima and Obiora used plastic ones while the rest of us had plain glass plates, bereft of dainty flowers or silver lines. Laughter floated over my head. Words spurted from everyone, often not seeking and not getting any response. We always spoke with a purpose back home, especially at the table, but my cousins seemed to simply speak and speak and speak.

'Mom, *biko*, give me the neck,' Amaka said.

'Didn't you talk me out of the neck the last time, *gbo*?' Aunty Ifeoma asked, and then she picked up the chicken neck on her plate and reached across to place it on Amaka's plate.

'When was the last time we ate chicken?' Obiora asked.

'Stop chewing like a goat, Obiora!' Aunty Ifeoma said.

'Goats chew differently when they ruminate and when they eat, Mom. Which do you mean?'

I looked up to watch Obiora chewing.

'Kambili, is something wrong with the food?' Aunty Ifeoma asked, startling me. I had felt as if I were not there, that I was just observing a table where you could say anything at any time to anyone, where the air was free for you to breathe as you wished.

'I like the rice, Aunty, thank you.'

'If you like the rice, eat the rice,' Aunty Ifeoma said.

'Maybe it is not as good as the fancy rice she eats at home,' Amaka said.

'Amaka, leave your cousin alone,' Aunty Ifeoma said.

I did not say anything else until lunch was over, but I listened to every word spoken, followed every cackle of laughter and line of banter. Mostly, my cousins did the talking and Aunty Ifeoma sat back and watched them, eating slowly. She looked like a football coach who had done a good job with her team and was satisfied to stand next to the eighteen-yard box and watch.

After lunch, I asked Amaka where I could ease myself, although I knew that the toilet was the door opposite the bedroom. She seemed irritated by my question and gestured vaguely toward the hall, asking, 'Where else do you think?'

The room was so narrow I could touch both walls if I stretched out my hands. There were no soft rugs, no furry cover for the toilet seat and lid like we had back home. An empty plastic bucket was near the toilet. After I urinated, I wanted to flush but the cistern was empty; the lever went limply up and down. I stood in the narrow room for a few minutes before leaving to look for Aunty Ifeoma. She was in the kitchen, scrubbing the sides of the kerosene stove with a soapy sponge.

'I will be very miserly with my new gas cylinders,' Aunty Ifeoma said, smiling, when she saw me. 'I'll use them only for special meals, so they will last long. I'm not packing away this kerosene stove just yet.'

I paused because what I wanted to say was so far removed from gas cookers and kerosene stoves. I could hear Obiora's laughter from the verandah.

'Aunty, there's no water to flush the toilet.'

'You urinated?'

'Yes.'

'Our water only runs in the morning, *o di egwu*. So we don't flush when we urinate, only when there is actually something to flush. Or sometimes, when the water does not run for a few days, we just close the lid until everybody has gone and then we flush with one bucket. It saves water.' Aunty Ifeoma was smiling ruefully.

'Oh,' I said.

Amaka had come in as Aunty Ifeoma spoke. I watched her walk to the refrigerator. 'I'm sure that back home you flush every hour, just to keep the water fresh, but we don't do that here,' she said.

'Amaka, *o gini*? I don't like that tone!' Aunty Ifeoma said.

'Sorry,' Amaka muttered, pouring cold water from a plastic bottle into a glass.

I moved closer to the wall darkened by kerosene smoke, wishing I could blend into it and disappear. I wanted to apologize to Amaka, but I was not sure what for.

'Tomorrow, we will take Kambili and Jaja around to show them the campus,' Aunty Ifeoma said, sounding so normal that I wondered if I had just imagined the raised voice.

'There's nothing to see. They will be bored.'

The phone rang then, loud and jarring, unlike the muted purr of ours back home. Aunty Ifeoma hurried to her bedroom to pick it up. 'Kambili! Jaja!' she called out a moment later. I knew it was Papa. I waited for Jaja to come in from the verandah so we could go in together. When we got to the phone, Jaja stood back and gestured that I speak first.

'Hello, Papa. Good evening,' I said, and then I wondered if he could tell that I had eaten after saying a too short prayer.

'How are you?'

'Fine, Papa.'

'The house is empty without you.'

'Oh.'

'Do you need anything?'

'No, Papa.'

'Call at once if you need anything, and I will send Kevin. I'll call every day. Remember to study and pray.'

'Yes, Papa.'

When Mama came on the line, her voice sounded louder than her usual whisper, or perhaps it was just the phone. She told me Sisi had forgotten we were away and cooked lunch for four.

When Jaja and I sat down to have dinner that evening, I thought about Papa and Mama, sitting alone at our wide dining table. We had the left-over rice and chicken. We drank water because the soft drinks bought in the afternoon were finished. I thought about the always full crates of Coke and Fanta and Sprite in the kitchen store back home and then quickly gulped my water down as if I could wash away the thoughts. I knew that if Amaka could read thoughts, mine would not please her. There was less talk and laughter at dinner because the TV was on and my cousins took their plates to the living room. The older two ignored the sofa and chairs to settle on the floor while Chima curled up on the sofa, balancing his plastic plate on his lap. Aunty Ifeoma asked Jaja and me to go and sit in the living room, too, so we could see the TV clearly. I waited to hear Jaja say no, that we did not mind sitting at the dining table, before I nodded in agreement.

Aunty Ifeoma sat with us, glancing often at the TV as she ate.

'I don't understand why they fill our television with second-rate Mexican shows and ignore all the potential our people have,' she muttered.

'Mom, please don't lecture now,' Amaka said.

'It's cheaper to import soap operas from Mexico,' Obiora said, his eyes still glued to the television.

Aunty Ifeoma stood up. 'Jaja and Kambili, we usually say the rosary every night before bed. Of course, you can stay up as long as you want afterward to watch TV or whatever else.'

Jaja shifted on his chair before pulling his schedule out of his pocket. 'Aunty, Papa's schedule says we should study in the evenings; we brought our books.'

Aunty Ifeoma stared at the paper in Jaja's hand. Then she started to laugh so hard that she staggered, her tall body bending like a whistling pine tree on a windy day. 'Eugene gave you a schedule to follow when you're here? *Nekwanu anya*, what does that mean?' Aunty Ifeoma laughed some more before she held out her hand and asked for the sheet of paper. When she turned to me, I brought mine, folded in crisp quarters, out of my skirt pocket.

'I will keep them for you until you leave.'

'Aunty . . ,' Jaja started.

'If you do not tell Eugene, eh, then how will he know that you did not follow the schedule, *gbo*? You are on holiday here and it is my house, so you will follow my own rules.'

I watched Aunty Ifeoma walk into her room with

our schedules. My mouth felt dry, my tongue clinging to the roof.

'Do you have a schedule at home that you follow every day?' Amaka asked. She lay face up on the floor, her head resting on one of the cushions from a chair.

'Yes,' Jaja said.

'Interesting. So now rich people can't decide what to do day by day, they need a schedule to tell them.'

'Amaka!' Obiora shouted.

Aunty Ifeoma came out holding a huge rosary with blue beads and a metal crucifix. Obiora turned off the TV as the credits started to slide down the screen. Obiora and Amaka went to get their rosaries from the bedroom while Jaja and I slipped ours out of our pockets. We knelt next to the cane chairs and Aunty Ifeoma started the first decade. After we said the last Hail Mary, my head snapped back when I heard the raised, melodious voice. Amaka was singing!

'*Ka m bunie afa gi enu . . .*'

Aunty Ifeoma and Obiora joined her, their voices melding. My eyes met Jaja's. His eyes were watery, full of suggestions. *No!* I told him, with a tight blink. It was not right. You did not break into song in the middle of the rosary. I did not join in the singing, and neither did Jaja. Amaka broke into song at the end of each decade, uplifting Igbo songs that made Aunty Ifeoma sing in echoes, like an opera singer drawing the words from the pit of her stomach.

After the rosary, Aunty Ifeoma asked if we knew any of the songs.

'We don't sing at home,' Jaja answered.

'We do here,' Aunty Ifeoma said, and I wondered if it was irritation that made her lower her eyebrows.

Obiora turned on the TV after Aunty Ifeoma said good night and went into her bedroom. I sat on the sofa, next to Jaja, watching the images on TV, but I couldn't tell the olive-skinned characters apart. I felt as if my shadow were visiting Aunty Ifeoma and her family, while the real me was studying in my room in Enugu, my schedule posted above me. I stood up shortly and went into the bedroom to get ready for bed. Even though I did not have the schedule, I knew what time Papa had penciled in for bed. I fell off to sleep wondering when Amaka would come in, if her lips would turn down at the corners in a sneer when she looked at me sleeping.

I dreamed that Amaka submerged me in a toilet bowl full of greenish-brown lumps. First my head went in, and then the bowl expanded so that my whole body went in, too. Amaka chanted, 'Flush, flush, flush,' while I struggled to break free. I was still struggling when I woke up. Amaka had rolled out of bed and was knotting her wrapper over her nightdress.

'We're going to fetch water at the tap,' she said. She did not ask me to come, but I got up, tightened my wrapper, and followed her.

Jaja and Obiora were already at the tap in the tiny backyard; old car tires and bicycle parts and broken trunks were piled in a corner. Obiora placed the containers under the tap, aligning the open mouths with the rushing water. Jaja offered to take the first filled container back to the kitchen, but Obiora said not to worry and took it in. While Amaka took the next, Jaja placed a smaller container under the tap and filled it. He had slept in the living room, he told me, on a mattress that Obiora unrolled from behind the bedroom door and covered with a wrapper. I listened to him and marveled at the wonder in his voice, at how much lighter the brown of his pupils was. I offered to carry the next container, but Amaka laughed and said I had soft bones and could not carry it.

When we finished, we said morning prayers in the living room, a string of short prayers punctuated by songs. Aunty Ifeoma prayed for the university, for the lecturers and administration, for Nigeria, and finally, she prayed that we might find peace and laughter today. As we made the sign of the cross, I looked up to seek out Jaja's face, to see if he, too, was bewildered that Aunty Ifeoma and her family prayed for, of all things, *laughter*.

We took turns bathing in the narrow bath-room, with half-full buckets of water, warmed for a while with a heating coil plunged into them. The spotless tub had a triangular hole at one corner, and the water groaned like a man in pain as it drained. I lathered over with my own sponge and soap – Mama had carefully packed my toiletries – and although I scooped the water with a shallow cup and poured it slowly over my body, I still felt slippery as I stepped on the old towel placed on the floor.

Aunty Ifeoma was at the dining table when I came out, dissolving a few spoonfuls of dried milk in a jug of cold water. 'If I let these children take the milk themselves, it will not last a week,' she said, before taking the tin of Carnation dried milk back to the safety of her room. I hoped that Amaka would not ask me if my mother did that, too, because I would stutter if I had to tell her that we took as much creamy Peak milk as we wanted back home. Breakfast was okpa that Obiora had dashed out to buy from somewhere nearby. I had never had okpa for a meal, only for a snack when we sometimes bought the steam-cooked cowpea-and-palm-oil cakes on the drive to Abba. I watched Amaka and Aunty Ifeoma cut up the moist yellow cake and did the same. Aunty Ifeoma asked us to hurry up. She wanted to show Jaja and me the campus and get back in time to cook. She had invited Father Amadi to dinner.

'Are you sure there's enough fuel in the car, Mom?' Obiora asked.

'Enough to take us around campus, at least. I really hope fuel comes in the next week, otherwise when we resume, I will have to walk to my lectures.'

'Or take *okada*,' Amaka said, laughing.

'I will try that soon at this rate.'

'What are *okada*?' Jaja asked. I turned to stare at him, surprised. I did not think he would ask that question or any other question.

'Motorcycles,' Obiora said. 'They have become more popular than taxis.'

Aunty Ifeoma stopped to pluck at some browned leaves in the garden as we walked to the car, muttering that the harmattan was killing her plants.

Amaka and Obiora groaned and said, 'Not the garden now, Mom.'

'That's a hibiscus, isn't it, Aunty?' Jaja asked, staring at a plant close to the barbed wire fencing. 'I didn't know there were purple hibiscuses.'

Aunty Ifeoma laughed and touched the flower, colored a deep shade of purple that was almost blue. 'Everybody has that reaction the first time. My good friend Phillipa is a lecturer in botany. She did a lot of experimental work while she was here. Look, here's white ixora, but it doesn't bloom as fully as the red.'

Jaja joined Aunty Ifeoma, while we stood watching them.

'*O maka*, so beautiful,' Jaja said. He was running a finger over a flower petal. Aunty Ifeoma's laughter lengthened to a few more syllables.

'Yes, it is. I had to fence my garden because the neighborhood children came in and plucked many of the more unusual flowers. Now I only let in the altar girls from our church or the Protestant church.'

'Mom, *o zugo*. Let's go,' Amaka said. But Aunty Ifeoma spent a little longer showing Jaja her flowers before we piled into the station wagon and she drove off. The street she turned into was steep and she switched the ignition off and let the car roll, loose bolts rattling. 'To save fuel,' she said, turning briefly to Jaja and me.

The houses we drove past had sunflower hedges, and the palm-size flowers brightened the foliage in big yellow polka dots. The hedges had many gaping holes, so I could see the backyards of the houses – the metal water tanks balanced on unpainted cement blocks, the old tire swings hanging from guava trees, the clothes spread out on lines tied tree to tree. At the end of the street, Aunty Ifeoma turned the ignition on because the road had become level.

'That's the university primary school,' she said. 'That's where Chima goes. It used to be so much better, but now look at all the missing louvers in the windows, look at the dirty buildings.'

The wide schoolyard, enclosed by a trimmed whistling pine hedge, was cluttered with long buildings as if they had all sprung up at will, unplanned. Aunty Ifeoma pointed at a building next to the school, the Institute of African Studies, where her office was and where she taught most of her classes. The building was old; I could tell from the color and from the windows, coated with the dust of so many harmattans that they would never shine again. Aunty Ifeoma drove through a roundabout planted with pink periwinkle flowers and lined with bricks painted alternating black and white. On the side of the road, a field stretched out like green bed linen, dotted by mango trees with faded leaves struggling to retain their color against the drying wind.

'That's the field where we have our bazaars,' Aunty Ifeoma said. 'And over there are female hostels. There's Mary Slessor Hall. Over there is Okpara Hall, and this is Bello Hall, the most famous hostel, where Amaka has sworn she will live when she enters the university and launches her activist movements.'

Amaka laughed but did not dispute Aunty Ifeoma.

'Maybe you two will be together, Kambili.'

I nodded stiffly, although Aunty Ifeoma could not see me. I had never thought about the university, where I would go or what I would study. When the time came, Papa would decide.

Aunty Ifeoma horned and waved at two balding men in tie-dye shirts standing at a corner as she turned. She switched the ignition off again, and the car hurtled down the street. Gmelina and dogonyaro trees stood firmly on either side. The sharp, astringent scent of the dogonyaro leaves filled the car, and Amaka breathed deeply and said they cured malaria. We were in a residential area, driving past bungalows in wide compounds with rose bushes and faded lawns and fruit trees. The street gradually lost its tarred smoothness and its cultivated hedges, and the houses became low and narrow, their front doors so close together that you could stand at one, stretch out, and touch the next door. There was no pretense at hedges here, no pretense at separation or privacy, just low buildings side by side amid a scattering of stunted shrubs and cashew trees. These were the junior-staff quarters, where the secretaries and drivers lived, Aunty Ifeoma explained, and Amaka added, 'If they are lucky enough to get it.'

We had just driven past the buildings when Aunty Ifeoma pointed to the right and said, 'There is Odim hill. The view from the top is breathtaking, when you stand there, you see just how God laid out the hills and valleys, *ezi okwu*.'

When she made a U-turn and went back the way we had come, I let my mind drift, imagining God laying out the hills of Nsukka with his wide white hands, crescent-moon shadows underneath his nails just like Father Benedict's. We drove past the sturdy trees around the faculty of engineering, past the vast mango-filled fields around the female hostels. Aunty Ifeoma turned the opposite way when she got close to her street. She wanted to show us the other side of Marguerite Cartwright Avenue, where the seasoned professors lived, with the duplexes hemmed in by gravely driveways.

'I hear that when they first built these houses, some of the white professors – all the professors were white back then – wanted chimneys and fire-places,' Aunty Ifeoma said, with the same kind of indulgent laugh that Mama let out when she talked about people who went to witch doctors.

She then pointed to the vice chancellor's lodge, to the high walls surrounding it, and said it used to have well-tended hedges of cherry and ixora until rioting students jumped over the hedges and burned a car in the compound.

'What was the riot about?' Jaja asked.

'Light and water,' Obiora said, and I looked at him.

'There was no light and no water for a month,' Aunty Ifeoma added. 'The students said they could not study and asked if the exams could be rescheduled, but they were refused.'

'The walls are hideous,' Amaka said, in English, and I wondered what she would think of our compound walls back home, if she ever visited us. The V.C.'s walls were not very high; I could see the big duplex that nestled behind a canopy of trees with greenish-yellow leaves. 'Putting up walls is a superficial fix, anyway,' she continued. 'If I were the V.C., the students would not riot. They would have water and light.'

'If some Big Man in Abuja has stolen the money, is the V.C. supposed to vomit money for Nsukka?' Obiora asked. I turned to watch him, imagining myself at fourteen, imagining myself now.

'I wouldn't mind somebody vomiting some money for me right now,' Aunty Ifeoma said, laughing in that proud-coach-watching-the-team way. 'We'll go into town to see if there is any decently priced *ube* in the market. I know Father Amadi likes *ube*, and we have some corn at home to go with it.'

'Will the fuel make it, Mom?' Obiora asked.

'*Amarom*, we can try.'

Aunty Ifeoma rolled the car down the road that led to the university entrance gates. Jaja turned to the statue of the preening lion as we drove past it, his lips moving soundlessly. *To restore the dignity of man.* Obiora was reading the plaque, too. He let out a short cackle and asked, 'But when did man lose his dignity?'

Outside the gate, Aunty Ifeoma started the ignition again. When the car shuddered without starting, she muttered, 'Blessed Mother, please not now,' and tried again. The car only whined. Somebody horned behind us, and I turned to look at the woman in the yellow Peugeot 504. She came out and walked toward us; she wore a pair of culottes that flapped around her calves, which were lumpy like sweet potatoes.

'My own car stopped near Eastern Shop yesterday.' The woman stood at Aunty Ifeoma's window, her hair in a riotous curly perm swaying in the wind. 'My son sucked one liter from my husband's car this morning, just so I can get to the market. *O di egwu.* I hope fuel comes soon.'

'Let us wait and see, my sister. How is the family?' Aunty Ifeoma asked.

'We are well. Go well.'

'Let's push it,' Obiora suggested, already opening the car door.

'Wait.' Aunty Ifeoma turned the key again, and the car shook and then started. She drove off, with a screech, as if she did not want to slow down and give the car another chance to stop.

We stopped beside an ube hawker by the roadside, her bluish fruits displayed in pyramids on an enamel tray. Aunty Ifeoma gave Amaka some crumpled notes from her purse. Amaka bargained with the trader for a while, and then she smiled and pointed at the pyramids she wanted. I wondered what it felt like to do that.

Back in the flat, I joined Aunty Ifeoma and Amaka in the kitchen while Jaja went off with Obiora to play football with the children from the flats upstairs. Aunty Ifeoma got one of the huge yams we had brought from home. Amaka spread newspaper sheets on the floor to slice the tuber; it was easier than picking it up and placing it on the counter. When Amaka put the yam slices in a plastic bowl, I offered to help peel them and she silently handed me a knife.

'You will like Father Amadi, Kambili,' Aunty Ifeoma said. 'He's new at our chaplaincy, but he is so popular with everybody on campus already. He has invitations to eat in everybody's house.'

'I think he connects with our family the most,' Amaka said.

Aunty Ifeoma laughed. 'Amaka is so protective of him.'

'You are wasting yam, Kambili,' Amaka snapped. 'Ah! Ah! Is that how you peel yam in your house?'

I jumped and dropped the knife. It fell an inch

away from my foot. 'Sorry,' I said, and I was not sure if it was for dropping the knife or for letting too much creamy white yam go with the brown peel.

Aunty Ifeoma was watching us. 'Amaka, *ngwa*, show Kambili how to peel it.'

Amaka looked at her mother with her lips turned down and her eyebrows raised, as if she could not believe that anybody had to be told how to peel yam slices properly. She picked up the knife and started to peel a slice, letting only the brown skin go. I watched the measured movement of her hand and the increasing length of the peel, wishing I could apologize, wishing I knew how to do it right. She did it so well that the peel did not break, a continuous twirling soil-studded ribbon.

'Maybe I should enter it in your schedule, how to peel a yam,' Amaka muttered.

'Amaka!' Aunty Ifeoma shouted. 'Kambili, get me some water from the tank outside.'

I picked up the bucket, grateful for Aunty Ifeoma, for the chance to leave the kitchen and Amaka's scowling face. Amaka did not talk much the rest of the afternoon, until Father Amadi arrived, in a whiff of an earthy cologne. Chima jumped on him and held on. He shook Obiora's hand. Aunty Ifeoma and Amaka gave him brief hugs, and then Aunty Ifeoma introduced Jaja and me.

'Good evening,' I said and then added, 'Father.' It felt almost sacrilegious addressing this boyish man – in an open-neck T-shirt and jeans faded so much I could not tell if they had been black or dark blue – as Father.

'Kambili and Jaja,' he said, as if he had met us before. 'How are you enjoying your first visit to Nsukka?'

'They hate it,' Amaka said, and I immediately wished she hadn't.

'Nsukka has its charms,' Father Amadi said, smiling. He had a singer's voice, a voice that had the same effect on my ears that Mama working Pears baby oil into my hair had on my scalp. I did not fully comprehend his English-laced Igbo sentences at dinner because my ears followed the sound and not the sense of his speech. He nodded as he chewed his yam and greens, and he did not speak until he had swallowed a mouthful and sipped some water. He was at home in Aunty Ifeoma's house; he knew which chair had a protruding nail and could pull a thread off your clothes. 'I thought I knocked that nail in,' he said, then talked about football with Obiora, the journalist the government had just arrested with Amaka, the Catholic women's organization with Aunty Ifeoma, and the neighborhood video game with Chima.

My cousins chattered as much as before, but they waited until Father Amadi said something first and then pounced on it in response. I thought of the fattened chickens Papa sometimes bought for our offertory procession, the ones we took to the altar in addition to communion wine and yams

157

and sometimes goats, the ones we let stroll around the backyard until Sunday morning. The chickens rushed at the pieces of bread Sisi threw to them, disorderly and enthusiastic. My cousins rushed at Father Amadi's words in the same way.

Father Amadi included Jaja and me in the conversation, asking us questions. I knew the questions were meant for both of us because he used the plural 'you,' *unu*, rather than the singular, *gi*, yet I remained silent, grateful for Jaja's answers. He asked where we went to school, what subjects we liked, if we played any sports. When he asked what church we went to in Enugu, Jaja told him.

'St Agnes? I visited there once to say Mass,' Father Amadi said.

I remembered then, the young visiting priest who had broken into song in the middle of his sermon, whom Papa had said we had to pray for because people like him were trouble for the church. There had been many other visiting priests through the months, but I knew it was him. I just knew. And I remembered the song he had sung.

'Did you?' Aunty Ifeoma asked. 'My brother, Eugene, almost single-handedly finances that church. Lovely church.'

'*Chelukwa.* Wait a minute. Your brother is Eugene Achike? The publisher of the *Standard*?'

'Yes, Eugene is my elder brother. I thought I'd mentioned it before.' Aunty Ifeoma's smile did not quite brighten her face.

'*Ezi okwu?* I didn't know.' Father Amadi shook

his head. 'I hear he's very involved in the editorial decisions. The *Standard* is the only paper that dares to tell the truth these days.'

'Yes,' Aunty Ifeoma said. 'And he has a brilliant editor, Ade Coker, although I wonder how much longer before they lock him up for good. Even Eugene's money will not buy everything.'

'I was reading somewhere that *Amnesty World* is giving your brother an award,' Father Amadi said. He was nodding slowly, admiringly, and I felt myself go warm all over, with pride, with a desire to be associated with Papa. I wanted to say something, to remind this handsome priest that Papa wasn't just Aunty Ifeoma's brother or the *Standard*'s publisher, that he was my father. I wanted some of the cloudlike warmth in Father Amadi's eyes to rub off on me, settle on me.

'An award?' Amaka asked, bright-eyed. 'Mom, we should at least buy the *Standard* once in a while so we'll know what is going on.'

'Or we could ask for free copies to be sent to us, if prides were swallowed,' Obiora said.

'I didn't even know about the award,' Aunty Ifeoma said. 'Not that Eugene would tell me anyway, *igasikwa*. We can't even have a conversation. After all, I had to use a pilgrimage to Aokpe to get him to say yes to the children's visiting us.'

'So you plan to go to Aokpe?' Father Amadi asked.

'I was not really planning to. But I suppose we will have to go now, I will find out the next apparition date.'

'People are making this whole apparition thing up. Didn't they say Our Lady was appearing at Bishop Shanahan Hospital the other time? And then that she was appearing in Transekulu?' Obiora asked.

'Aokpe is different. It has all the signs of Lourdes,' Amaka said. 'Besides, it's about time Our Lady came to Africa. Don't you wonder how come she always appears in Europe? She was from the Middle East, after all.'

'What is she now, the Political Virgin?' Obiora asked, and I looked at him again. He was a bold, male version of what I could never have been at fourteen, what I still was not.

Father Amadi laughed. 'But she's appeared in Egypt, Amaka. At least people flocked there, like they are flocking to Aokpe now. *O bugodi*, like migrating locusts.'

'You don't sound like you believe, Father.' Amaka was watching him.

'I don't believe we have to go to Aokpe or anywhere else to find her. She is here, she is within us, leading us to her Son.' He spoke so effortlessly, as if his mouth were a musical instrument that just let sound out when touched, when opened.

'But what about the Thomas inside us, Father? The part that needs to see to believe?' Amaka asked. She had that expression that made me wonder if she was serious or not.

Father Amadi did not respond; instead he made a face, and Amaka laughed, the gap between her teeth wider, more angular, than Aunty Ifeoma's, as if someone had pried her two front teeth apart with a metal instrument.

After dinner, we all retired to the living room, and Aunty Ifeoma asked Obiora to turn the TV off so we could pray while Father Amadi was here. Chima had fallen asleep on the sofa, and Obiora leaned against him throughout the rosary. Father Amadi led the first decade, and at the end, he started an Igbo praise song. While they sang, I opened my eyes and stared at the wall, at the picture of the family at Chima's baptism. Next to it was a grainy copy of the pietà, the wooden frame cracked at the corners. I pressed my lips together, biting my lower lip, so my mouth would not join in the singing on its own, so my mouth would not betray me.

We put our rosaries away and sat in the living room eating corn and ube and watching *Newsline* on television. I looked up to find Father Amadi's eyes on me, and suddenly I could not lick the ube flesh from the seed. I could not move my tongue, could not swallow. I was too aware of his eyes, too aware that he was looking at me, watching me. 'I haven't seen you laugh or smile today, Kambili,' he said, finally.

I looked down at my corn. I wanted to say I was sorry that I did not smile or laugh, but my words would not come, and for a while even my ears could hear nothing.

'She is shy,' Aunty Ifeoma said.

I muttered a word I knew was nonsense and stood up and walked into the bedroom, making sure to close the door that led to the hallway. Father Amadi's musical voice echoed in my ears until I fell asleep.

Laughter always rang out in Aunty Ifeoma's house, and no matter where the laughter came from, it bounced around all the walls, all the rooms. Arguments rose quickly and fell just as quickly. Morning and night prayers were always peppered with songs, Igbo praise songs that usually called for hand clapping. Food had little meat, each person's piece the width of two fingers pressed close together and the length of half a finger. The flat always sparkled – Amaka scrubbed the floors with a stiff brush, Obiora did the sweeping, Chima plumped up the cushions on the chairs. Everybody took turns washing plates. Aunty Ifeoma included Jaja and me in the plate-washing schedule, and after I washed the garri-encrusted lunch plates, Amaka picked them off the tray where I had placed them to dry and soaked them in water.

'Is this how you wash plates in your house?' she asked. 'Or is plate washing not included in your fancy schedule?'

I stood there, staring at her, wishing Aunty Ifeoma were there to speak for me. Amaka glared

163

at me for a moment longer and then walked away. She said nothing else to me until her friends came over that afternoon, when Aunty Ifeoma and Jaja were in the garden and the boys were playing football out front. 'Kambili, these are my friends from school,' she said, casually.

The two girls said hello, and I smiled. They had hair as short as Amaka's, wore shiny lipstick and trousers so tight I knew they would walk differently if they were wearing something more comfortable. I watched them examine themselves in the mirror, pore over an American magazine with a brown-skinned, honey-haired woman on the cover, and talk about a math teacher who didn't know the answers to his own tests, a girl who wore a miniskirt to evening lesson even though she had fat yams on her legs, and a boy who was fine. 'Fine, *sha*, not attractive,' one of them stressed. She wore a dangling earring on one ear and a shiny, false gold stud on the other.

'Is it all your hair?' the other one asked, and I did not realize she was referring to me, until Amaka said, 'Kambili!'

I wanted to tell the girl that it was all my hair, that there were no attachments, but the words would not come. I knew they were still talking about hair, how long and thick mine looked. I wanted to talk with them, to laugh with them so much that I would start to jump up and down in one place the way they did, but my lips held stubbornly together. I did not want to stutter, so I started to cough and then ran out and into the toilet.

That evening, as I set the table for dinner, I heard Amaka say, 'Are you sure they're not abnormal, mom? Kambili just behaved like an *atulu* when my friends came.' Amaka had neither raised nor lowered her voice, and it drifted clearly in from the kitchen.

'Amaka, you are free to have your opinions, but you must treat your cousin with respect. Do you understand that?' Aunty Ifeoma replied in English, her voice firm.

'I was just asking a question.'

'Showing respect is not calling your cousin a sheep.'

'She behaves funny. Even Jaja is strange. Something is not right with them.'

My hand shook as I tried to straighten a piece of the table surface that had cracked and curled tightly around itself. A line of tiny ginger-colored ants marched near it. Aunty Ifeoma had told me not to bother the ants, since they hurt no one and you could never really get rid of them anyway; they were as old as the building itself.

I looked across at the living room to see if Jaja had heard Amaka over the sound of the television. But he was engrossed in the images on the screen, lying on the floor next to Obiora. He looked as though he had been lying there watching TV his whole life, It was the same way he looked in Aunty Ifeoma's garden the next morning, as though it were something he had been doing for a long time rather than the few days we had been here.

Aunty Ifeoma asked me to join them in the garden, to carefully pick out leaves that had started to wilt on the croton plants.

'Aren't they pretty?' Aunty Ifeoma asked. 'Look at that, green and pink and yellow on the leaves. Like God playing with paint brushes.'

'Yes,' I said. Aunty Ifeoma was looking at me, and I wondered if she was thinking that my voice lacked the enthusiasm of Jaja's when she talked about her garden.

Some of the children from the flats upstairs came down and stood watching us. They were about five, all a blur of food-stained clothes and fast words. They talked to one another and to Aunty Ifeoma, and then one of them turned and asked me what school I went to in Enugu. I stuttered and gripped hard at some fresh croton leaves, pulling them off, watching the viscous liquid drip from their stalks. After that, Aunty Ifeoma said I could go inside if I wanted to. She told me about a book she had just finished reading: it was on the table in her room and she was sure I would like it. So I went in her room and took a book with a faded blue cover, called *Equiano's Travels, or the Life of Gustavus Vassa the African.*

I sat on the verandah, with the book on my lap, watching one of the children chase a butterfly in the front yard. The butterfly dipped up and down, and its black-spotted yellow wings flapped slowly, as if teasing the little girl. The girl's hair, held atop her head like a ball of wool, bounced as she ran. Obiora was sitting on the verandah, too, but outside the shade, so he squinted behind his thick glasses to keep the sun out of his eyes. He was watching the girl and the butterfly while repeating the name Jaja slowly, placing the stress on both syllables, then on the first, then on the second. '*Aja* means sand or oracle, but *Jaja*? What kind of name is Jaja? It is not Igbo,' he finally pronounced.

'My name is actually Chukwuka. Jaja is a childhood nickname that stuck.' Jaja was on his knees. He wore only a pair of denim shorts, and the muscles on his back rippled, smooth and long like the ridges he weeded.

'When he was a baby, all he could say was Ja-Ja. So everybody called him Jaja,' Aunty Ifeoma said. She turned to Jaja and added, 'I told your mother that it was an appropriate nickname, that you would take after Jaja of Opobo.'

'Jaja of Opobo? The stubborn king?' Obiora asked.

'Defiant,' Aunt Ifeoma said. 'He was a defiant king.'

'What does defiant mean, Mommy? What did the king do?' Chima asked. He was in the garden, doing something on his knees, too, although Aunty Ifeoma often told him '*Kwusia*, don't do that' or 'If you do that again, I will give you a knock.'

'He was king of the Opobo people,' Aunty Ifeoma said, 'and when the British came, he refused to let them control all the trade. He did not sell his soul for a bit of gunpowder like the other kings did, so the British exiled him to the West Indies. He never returned to Opobo.' Aunt Ifeoma continued watering the row of tiny banana-colored flowers that clustered in bunches. She held a metal watering can in her hand, tilting it to let the water out through the nozzle. She had already used up the biggest container of water we fetched in the morning.

'That's sad. Maybe he should not have been defiant,' Chima said. He moved closer to squat next to Jaja. I wondered if he understood what 'exiled' and 'sold his soul for a bit of gunpowder' meant. Aunty Ifeoma spoke as though she expected that he did.

'Being defiant can be a good thing sometimes,' Aunty Ifeoma said. 'Defiance is like marijuana – it is not a bad thing when it is used right.'

The solemn tone, more than the sacrilege of what she said, made me look up. Her conversation was with Chima and Obiora, but she was looking at Jaja.

Obiora smiled and pushed his glasses up. 'Jaja of Opobo was no saint, anyway. He sold his people into slavery, and besides, the British won in the end. So much for the defiance.'

'The British won the war, but they lost many battles,' Jaja said, and my eyes skipped over the rows of text on the page. How did Jaja do it? How could he speak so easily? Didn't he have the same bubbles of air in his throat, keeping the words back, letting out only a stutter at best? I looked up to watch him, to watch his dark skin covered with beads of sweat that gleamed in the sun. I had never seen his arm move this way, never seen this piercing light in his eyes that appeared when he was in Aunty Ifeoma's garden.

'What happened to your little finger?' Chima asked. Jaja looked down, too, as if he were just then noticing the gnarled finger, deformed like a dried stick.

'Jaja had an accident,' Aunty Ifeoma said, quickly. 'Chima, go and get me the container of water. It is almost empty, so you can carry it.'

I stared at Aunty Ifeoma, and when her eyes met mine, I looked away. She knew. She knew what had happened to Jaja's finger.

When he was ten, he had missed two questions on his catechism test and was not named the best in his First Holy Communion class. Papa took him upstairs and locked the door. Jaja, in tears, came out supporting his left hand with his right, and Papa drove him to St Agnes hospital. Papa was crying, too, as he carried Jaja in his arms like a baby all the way to the car. Later, Jaja told me that Papa had avoided his right hand because it is the hand he writes with.

'This is about to bloom,' Aunt Ifeoma said to Jaja, pointing at an ixora bud. 'Another two days and it will open its eyes to the world.'

'I probably won't see it,' Jaja said. 'We'll be gone by then.'

Aunty Ifeoma smiled. 'Don't they say that time flies when you are happy?'

The phone rang then, and Aunty Ifeoma asked me to pick it up, since I was closest to the front door. It was Mama. I knew something was wrong right away, because it was Papa who always placed the call. Besides, they did not call in the afternoon.

'Your father is not here,' Mama said. Her voice sounded nasal, as if she needed to blow her nose. 'He had to leave this morning.'

'Is he well?' I asked.

'He is well.' She paused, and I could hear her talking to Sisi. Then she came back to the phone and said that yesterday soldiers had gone to the small, nondescript rooms that served as the offices of the *Standard*. Nobody knew how they had found out where the offices were. There were so many soldiers that the people on that street told Papa it reminded them of pictures from the front during the civil war. The soldiers took every copy of the entire press run, smashed furniture and printers, locked the offices, took the keys, and boarded up the doors and windows. Ade Coker was in custody again.

'I worry about your father,' Mama said, before I gave the phone to Jaja. 'I worry about your father.'

Aunty Ifeoma seemed worried, too, because after the phone call, she went out and bought a copy of the *Guardian* although she never bought newspapers. They cost too much; she read them at the paper stands when she had the time. The story of soldiers closing down the *Standard* was tucked into the middle page, next to advertisements for women's shoes imported from Italy.

'Uncle Eugene would have run it on the front page of his paper,' Amaka said, and I wondered if the inflection in her voice was pride.

When Papa called later, he asked to talk to Aunty Ifeoma first. Afterward he talked to Jaja and then me. He said he was fine, that everything was fine, that he missed us and loved us very much. He did not mention the *Standard* or what had happened to the editorial offices. After we hung up, Aunty Ifeoma said, 'Your father wants you to stay here a few days longer,' and Jaja smiled so widely I saw dimples I did not even know he had.

The phone rang early, before any of us had taken a morning bath. My mouth went dry because I was sure it was about Papa, that something had happened to him. The soldiers had gone to the house; they had shot him to make sure he would never publish anything again. I waited for Aunty Ifeoma to call Jaja and me, though I tightened my fist and willed her not to. She stayed for a few moments on the phone, and when she came out, she looked downcast. Her laughter did not ring out as often for the rest of the day, and she snapped at Chima when he wanted to sit next to her, saying, 'Leave me alone! *Nekwa anya*, you are no longer a baby.' One half of her lower lip disappeared into her mouth, and her jaw quivered as she chewed.

Father Amadi dropped by during dinner. He pulled a chair from the living room and sat, sipping water from a glass Amaka had brought him.

'I played football at the stadium and afterward I took some of the boys to town, for *akara* and fried yams,' he said, when Amaka asked what he had done today.

'Why didn't you tell me you would be playing today, Father?' Obiora asked.

'I'm sorry I forgot to, but I will pick you and Jaja up next weekend so we can play.' The music of his voice lowered in apology. I could not help staring at him, because his voice pulled me and because I did not know a priest could play football. It seemed so ungodly, so common. Father Amadi's eyes met mine across the table, and I looked away quickly.

'Perhaps Kambili will play with us also,' he said.

Hearing my name in his voice, in that melody, made me feel taut inside. I filled my mouth, as if I might have said something but for the food I had to chew. 'Amaka used to play with us when I first came here, but now she spends her time listening to African music and dreaming unrealistic dreams.'

My cousins laughed, Amaka the loudest, and Jaja smiled. But Aunty Ifeoma did not laugh. She chewed her food in little bites; her eyes were distant.

'Ifeoma, is something wrong?' Father Amadi asked.

She shook her head and sighed, as though she had just realized that she was not alone. 'I got a message from home today. Our father is sick. They said he did not rise well three mornings in a row. I want to bring him here.'

*'Ezi okwu?'* Father Amadi's brows furrowed. 'Yes, you should bring him here.'

'Papa-Nnukwu is sick?' Amaka asked shrilly. 'Mom, when did you know?'

'This morning, his neighbor called. She is a good woman, Nwamgba, she went all the way to Ukpo to find a phone.'

'You should have told us!' Amaka shouted.

*'O gini?* Have I not told you now?' Aunty Ifeoma snapped.

'When can we go to Abba, Mom?' Obiora asked, calmly, and at that moment, as in many others I had observed since we came, he seemed so much older than Jaja.

'I don't have enough fuel in the car to reach even Ninth Mile, and I don't know when fuel will come. I cannot afford to charter a taxi. If I take public transport, how will I bring back a sick old man in those buses so packed with people your face is in the next person's smelly armpit?' Aunty Ifeoma shook her head. 'I am tired. I am so tired . . .'

'We have some emergency fuel reserves in the chaplaincy,' Father Amadi said quietly. 'I am sure I could get you a gallon. *Ekwuzina*, don't sound that way.'

Aunty Ifeoma nodded and thanked Father Amadi. But her face did not brighten, and later, when we said the rosary, her voice did not rise when she sang. I struggled to meditate on the joyful Mysteries, all the time wondering where Papa-Nnukwu would sleep when he came. There were few choices in the small flat – the living room was already full with the boys, and Aunt Ifeoma's room was so busy, serving as food store and library and bedroom for her and Chima. It would have to be the other bedroom, Amaka's – and mine. I wondered if I would have to confess that I had shared a room with a heathen. I paused then, in my meditation, to pray that Papa would never find out that Papa-Nnukwu had visited and that I had shared a room with him.

At the end of the five decades, before we said the Hail Holy Queen, Aunty Ifeoma prayed for Papa-Nnukwu. She asked God to stretch a healing

174

hand over him as he had stretched over the apostle Peter's mother-in-law. She asked the Blessed Virgin to pray for him. She asked the angels to take charge of him.

My 'Amen' was a little delayed, a little surprised. When Papa prayed for Papa-Nnukwu, he asked only that God convert him and save him from the raging fires of hell.

Father Amadi came early the next morning, looking even more unpriestly than before, in khaki shorts that stopped just below his knees. He had not shaved, and in the clear morning sunlight, his stubble looked like tiny dots drawn on his jaw. He parked his car next to Aunty Ifeoma's station wagon and took out a can of petrol and a garden hose that had been cut to a quarter of its length.

'Let me do the sucking, Father,' Obiora said.

'Make sure you don't swallow,' Father Amadi said. Obiora inserted one end of the hose in the can and then enclosed the other end in his mouth. I watched his cheeks inflate like a balloon and then deflate. He swiftly took the hose out of his mouth and inserted it into the stations wagon's petrol tank. He was sputtering and coughing.

'Did you swallow too much?' Father Amadi asked, tapping Obiora's back.

'No,' Obiora said, between coughs. He looked proud.

'Well done. *Imana*, you know sucking fuel is a skill

175

you need these days,' Father Amadi said. His wry smile did little to mar the perfect clay smoothness of his features. Aunty Ifeoma came out dressed in a plain black boubou. She wore no shiny lipstick, and her lips looked chapped. She hugged Father Amadi. 'Thank you, Father.'

'I can drive you to Abba later this afternoon, after my office hours.'

'No, Father. Thank you. I will go with Obiora.'

Aunty Ifeoma drove off with Obiora in the front seat, and Father Amadi left soon after. Chima went upstairs to the neighbor's flat. Amaka went into her room and turned on her music, high enough that I heard it clearly from the verandah. I could tell her culturally conscious musicians apart now. I could distinguish the pure tones of Onyeka Onwenu, the brash power of Fela, the soothing wisdom of Osadebe. Jaja was in the garden with Aunt Ifeoma's shears, and I sat with the book I was almost finished reading, watching him. He held the shears with both hands, above his head, clipping away.

'Do you think we're abnormal?' I asked, in a whisper.

'*Gini?*'

'Amaka said we're abnormal.'

Jaja looked at me, then away, toward the line of garages in the front yard. 'What does abnormal mean?' he asked, a question that did not need or want an answer, and then went back to trimming the plants.

Aunty Ifeoma came back in the afternoon when the buzz of a bee around the garden was almost lulling me to sleep. Obiora helped Papa-Nnukwu out of the car, Papa-Nnukwu leaning against him as they walked into the flat. Amaka ran out and pressed her side lightly to Papa-Nnukwu's. His eyes drooped, his lids looked as though they had weights placed on them, but he smiled and said something that made Amaka laugh.

'Papa-Nnukwu, *nno*,' I said.

'Kambili,' he said, weakly.

Aunty Ifeoma wanted Papa-Nnukwu to lie down on Amaka's bed, but he said he preferred the floor. The bed was too springy. Obiora and Jaja dressed the spare mattress and placed it on the floor, and Aunty Ifeoma helped Papa-Nnukwu lower himself onto it. His eyes closed almost at once, although the lid of his going-blind eye remained slightly open, as if he were stealing a peek at all of us from the land of tired, ill sleep. He seemed taller lying down, occupying the length of the mattress, and I remembered what he had said about simply reaching out to pluck icheku from the tree, in his youth. The only icheku tree I had seen was huge, with branches grazing the roof of a duplex. Still, I believed Papa-Nnukwu, that he had simply raised his hands to pluck the black icheku pods from the branches.

'I'll make *ofe nsala* for dinner. Papa-Nnukwu likes that,' Amaka said.

177

'I hope he will eat. Chinyelu said even water has been hard for him to take in the last two days.' Aunty Ifeoma was watching Papa-Nnukwu. She bent and flicked gently at the rough white calluses on his feet. Narrow lines ran across his soles, like cracks in a wall.

'Will you take him to the medical center today or tomorrow morning, Mom?' Amaka asked.

'Have you forgotten, *imarozi*, that the doctors went on strike just before Christmas? I called Doctor Nduoma before I left, though, and he said he will come by this evening.'

Doctor Nduoma lived on Marguerite Cartwright Avenue, too, down the street, in one of the duplexes with BEWARE OF DOGS signs and wide lawns. He was director of the medical center, Amaka told Jaja and me, as we watched him get out of his red Peugeot 504 a few hours later. But since the doctors' strike had started, he had run a small clinic in town. The clinic was cramped, Amaka said. She had gotten her chloroquine injections there the last time she had malaria, and the nurse had boiled water on a smoky kerosene stove. Amaka was pleased that Doctor Nduoma had come to the house; the fumes alone in the stuffy clinic could choke Papa-Nnukwu, she said.

Doctor Nduoma had a permanent smile plastered on his face, as though he would break bad news to a patient with a smile. He hugged Amaka, and then shook hands with Jaja and me.

Amaka followed him into her bedroom to look at Papa-Nnukwu.

'Papa-Nnukwu is so skinny now,' Jaja said. We were sitting side by side on the verandah. The sun had fallen and there was a light breeze. Many of the children from the flats were playing football in the compound. From a flat upstairs, an adult yelled, '*Nee anya*, if you children make patches on the garage walls with that ball, I will cut off your ears!' The children laughed as the football hit the garage walls; the dust-covered ball left the walls polka-dotted brown.

'Do you think Papa will find out?' I asked.

'What?'

I laced my fingers together. How could Jaja not know what I meant? 'That Papa-Nnukwu is here with us. In the same house.'

'I don't know.'

Jaja's tone made me turn and stare at him. His brows were not knotted in worry, as I was sure mine were. 'Did you tell Aunty Ifeoma about your finger?' I asked. I should not have asked. I should have let it be. But there, it was out. It was only when I was alone with Jaja that the bubbles in my throat let my words come out.

'She asked me, and I told her.' He was tapping his foot on the verandah floor in an energetic rhythm.

I stared at my hands, at the short nails that Papa used to cut to a chafing shortness, when I would sit between his legs and his cheek would brush mine gently, until I was old enough to do it myself – and I always cut them to a chafing shortness, too. Had Jaja forgotten that we never told, that there was so much that we never told? When people asked, he always said his finger was 'something' that had happened at home. That way, it was not a lie and it let them imagine some accident, perhaps involving a heavy door. I wanted to ask Jaja why he had told Aunty Ifeoma, but I knew there was no need to, that this was one question he did not know the answer to.

'I am going to wipe down Aunty Ifeoma's car,' Jaja said, getting up. 'I wish the water ran so I could wash it. It is so dusty.'

I watched him walk into the flat. He had never washed a car at home. His shoulders seemed broader, and I wondered if it was possible for a teenager's shoulders to broaden in a week. The mild breeze was heavy with the smell of dust and the bruised leaves Jaja had cut. From the kitchen, the spices in Amaka's ofe nsala tickled my nose. I realized then that Jaja had been tapping his feet to the beat of an Igbo song that Aunty Ifeoma and my cousins sang at evening rosary.

I was still sitting on the verandah, reading, when Doctor Nduoma left. He talked and laughed as Aunty Ifeoma walked him to his car, telling her how tempted he was to ignore the patients waiting in his clinic so he could take her up on her offer

180

of dinner. 'That soup smells like something Amaka washed her hands well to cook,' he said.

Aunty Ifeoma came to the verandah and watched him drive off.

'Thank you, *nna m*,' she called out to Jaja, who was cleaning her car parked in front of the flat. I had never heard her call Jaja '*nna m*,' 'my father' – it was what she sometimes called her sons.

Jaja came up to the verandah. 'It's nothing, Aunty.' He lifted his shoulders as he stood there, like someone proudly wearing clothes that were not his size. 'What did the doctor say?'

'He wants us to get some tests done. I will take your Papa-Nnukwu to the medical center tomorrow, at least the labs there are still open.'

Aunty Ifeoma took Papa-Nnukwu to the University Medical Center in the morning and came back shortly afterward, her mouth set in a full pout. The lab staff was on strike, too, so Papa-Nnukwu could not have the tests done. Aunty Ifeoma stared at the middle distance and said she would have to find a private lab in town and, in a lower voice, said the private labs jacked up their fees so much that a simple typhoid fever test cost more than the medicine for the fever. She would have to ask Dr Nduoma if she really had to have all the tests done. She would not have paid a kobo at the medical center; at least there was still that benefit to being a lecturer. She left Papa-Nnukwu to rest and went out to buy the medicine that Doctor Nduoma had prescribed, worry lines etched in her forehead.

That evening, though, Papa-Nnukwu felt well enough to get up for dinner, and the knots on Aunty Ifeoma's face loosened a little. We had leftover ofe nsala and garri, pounded to a sticky softness by Obiora.

'Eating *garri* at night is not right,' Amaka said. But she was not scowling as she usually did when she complained; instead, she had that fresh smile that showed the gap in her teeth, the smile she seemed to always have when Papa-Nnukwu was around. 'It rests heavy in your stomach when you eat it at night.'

Papa-Nnukwu clucked. 'What did our fathers eat at night in their time, *gbo*? They ate pure cassava. *Garri* is for you modern ones. It does not even have the flavor of pure cassava.'

'But you have to eat all of yours, anyway, *nna anyi*.' Aunty Ifeoma reached over and plucked a morsel from Papa-Nnukwu's garri; she dug a hole in it with one finger, inserted a white medicine tablet, and then molded the morsel into a smooth ball. She placed it on Papa-Nnukwu's plate. She did the same with four other tablets. 'He will not take the medicine unless I do this,' she said in English. 'He says tablets are bitter, but you should taste the kola nuts he chews happily – they taste like bile.'

My cousins laughed.

'Morality, as well as the sense of taste, is relative,' Obiora said.

'Eh? What are you saying about me, *gbo*?' Papa-Nnukwu asked.

'*Nna anyi*, I want to see you swallow them,' Aunty Ifeoma said.

Papa-Nnukwu dutifully picked up each molded morsel, dunked it in soup, and swallowed. When the five were gone, Aunty Ifeoma asked him to drink some water so the tablets could break down and start to help his body heal. He took a gulp of water and set the glass down. 'When you become old, they treat you like a child,' he muttered.

Just then the TV made a scratchy sound like pouring dry sand on paper and the lights went off. A blanket of darkness covered the room.

'Hei,' Amaka groaned. 'This is not a good time for NEPA to take light. I wanted to watch something on TV.'

Obiora moved through the darkness to the two kerosene lamps that stood at the corner of the room and lit them. I smelled the kerosene fumes almost immediately; they made my eyes water and my throat itch.

'Papa-Nnukwu, tell us a folk story, then, just like we do in Abba,' Obiora said. 'It is better than TV anyway.'

'*O di mma*. But first, you have not told me how those people in the TV climb into it.'

My cousins laughed. It was something Papa-Nnukwu said often to make them laugh. I could tell from the way they started to laugh even before he finished speaking.

'Tell us the story of why the tortoise has a cracked shell!' Chima piped up.

'I would like to know why the tortoise features so much in our people's stories,' Obiora said in English.

'Tell us the story of why the tortoise has a cracked shell!' Chima repeated.

Papa-Nnukwu cleared his throat. 'Long ago, when animals talked and lizards were few, there was a big famine in the land of the animals. Farms dried up and the soil cracked. Hunger killed many of the animals and the ones left behind did not even have the strength to dance the mourning dance at funerals. One day all the male animals had a meeting to decide what could be done, before hunger wiped out the whole village.

'They all staggered to the meeting, bony and weak. Even Lion's roar was now like the whine of a mouse. Tortoise could hardly carry his shell. It was only Dog that looked well. His fur shone with good health and you could not see the bones under his skin because they were padded with flesh. The animals all asked Dog how he remained so well in the midst of famine. 'I have been eating feces like I always do,' Dog answered.

'The other animals used to laugh at Dog because he and his family were known to eat feces. None of the other animals could imagine themselves eating feces. Lion took control of the meeting and said, 'Since we cannot eat feces like Dog, we must think of a way to feed ourselves.'

'The animals thought long and hard until Rabbit suggested that all the animals kill their mothers and eat them. Many of the animals disagreed with this, they still remembered the sweetness of their mothers' breast milk. But finally they all agreed that it was the best alternative, since they would all die anyway if nothing was done.'

'I could never eat Mommy,' Chima said, giggling.

'It might not be a good idea, that tough skin,' Obiora said.

'The mothers did not mind being sacrificed,' Papa-Nnukwu continued. 'And so each week a mother was killed and the animals shared the meat. Soon they were all looking well again. Then, a few days before it was time for Dog's mother to be killed, Dog ran out wailing the mourning song for his mother. She had died of the disease. The other animals sympathized with Dog and offered to help bury her. Since she had died of the disease, they could not eat her. Dog refused any help and said he would bury her himself. He was distraught that she would not have the honor of dying like the other mothers who were sacrificed for the village.

'Only a few days later, Tortoise was on his way to his parched farm to see if there were any dried vegetables to be harvested. He stopped to ease himself near a bush, but because the bush was wilted it did not give good cover. He was able to see across the bush and he saw Dog, looking up and singing. Tortoise wondered if perhaps

185

Dog's grief had made him go mad. Why was Dog singing to the sky? Tortoise listened and heard what Dog was singing: "*Nne, Nne*, Mother, Mother."'

'*Njemanze!*' my cousins chorused.

'"*Nne, Nne*, I have come."'

'*Njemanze!*'

'"*Nne, Nne*, let down the rope. I have come."'

'*Njemanze!*'

'Tortoise came out then and challenged Dog. Dog admitted that his mother had not really died, that she had gone to the sky where she lived with wealthy friends. It was because she fed him daily from the sky that he looked so well. "Abomination!" Tortoise bellowed. 'So much for eating feces! Wait until the rest of the village hears what you have done.'

'Of course, Tortoise was as cunning as always. He had no intention of telling the village. He knew that Dog would offer to take him to the sky, too. When Dog did, Tortoise pretended to think about it before accepting. But saliva had already started to run down his cheeks. Dog sang the song again and a rope descended from the sky and the two animals went up.

'Dog's mother was not pleased that her son had brought a friend but she served them well anyway. Tortoise ate like an animal with no home training. He ate almost all of the *fufu* and *onugbu* soup and poured a full horn of palm wine down his throat when his mouth was full of food. After the meal they descended the rope. Tortoise told Dog he would tell no one as long as Dog took him to the sky every day until the rains came and the famine ended. Dog agreed – what else could he do? The more Tortoise ate in the sky, the more he wanted, until one day he decided that he would go to the sky by himself so that he would get to eat Dog's portion as well as his. He went to the spot by the dry bush and started singing, mimicking Dog's voice. The rope started to fall. Just then, Dog came by and saw what was happening. Furious, Dog started to sing loudly. "*Nne, Nne,* Mother, Mother."'

'*Njemanze!*' my cousins chorused.

' "*Nne, Nne,* it is not your son coming up."'

'*Njemanze!*'

' "*Nne, Nne,* cut the rope. It is not your son coming up. It is the cunning Tortoise."'

'*Njemanze!*'

'Right away, Dog's mother cut the rope and Tortoise, already halfway to the sky, came hurtling down. Tortoise fell on a pile of stones and cracked his shell. To this day, the Tortoise has a cracked shell.'

Chima chortled. 'The tortoise has a cracked shell!'

'Don't you wonder how only Dog's mother got up to the sky in the first place?' Obiora asked in English.

'Or who the wealthy friends in the sky were,' Amaka said.

'Probably Dog's ancestors,' Obiora said.

187

My cousins and Jaja laughed, and Papa-Nnukwu laughed, too, a gentle chuckle, as if he had understood the English, then leaned back and closed his eyes. I watched them and wished that I had joined in chanting the *Njemanze!* response.

Papa-Nnukwu had woken up before everyone else. He wanted to have breakfast sitting on the verandah, to watch the morning sun. And so Aunty Ifeoma asked Obiora to spread a mat on the verandah, and we all sat and had breakfast with Papa-Nnukwu, listening to him talk about the men who tapped palm wine in the village, how they left at dawn to climb up the palm trees because the trees gave sour wine after the sun rose. I could tell that he missed the village, that he missed seeing those palm trees the men climbed, with a raffia belt encircling them and the tree trunk.

Although we had bread and okpa and Bournvita for breakfast, Aunty Ifeoma made a little fufu to bury Papa-Nnukwu's tablets in, soft spherical coffins that she carefully watched Papa-Nnukwu swallow. The cloud had lifted from her face.

'He will be fine,' she said, in English. 'Soon he will start nagging about wanting to go back to the village.'

'He must stay for a while,' Amaka said. 'Maybe he should live here, Mom. I don't think that girl Chinyelu takes proper care of him.'

'*Igasikwa!* He will never agree to live here.'

'When will you take him to do the tests?'

'Tomorrow. Doctor Nduoma said I can have two tests done instead of all four. The private labs in town always want full payment, so I will have to go to the bank first. I don't think I will finish in time to take him today, with all those lines at the bank.'

A car drove into the compound then, and even before Amaka asked, 'Is that Father Amadi?' I knew it was him. I had seen the small Toyota hatchback only twice before, but I could point it out anywhere. My hands started to shake.

'He said he would stop by and see your Papa-Nnukwu,' Aunty Ifeoma said.

Father Amadi wore his soutane, long-sleeved and loose-fitting, with a loose black rope slanted around his waist. Even in the priestly garb, his loping, comfortable gait pulled my eyes and held them. I turned and dashed into the flat. I could see the front yard clearly from the window in the bedroom, which had a few louvers missing. I pressed my face close to the window, close to the small tear in the mosquito netting that Amaka blamed for letting in every moth that flapped around the light bulb at night. Father Amadi was standing by the window, close enough for me to see the way his hair lay in wavy curls on his head, like the ripples in a stream.

'His recovery has been so swift, Father, *Chukwu aluka*,' Aunty Ifeoma said.

'Our God is faithful, Ifeoma,' he said happily, as though Papa-Nnukwu were his own relative. Then he told her that he was on his way to Isienu, to visit a friend who had just got back from missionary work in Papua New Guinea. He turned to Jaja and Obiora and said, 'I will come by this evening to pick you up. We'll play in the stadium with some of the boys from the seminary.'

'Okay, Father.' Jaja's voice was strong.

'Where is Kambili?' he asked.

I looked down at my chest, which was heaving now. I did not know why, but I was grateful that he had said my name, that he remembered my name.

'I think she is inside,' Aunty Ifeoma said.

'Jaja, tell her she can come with us if she likes.'

When he came back that evening, I pretended I was taking a siesta. I waited to hear his car drive off, with Jaja and Obiora inside, before I came out into the living room. I had not wanted to go with them, and yet when I could no longer hear the sound of his car, I wished I could run after it.

Amaka was in the living room with Papa-Nnukwu, slowly oiling the few tufts of hair on his head with Vaseline. Afterward, she smoothed talcum powder on his face and chest.

'Kambili,' Papa-Nnukwu said, when he saw me. 'Your cousin paints well. In the old days, she would have been chosen to decorate the shrines of our gods.' He sounded dreamy. Some of his medications probably made him drowsy. Amaka did not look at me; she gave his hair one last pat – a caress, really – and then sat down on the floor in front of him. I followed the swift movements of her hand as she moved the brush from palette to paper and then back again. She painted so quickly that I thought it would all be a muddle on the paper, until I looked and saw the form clearly taking shape – a lean, graceful form. I could hear the ticking of the clock on the wall, the one with the picture of the Pope leaning on his staff. The silence was delicate. Aunty Ifeoma was scraping a burnt pot in the kitchen, and the *kroo-kroo-kroo* of the metal spoon on the pot seemed intrusive. Amaka and Papa-Nnukwu spoke sometimes, their voices low, twining together. They understood each other, using the sparest words. Watching them, I felt a longing for something I knew I would never have. I wanted to get up and leave, but my legs did not belong to me, did not do what I wanted them to. Finally, I pushed myself up and went into the kitchen; neither Papa-Nnukwu nor Amaka noticed when I left.

Aunty Ifeoma sat on a low stool, pulling the brown skin off hot cocoyams, throwing the sticky, rounded tubers in the wooden mortar and stopping to cool her hands in a bowl of cold water.

'Why do you look that way, *o gini*?' she asked.

'What way, Aunty?'

'There are tears in your eyes.'

I felt my wet eyes. 'Something must have flown into my eyes.'

Aunty Ifeoma looked doubtful. 'Help me with the cocoyams,' she said, finally.

I pulled a low stool close to her and sat down. The skins seemed to slip off easily enough for Aunty Ifeoma, but when I pressed one end of a tuber, the rough brown skin stayed put and the heat stung my palms.

'Soak your hand in water first.' She demonstrated where and how to press, to have the skin come sliding off. I watched her pound the cocoyams, dipping the pestle often into the bowl of water so the cocoyam wouldn't stick too much to it. Still, the sticky white mash clung to the pestle, to the mortar, to Aunty Ifeoma's hand. She was pleased, though, because it would thicken the onugbu soup well.

'See how well your Papa-Nnukwu is doing?' she asked. 'He has been sitting up so long for Amaka to paint him. It's a miracle. Our Lady is faithful.'

'How can Our Lady intercede on behalf of a heathen, Aunty?'

Aunty Ifeoma was silent as she ladled the thick cocoyam paste into the soup pot; then she looked up and said Papa-Nnukwu was not a heathen but a traditionalist, that sometimes what was different was just as good as what was familiar, that when Papa-Nnukwu did his itu-nzu, his declaration of innocence, in the morning, it was the same as our saying the rosary. She said a few other things, but I was not really listening, because I heard Amaka laughing in the living room with Papa-Nnukwu, and

193

I wondered what they were laughing about, and whether they would stop laughing if I went in there.

When Aunty Ifeoma woke me up, the room was dim and the shrills of the night crickets were dying away. A rooster's crow drifted through the window above my bed.

'*Nne.*' Aunty Ifeoma patted my shoulder. 'Your Papa-Nnukwu is on the verandah. Go and watch him.'

I felt wide awake, although I had to pry my eyes open with my fingers. I remembered Aunty Ifeoma's words from the day before, about Papa-Nnuwku being a traditionalist and not a heathen. Still, I was not sure why she wanted me to go and watch him on the verandah.

'*Nne*, remember to be quiet. Just watch him.' Aunty Ifeoma whispered to avoid waking Amaka.

I tied my wrapper around my chest, over my pink-and-white flowered nightgown, and padded out of the room. The door that led to the verandah was half open, and the purplish tinge of early dawn trickled into the living room. I did not want to turn the light on because Papa-Nnukwu would notice, so I stood by the door, against the wall.

Papa-Nnukwu was on a low wooden stool, his legs bent into a triangle. The loose knot of his wrapper had come undone, and the wrapper had slipped off his waist to cover the stool, its faded blue edges grazing the floor. A kerosene lamp, turned to its lowest, was right next to him. The flickering light cast a topaz glow over the narrow verandah, over the stubby gray hairs on Papa-Nnukwu's chest, over the loose, soil-colored skin on his legs. He leaned down to draw a line on the floor with the nzu in his hand. He was speaking, his face down as if addressing the white chalk line, which now looked yellow. He was talking to the gods or the ancestors; I remembered Aunty Ifeoma saying that the two could be interchanged.

'Chineke! I thank you for this new morning! I thank you for the sun that rises.' His lower lip quivered as he spoke. Perhaps that was why his Igbo words flowed into each other, as if writing his speech would result in a single long word. He bent down to draw another line, quickly, with a fierce determination that shook the flesh on his arm, which was hanging low like a brown leather pouch. 'Chineke! I have killed no one, I have taken no one's land, I have not committed adultery.' He leaned over and drew the third line. The stool squeaked. 'Chineke! I have wished others well. I have helped those who have nothing with the little that my hands can spare.'

A cock was crowing, a drawn-out, plaintive sound that seemed very close by.

'Chineke! Bless me. Let me find enough to fill my stomach. Bless my daughter, Ifeoma. Give her enough for her family.' He shifted on the stool. His navel had once jutted out, I could tell, but now it looked like a wrinkled eggplant, drooping.

'Chineke! Bless my son, Eugene. Let the sun not

195

set on his prosperity. Lift the curse they have put on him.' Papa-Nnukwu leaned over and drew one more line. I was surprised that he prayed for Papa with the same earnestness that he prayed for himself and Aunty Ifeoma.

'Chineke! Bless the children of my children. Let your eyes follow them away from evil and towards good.' Papa-Nnukwu smiled as he spoke. His few front teeth seemed a deeper yellow in the light, like fresh corn kernels. The wide gaps in his gums were tinged a subtle tawny color. 'Chineke! Those who wish others well, keep them well. Those who wish others ill, keep them ill.' Papa-Nnukwu drew the last line, longer than the rest, with a flourish. He was done.

When Papa-Nnukwu rose and stretched, his entire body, like the bark of the gnarled gmelina tree in our yard, captured the gold shadows from the lamp flame in its many furrows and ridges. Even the age spots that dotted his hands and legs gleamed. I did not look away, although it was sinful to look upon another person's nakedness. The rumples in Papa-Nnukwu's belly did not seem so many now, and his navel rose higher, still enclosed between folds of skin. Between his legs hung a limp cocoon that seemed smoother, free of the wrinkles that crisscrossed the rest of his body like mosquito netting. He picked up his wrapper and tied it around his body, knotting it at his waist. His nipples were like dark raisins nestled among the sparse gray tufts of hair on his chest. He was still smiling as I quietly turned and went back to the bedroom. I never smiled after we said the rosary back home. None of us did.

Papa-Nnukwu was back on the verandah after breakfast, sitting on the stool, with Amaka settled on a plastic mat at his feet. She scrubbed his foot gently with a pumice stone, soaked it in a plastic bowl of water, rubbed it over with Vaseline, and then moved to the other foot. Papa-Nnukwu complained that she would make his feet too tender, that even soft stones would pierce his soles now because he never wore sandals in the village, though Aunty Ifeoma made him wear them here. But he did not ask Amaka to stop.

'I am going to paint him out here on the verandah, in the shade. I want to catch the sunlight on his skin,' Amaka said, when Obiora joined them.

Aunty Ifeoma came out, dressed in a blue wrapper and blouse. She was going to the market with Obiora, who she said figured out change faster than a trader with a calculator. 'Kambili, I want you to help me do the *orah* leaves, so I can start the soup when I come back,' she said.

'*Orah* leaves?' I asked, swallowing.

'Yes. Don't you know how to prepare *orah*?'

I shook my head. 'No, Aunty.'

'Amaka will do it, then,' Aunty Ifeoma said. She unfolded and refolded her wrapper around her waist, knotting it at her side.

'Why?' Amaka burst out. 'Because rich people

do not prepare *orah* in their houses? Won't she participate in eating the *orah* soup?'

Aunty Ifeoma's eyes hardened – she was not looking at Amaka, she was looking at me. '*O ginidi*, Kambili, have you no mouth? Talk back to her!'

I watched a wilted African lily fall from its stalk in the garden. The crotons rustled in the late morning breeze. 'You don't have to shout, Amaka,' I said, finally. 'I don't know how to do the *orah* leaves, but you can show me.' I did not know where the calm words had come from. I did not want to look at Amaka, did not want to see her scowl, did not want to prompt her to say something else to me, because I knew I could not keep up. I thought I was imagining it when I heard the cackling, but then I looked at Amaka – and sure enough, she was laughing.

'So your voice can be this loud, Kambili,' she said.

She showed me how to prepare the orah leaves. The slippery, light green leaves had fibrous stalks that did not become tender from cooking and so had to be carefully plucked out. I balanced the tray of vegetables on my lap and set to work, plucking the stalks and putting the leaves in a bowl at my feet. I was done by the time Aunty Ifeoma drove in, about an hour later, and sank onto a stool, fanning herself with a newspaper. Sweat streaks had washed away her pressed powder in parallel lines of darker-colored skin down the sides of her face. Jaja and Obiora were bringing in the

198

foodstuffs from the car, and Aunty Ifeoma asked Jaja to place the bunch of plantains on the verandah floor.

'Amaka, *ka*? Guess how much?' she asked.

Amaka stared at the bunch critically before she guessed an amount. Aunty Ifeoma shook her head and said that the plantains had cost forty naira more than what Amaka guessed.

'Hei! For this small thing?' Amaka shouted.

'The traders say it is hard to transport their food because there is no fuel, so they add on the costs of transportation, *o di egwu*,' Aunty Ifeoma said.

Amaka picked up the plantains and pressed each between her fingers, as if she would figure out why they cost so much by doing that. She took them inside just as Father Amadi drove in and parked in front of the flat. His windscreen caught the sun and glittered. He bounded up the few stairs to the verandah, holding his soutane up like a bride holding a wedding dress. He greeted Papa-Nnukwu first, before hugging Aunty Ifeoma and shaking hands with the boys. I extended my hand so that we could shake, my lower lip starting to tremble.

'Kambili,' he said, holding my hand a little longer than the boys'.

'Are you going somewhere, Father?' Amaka asked, coming onto the verandah. 'You must be baking in that soutane.'

'I am going over to give some things to a friend

of mine, the priest who came back from Papua New Guinea. He returns next week.'

'Papua New Guinea. How did he say the place is, eh?' Amaka asked.

'He was telling a story of crossing a river by canoe, with crocodiles right underneath. He said he is not sure which happened first, hearing the teeth of the crocodiles snapping or discovering that he had wet his trousers.'

'They had better not send you to a place like that,' Aunty Ifeoma said with a laugh, still fanning herself and sipping from a glass of water.

'I don't even want to think about your leaving, Father,' Amaka said. 'You still don't have an idea where and when, *okwia*?'

'No. Sometime next year, perhaps.'

'Who is sending you?' Papa-Nnukwu asked, in his sudden way that made me realize he had been following every word spoken in Igbo.

'Father Amadi belongs to a group of priests, *ndi* missionary, and they go to different countries to convert people,' Amaka said. She hardly peppered her speech with English words when she spoke to Papa-Nnukwu, as the rest of us inadvertently did.

'*Ezi okwu?*' Papa-Nnukwu looked up, his milky eye on Father Amadi. 'Is that so? Our own sons now go to be missionaries in the white man's land?'

'We go to the white man's land and the black man's land, sir,' Father Amadi said. 'Any place that needs a priest.'

'It is good, my son. But you must never lie to them. Never teach them to disregard their fathers.' Papa-Nnukwu looked away, shaking his head.

'Did you hear that, Father?' Amaka asked. 'Don't lie to those poor ignorant souls.'

'It will be hard not to, but I will try,' Father Amadi said, in English. His eyes crinkled at the corners when he smiled.

'You know, Father, it's like making *okpa*,' Obiora said. 'You mix the cowpea flour and palm oil, then you steam-cook for hours. You think you can ever get just the cowpea flour? Or just the palm oil?'

'What are you talking about?' Father Amadi asked.

'Religion and oppression,' Obiora said.

'You know there is a saying that it is not just the naked men in the market who are mad?' Father Amadi asked. 'That streak of madness has returned and is disturbing you again, *okwia*?'

Obiora laughed, and so did Amaka, in that loud way it seemed only Father Amadi could get out of her.

'Spoken like the true missionary priest, Father,' Amaka said. 'When people challenge you, label them mad.'

'See how your cousin sits quiet and watches?' Father Amadi asked, gesturing to me. 'She does not waste her energy in picking never-ending arguments. But there is a lot going on in her mind, I can tell.'

I stared at him. Round, wet patches of sweat encircled his underarms, darkening the white of his soutane. His eyes rested on my face and I looked away. It was too disturbing, locking eyes with him; it made me forget who was nearby, where I was sitting, what color my skirt was. 'Kambili, you did not want to come out with us the last time.'

'I . . . I . . . I was asleep.'

'Well, today, you're coming with me. Just you,' Father Amadi said. 'I will come and pick you up on my way back from town. We're going to the stadium for football. You can play or watch.'

Amaka started to laugh. 'Kambili looks frightened to death.' She was looking at me, but it was not the look I was used to, the one where her eyes held me guilty of things I did not know. It was a different, softer look.

'There is nothing to be frightened about, *nne*. You will have fun at the stadium,' Aunty Ifeoma said, and I turned to stare blankly at her, too. Tiny beads of sweat, like pimples, covered her nose. She seemed so happy, so at peace, and I wondered how anybody around me could feel that way when liquid fire was raging inside me, when fear was mingling with hope and clutching itself around my ankles.

After Father Amadi left, Aunty Ifeoma said, 'Go and get ready so you don't keep him waiting when he gets back. Shorts are best because even if you don't play, it will get hotter before the sun falls and most of the spectator stands don't have roofs.'

'Because they have spent ten years building that stadium. The money has gone into peoples' pockets,' Amaka muttered.

'I don't have shorts, Aunty,' I said.

Aunty Ifeoma did not ask why, perhaps because she already knew. She asked Amaka to lend me a pair of shorts. I expected Amaka to sneer, but she gave me a pair of yellow shorts as if it were normal that I did not have any. I took my time putting on the shorts, but I did not stand in front of the mirror for too long, as Amaka did, because guilt would nibble at me. Vanity was a sin. Jaja and I looked in the mirror just long enough to make sure our buttons were done right.

I heard the Toyota drive up to the front of the flat awhile later. I took Amaka's lipstick from the top of the dresser and ran it over my lips. It looked strange, not as glamorous as it did on Amaka; it did not even have the same bronze shimmer. I wiped it off. My lips looked pale, a dour brown. I ran the lipstick over my lips again, and my hands shook.

'Kambili! Father Amadi is horning outside for you,' Aunty Ifeoma called. I wiped the lipstick away with the back of my hand and left the room.

Father Amadi's car smelled like him, a clean scent that made me think of a clear azure sky. His shorts had seemed longer the last time I saw him in them, well past his knees. But now they climbed up to expose a muscular thigh sprinkled with dark hair. The space between us was too small, too tight. I was always a penitent when I was close to a priest at confession. But it was hard to feel penitent now, with Father Amadi's cologne deep in my lungs. I felt guilty instead because I could not focus on my sins, could not think of anything except how near he was. 'I sleep in the same room as my grandfather. He is a heathen,' I blurted out.

He turned to me briefly, and before he looked away, I wondered if the light in his eyes was amusement. 'Why do you say that?'

'It is a sin.'

'Why is it a sin?'

I stared at him. I felt that he had missed a line in his script. 'I don't know.'

'Your father told you that.'

I looked away, out the window. I would not implicate Papa, since Father Amadi obviously disagreed.

'Jaja told me a little about your father the other day, Kambili.'

I bit my lower lip. What had Jaja said to him? What was wrong with Jaja, anyway? Father Amadi said nothing else until we got to the stadium and he quickly scanned the few people running on the tracks. His boys were not here yet, so the football field was empty. We sat on the stairs, in one of the two spectator stands that had a roof.

'Why don't we play set ball before the boys come?' he asked.

'I don't know how to play.'

'Do you play handball?'

'No.'

'What about volleyball?'

I looked at him and then away. I wondered if Amaka would ever paint him, would ever capture the clay-smooth skin, the straight eyebrows, which were slightly raised as he watched me. 'I played volleyball in class one,' I said. 'But I stopped playing because I . . . I was not that good and nobody liked to pick me.' I kept my eyes focused on the bleak, unpainted spectator stands, abandoned for so long that tiny plants had started to push their green heads through the cracks in the cement.

'Do you love Jesus?' Father Amadi asked, standing up.

I was startled. 'Yes. Yes, I love Jesus.'

'Then show me. Try and catch me, show me you love Jesus.'

He had hardly finished speaking before he dashed off and I saw the blue flash of his tank top. I did not stop to think; I stood up and ran after him. The wind blew in my face, into my eyes, across my ears. Father Amadi was like blue wind, elusive. I did not catch up until he stopped near the football goal post. 'So you don't love Jesus,' he teased.

'You run too fast,' I said, panting.

'I will let you rest, and then you can have another chance to show me you love the Lord.'

We ran four more times. I did not catch him. We

flopped down on the grass, finally, and he pushed a water bottle into my hand. 'You have good legs for running. You should practice more,' he said.

I looked away. I had never heard anything like that before. It seemed too close, too intimate, to have his eyes on my legs, on any part of me.

'Don't you know how to smile?' he asked.

'What?'

He reached across, tugged lightly at the sides of my lips. 'Smile.'

I wanted to smile, but I could not. My lips and cheeks were frozen, unthawed by the sweat running down the sides of my nose. I was too aware that he was watching me.

'What is that reddish stain on your hand?' he asked.

I looked down at my hand, at the smudge of hastily wiped lipstick that still clung to the sweaty back of my hands. I had not realized how much I had put on. 'It's . . . a stain,' I said, feeling stupid.

'Lipstick?'

I nodded.

'Do you wear lipstick? Have you ever worn lipstick?'

'No,' I said. Then I felt the smile start to creep over my face, stretching my lips and cheeks, an embarrassed and amused smile. He knew I had tried to wear lipstick for the first time today. I smiled. I smiled again.

'Good evening, Father!' echoed all around, and eight boys descended on us. They were all about my age, with shorts that had holes in them and shirts washed so often I didn't know what color they had originally been and similar crusty spots from insect bites on their legs. Father Amadi took his tank top off and dropped it on my lap before joining the boys on the football field. With his upper body bare, his shoulders were a broad square. I did not look down at his tank top on my lap as I inched my hand ever so slowly toward it. My eyes were on the football field, on Father Amadi's running legs, on the flying white-and-black football, on the many legs of the boys, which all looked like one leg. My hand had finally touched the top on my lap, moving over it tentatively as though it could breathe, as though it were a part of Father Amadi, when he blew a whistle for a water break. He brought peeled oranges and water wrapped into tight cone shapes in plastic bags from his car. They all settled down on the grass to eat the oranges, and I watched Father Amadi laugh loudly with his head thrown back, leaning to rest his elbows on the grass. I wondered if the boys felt the same way I did with him, that they were all he could see.

I held on to his tank top while I watched the rest of the play. A cool wind had started to blow, chilling the sweat on my body, when Father Amadi blew the final whistle, three times with the last time drawn out. Then the boys clustered around him, heads bowed, while he prayed. 'Good-bye, Father!' echoed around as he made his way toward me. There was something confident about his gait, like a rooster in charge of all the neighborhood hens.

In the car, he played a tape. It was a choir singing Igbo worship songs. I knew the first song: Mama sang it sometimes when Jaja and I brought our report cards home. Father Amadi sang along. His voice was smoother than the lead singer's on the tape. When the first song ended, he lowered the volume and asked, 'Did you enjoy the game?'

'Yes.'

'I see Christ in their faces, in the boys' faces.'

I looked at him. I could not reconcile the blond Christ hanging on the burnished cross in St Agnes and the sting-scarred legs of those boys.

'They live in Ugwu Oba. Most of them don't go to school anymore because their families can't afford it. Ekwueme – remember him, in the red shirt?'

I nodded, although I could not remember. All the shirts had seemed similar and colorless.

'His father was a driver here in the university. But they retrenched him, and Ekwueme had to drop out of Nsukka High School. He is working as a bus conductor now, and he is doing very well. They inspire me, those boys.' Father Amadi stopped talking to join in the chorus. *I na-asi m esona ya! I na-asi m esona ya!*

I nodded in time to the chorus. We really did not need the music, though, because his voice was melody enough. I felt that I was at home, that I

208

was where I had been meant to be for a long time. Father Amadi sang for a while; then he lowered the volume to a whisper again. 'You haven't asked me a single question,' he said.

'I don't know what to ask.'

'You should have learned the art of questioning from Amaka. Why does the tree's shoot go up and the root down? Why is there a sky? What is life? Just why?'

I laughed. It sounded strange, as if I were listening to the recorded laughter of a stranger being played back. I was not sure I had ever heard myself laugh.

'Why did you become a priest?' I blurted out, then wished I had not asked, that the bubbles in my throat had not let that through. Of course he had gotten the call, the same call that all the Reverend Sisters in school talked about when they asked us to always listen for the call when we prayed. Sometimes I imagined God calling me, his rumbling voice British-accented. He would not say my name right; like Father Benedict, he would place the emphasis on the second syllable rather than the first.

'I wanted to be a doctor at first. Then I went to church once and heard this priest speak and I was changed forever,' Father Amadi said.

'Oh.'

'I was joking,' Father Amadi glanced at me. He looked surprised I did not realize that it was a joke. 'It's a lot more complicated than that,

Kambili. I had many questions, growing up. The priesthood came closest to answering them.'

I wondered what questions they were and if Father Benedict, too, had those questions. Then I thought, with a fierce, unreasonable sadness, how Father Amadi's smooth skin would not be passed on to a child, how his square shoulders would not balance the legs of his toddler son who wanted to touch the ceiling fan.

'*Ewo*, I am late for a chaplaincy council meeting,' he said, looking at the clock. 'I'll drop you off and leave right away.'

'I'm sorry.'

'Why? I've spent an enjoyable afternoon with you. You must come with me to the stadium again. I will tie your hands and legs up and carry you if I have to.' He laughed.

I stared at the dashboard, at the blue-and-gold Legion of Mary sticker on it. Didn't he know that I did not want him to leave, ever? That I did not need to be persuaded to go to the stadium, or anywhere, with him? The afternoon played across my mind as I got out of the car in front of the flat. I had smiled, run, laughed. My chest was filled with something like bath foam. Light. The lightness was so sweet I tasted it on my tongue, the sweetness of an overripe bright yellow cashew fruit.

Aunty Ifeoma was standing behind Papa-Nnukwu on the verandah, rubbing his shoulders. I greeted them.

'Kambili, *nno*,' Papa-Nnukwu said. He looked tired; his eyes were dull.

'Did you enjoy yourself?' Aunty Ifeoma asked, smiling.

'Yes, Aunty.'

'Your father called this afternoon,' she said, in English.

I stared at her, studying the black mole above her lip, willing her to laugh her loud, cackling laugh and tell me it was a joke. Papa never called in the afternoon. Besides, he had called before he went to work, so why had he called again? Something had to be wrong.

'Somebody from the village – I'm sure it was a member of our extended family – told him that I had come to take your grandfather from the village,' Aunty Ifeoma said, still in English so Papa-Nnukwu would not understand. 'Your father said I should have told him, that he deserved to know that your grandfather was here in Nsukka. He went on and on about a heathen being in the same house as his children.' Aunty Ifeoma shook her head as if the way Papa felt were just a minor eccentricity. But it was not. Papa would be outraged that neither Jaja nor I had mentioned it when he called. My head was filling up quickly with blood or water or sweat. Whatever it was, I knew I would faint when my head got full.

'He said he would come here tomorrow to take you both back, but I calmed him down. I told him that I would take you and Jaja home the day after tomorrow, and I think he accepted that. Let's hope we find fuel,' Aunty Ifeoma said.

'Okay, Aunty.' I turned to go into the flat, feeling dizzy.

'Oh, and he has gotten his editor out of prison,' Aunty Ifeoma said. But I hardly heard her.

Amaka shook me although her movements had already woken me. I had been teetering on that boundary that divides sleep and wakefulness, imagining Papa coming to get us himself, imagining the rage in his red-tinged eyes, the burst of Igbo from his mouth.

'Let's go and fetch water. Jaja and Obiora are already out,' Amaka said, stretching. She said that every morning now. She let me carry one container in now, too.

'*Nekwa*, Papa-Nnukwu is still asleep. He will be upset that the medicines made him oversleep and he did not wake to watch the sun rise.' She bent and shook him gently.

'Papa-Nnukwu, Papa-Nnukwu, *kunie*.' She turned him over slowly when he did not stir. His wrapper had come undone to reveal a pair of white shorts with a frayed elastic band at the waist. 'Mom! Mom!' Amaka screamed. She moved a hand over Papa-Nnukwu's chest, feverishly, searching for a heart-beat. 'Mom!'

Aunty Ifeoma hurried into the room. She had not tied her wrapper over her nightdress, and I could make out the downward slope of her breasts, the

212

slight swell of her belly underneath the sheer fabric. She sank to her knees and clutched Papa-Nnukwu's body, shaking it.

'*Nna anyi! Nna anyi!*' Her voice was desperately loud, as if raising it would make Papa-Nnukwu hear better and respond. '*Nna anyi!*' When she stopped speaking, grasping Papa-Nnukwu's wrist, resting her head on his chest, the silence was broken only by the crow of the neighbor's cock. I held my breath – it suddenly seemed too loud for Aunty Ifeoma to hear Papa-Nnukwu's heartbeat.

'*Ewuu*, he has fallen asleep. He has fallen asleep,' Aunty Ifeoma said, finally. She buried her head on Papa-Nnukwu's shoulder, rocking back and forth.

Amaka pulled at her mother. 'Stop it, Mom. Give him mouth to mouth! Stop it!'

Aunty Ifeoma kept rocking, and for a moment, because Papa-Nnukwu's body moved back and forth as well, I wondered if Aunty Ifeoma was wrong and Papa-Nnukwu was only really asleep.

'*Nna m o!* My father!' Aunty Ifeoma's voice rang out so pure and high it seemed to come from the ceiling. It was the same tone, the same piercing depth, that I heard sometimes in Abba when mourners danced past our house, holding the photograph of a dead family member, shouting.

'*Nna m o!*' Aunty Ifeoma screamed, still clutching Papa-Nnukwu. Amaka made feeble attempts to pull her off. Obiora and Jaja dashed into the room. And I imagined our forebears a century ago, the

213

ancestors Papa-Nnukwu prayed to, charging in to defend their hamlet, coming back with lolling heads on long sticks.

'What is it, Mom?' Obiora asked. The bottom of his trousers clung to his leg where water from the tap had splashed on it.

'Papa-Nnukwu is alive,' Jaja said in English, with authority, as if doing so would make his words come true. The same tone God must have used when He said 'Let there be Light.' Jaja wore only the bottom of his pajamas, which was also splattered with water. For the first time, I noticed the sparse hair on his chest.

'*Nna m o!*' Aunty Ifeoma was still clutching Papa-Nnukwu.

Obiora started to breathe in a noisy, rasping way. He bent over Aunty Ifeoma and grasped her, slowly prying her away from Papa-Nnukwu's body. '*O zugo*, it is enough, Mom. He has joined the others.' His voice had a strange timbre. He helped Aunty Ifeoma up and led her to sit on the bed. She had the same blank look in her eyes that Amaka had, standing there, staring down at Papa-Nnukwu's form.

'I will call Doctor Nduoma,' Obiora said.

Jaja bent down and covered Papa-Nnukwu's body with the wrapper, but he did not cover his face even though the wrapper was long enough. I wanted to go over and touch Papa-Nnukwu, touch the white tufts of hair that Amaka oiled, smooth the wrinkled skin of his chest. But I would not. Papa would be outraged. I closed my eyes then so that if Papa asked if I had seen Jaja touch the body of a heathen – it seemed more grievous, touching Papa-Nnukwu in death – I could truthfully say no, because I had not seen everything that Jaja did. My eyes remained closed for a long time, and it seemed that my ears, too, were closed, because although I could hear the sound of voices, I did not make out what they said. When I finally opened my eyes, Jaja sat on the floor, next to Papa-Nnukwu's sheathed frame. Obiora sat on the bed with Aunty Ifeoma, who was speaking. 'Wake Chima up, so we can tell him before the people from the mortuary come.'

Jaja stood up to go and wake Chima. He wiped at the tears that slid down his cheeks as he went.

'I will clean where the *ozu* lay, Mom,' Obiora said. He let out sporadic choking sounds, crying deep in his throat. I knew that the reason he did not cry out loud was because he was the nwoke in the house, the man Aunty Ifeoma had by her side.

'No,' Aunty Ifeoma said. 'I will do it.' She stood up then and hugged Obiora, and they held on to each other for a long time. I went toward the bathroom, the word *ozu* ringing in my ears. Papa-Nnukwu was an ozu now, a corpse.

The bathroom door did not give when I tried to open it, and I pushed harder to make sure it was really locked. Sometimes it got stuck because of the way the wood expanded and contracted. Then I heard Amaka's sobbing. It was loud and throaty; she laughed the way she cried. She had not learned the art of silent crying; she had not needed to. I wanted to turn and go away, to leave her with her grief. But my underwear already felt wet, and I had to move my weight from leg to leg to hold the urine back.

'Amaka, please, I have to use the toilet,' I whispered, and when she did not respond, I repeated it loudly. I did not want to knock; knocking would intrude rudely on her tears. Finally, Amaka unlocked the door and opened it. I urinated as quickly as I could because I knew she stood just outside, waiting to go back in and sob behind the locked door.

The two men who came with Doctor Nduoma carried Papa-Nnukwu's stiffening body in their hands, one holding his underarms and the other his ankles. They could not get the stretcher from the medical center because the medical administrative staff was on strike, too. Doctor Nduoma said '*Ndo*' to all of us, the smile still on his face. Obiora said he wanted to accompany the ozu to the mortuary; he wanted to see them put the ozu in the fridge. But Aunty Ifeoma said no, he did not have to see Papa-Nnukwu put in the fridge. The word *fridge* floated around in my head. I knew where they put corpses in the mortuary was different, yet I imagined Papa-Nnukwu's body being folded into a home refrigerator, the kind in our kitchen.

Obiora agreed not to go to the mortuary, but he followed the men and watched closely as they loaded the ozu into the station wagon ambulance. He peered into the back of the car to make sure that there was a mat to lay the ozu on, that they would not just lay it down on the rusty floor.

After the ambulance drove off, followed by Doctor Nduoma in his car, I helped Aunty Ifeoma carry Papa-Nnukwu's mattress to the verandah. She scrubbed it thoroughly with Omo detergent and the same brush Amaka used to clean the bathtub.

'Did you see your Papa-Nnukwu's face in death, Kambili?' Aunty Ifeoma asked, leaning the clean mattress against the metal railings to dry.

I shook my head. I had not looked at his face.

'He was smiling,' she said. 'He was smiling.'

I looked away so Aunty Ifeoma would not see the tears on my face and so I would not see the tears on hers. There was not much talking in the flat; the silence was heavy and brooding. Even Chima curled up in a corner for much of the morning, quietly drawing pictures. Aunty Ifeoma boiled some yam slices, and we ate them dipped in palm oil that had chopped red peppers floating in it. Amaka came out of the bathroom hours after we had eaten, her eyes swollen, her voice hoarse.

'Go and eat, Amaka. I boiled yam,' Aunty Ifeoma said.

'I did not finish painting him. He said we would finish it today.'

'Go and eat, *inugo*,' Aunty Ifeoma repeated.

'He would be alive now if the medical center was not on strike,' Amaka said.

'It was his time,' Aunty Ifeoma said. 'Do you hear me? It was simply his time.'

Amaka stared at Aunty Ifeoma and then turned away. I wanted to hug her, to say *'ebezi na'* and wipe away her tears. I wanted to cry loudly, in front of her, with her. But I knew it might anger her. She was already angry enough. Besides, I did not have a right to mourn Papa-Nnukwu with her; he had been her Papa-Nnukwu more than mine. She had oiled his hair while I kept away and wondered what Papa would say if he knew. Jaja put his arm around her and led her into the kitchen. She shook free of him, as if to prove she did not need support, but she walked close to him. I stared after them, wishing I had done that instead of Jaja.

'Somebody just parked in front of our flat,' Obiora said. He had taken off his glasses to cry, but now he had them back on, and he pushed them up the bridge of his nose as he got up to look outside.

'Who is it?' Aunty Ifeoma asked, tiredly. She could not care less who it was.

'Uncle Eugene.'

I froze on my seat, felt the skin of my arms melding and becoming one with the cane arms of

218

the chair. Papa-Nnukwu's death had overshadowed everything, pushed Papa's face into a vague place. But that face had come alive now. It was at the door, looking down at Obiora. Those bushy eyebrows were not familiar; neither was that shade of brown skin. Perhaps if Obiora had not said, 'Uncle Eugene,' I would not have known that it was Papa, that the tall stranger in the well-tailored white tunic was Papa.

'Good afternoon, Papa,' I said, mechanically.

'Kambili, how are you? Where is Jaja?'

Jaja came out of the kitchen then and stood staring at Papa. 'Good afternoon, Papa,' he finally said.

'Eugene, I asked you not to come,' Aunty Ifeoma said, in the same tired tone of one who did not really care. 'I told you I would bring them back tomorrow,'

'I could not let them stay an extra day,' Papa said, looking around the living room, toward the kitchen and then the hallway, as if waiting for Papa-Nnukwu to appear in a puff of heathen smoke.

Obiora took Chima by the hand and went out to the verandah.

'Eugene, our father has fallen asleep,' Aunty Ifeoma said.

Papa stared at her for a while, surprise widening the narrow eyes that so easily became red-spotted. 'When?'

'This morning. In his sleep. They took him to the mortuary just hours ago.'

Papa sat down and slowly lowered his head into his hands, and I wondered if he was crying, if it would be acceptable for me to cry, too. But when he looked up, I did not see the traces of tears in his eyes. 'Did you call a priest to give him extreme unction?' he asked.

Aunty Ifeoma ignored him and continued to look at her hands, folded in her lap.

'Ifeoma, did you call a priest?' Papa asked.

'Is that all you can say, eh, Eugene? Have you nothing else to say, *gbo*? Our father has died! Has your head turned upside down? Will you not help me bury our father?'

'I cannot participate in a pagan funeral, but we can discuss with the parish priest and arrange a Catholic funeral.'

Aunty Ifeoma got up and started to shout. Her voice was unsteady. 'I will put my dead husband's grave up for sale, Eugene, before I give our father a Catholic funeral. Do you hear me? I said I will sell Ifediora's grave first! Was our father a Catholic? I ask you, Eugene, was he a Catholic? *Uchu gba gi!*' Aunty Ifeoma snapped her fingers at Papa; she was throwing a curse at him. Tears rolled down her cheeks. She made choking sounds as she turned and walked into her bedroom.

'Kambili and Jaja, come,' Papa said, standing up. He hugged us at the same time, tightly. He kissed the tops of our heads, before saying, 'Go and pack your bags.'

In the bedroom, most of my clothes were in the

bag already. I stood staring at the window with the missing louvers and the torn mosquito netting, wondering what it would be like if I tore through the small hole and leaped out.

'*Nne*.' Aunty Ifeoma came in silently and ran a hand over my cornrows. She handed me my schedule, still folded in crisp quarters.

'Tell Father Amadi that I have left, that we have left, say good-bye for us,' I said, turning. She had wiped the tears from her face, and she looked the same again, fearless.

'I will,' she said.

She held my hand in hers as we walked to the front door. Outside, the harmatten wind tore across the front yard, ruffling the plants in the circular garden, bending the will and branches of trees, coating the parked cars with more dust. Obiora carried our bags to the Mercedes, where Kevin waited with the boot open. Chima started to cry; I knew he did not want Jaja to leave.

'Chima, *o zugo*. You will see Jaja again soon. They will come again,' Aunty Ifeoma said, holding him close. Papa did not say yes to back up what Aunty Ifeoma had said. Instead, to make Chima feel better he said, '*O zugo*, it's enough,' hugged Chima, and stuffed a small wad of naira notes into Aunty Ifeoma's hand to buy Chima a present, which made Chima smile. Amaka blinked rapidly as she said good-bye, and I was not sure if it was from the gritty wind or to keep more tears back. The dust coating her eyelashes looked stylish, like cocoa-colored mascara. She pressed something wrapped in black cellophane into my hands, then turned and hurried back into the flat. I could see through the wrapping: it was the unfinished painting of Papa-Nnukwu. I hid it in my bag, quickly, and climbed into the car.

Mama was at the door when we drove into our compound. Her face was swollen and the area around her right eye was the black-purple shade of an overripe avocado. She was smiling. '*Umu m*, welcome. Welcome.' She hugged us at the same time, burying her head in Jaja's neck and then in mine. 'It seems so long, so much longer than ten days.'

'Ifeoma was busy tending to a heathen,' Papa said, pouring a glass of water from a bottle Sisi placed on the table. 'She did not even take them to Aokpe on pilgrimage.'

'Papa-Nnukwu is dead,' Jaja said.

Mama's hand flew to her chest. '*Chi m!* When?'

'This morning,' Jaja said. 'He died in his sleep.'

Mama wrapped her hands around herself. '*Ewuu*, so he has gone to rest, *ewuu*.'

'He has gone to face judgment,' Papa said, putting his glass of water down. 'Ifeoma did not have the sense to call a priest before he died. He might have converted before he died.'

'Maybe he didn't want to convert,' Jaja said.

'May he rest in peace,' Mama said quickly.

Papa looked at Jaja. 'What did you say? Is that

what you have learned from living in the same house as a heathen?'

'No,' Jaja said.

Papa stared at Jaja, then at me, shaking his head slowly as if we had somehow changed color. 'Go and bathe and come down for dinner,' he said.

As we went upstairs, Jaja walked in front of me and I tried to place my feet on the exact spots where he placed his. Papa's prayer before dinner was longer than usual: he asked God to cleanse his children, to remove whatever spirit it was that made them lie to him about being in the same house as a heathen. 'It is the sin of omission, Lord,' he said, as though God did not know. I said my 'amen' loudly. Dinner was beans and rice with chunks of chicken. As I ate, I thought how each chunk of chicken on my plate would be cut into three pieces in Aunty Ifeoma's house.

'Papa, may I have the key to my room, please?' Jaja asked, setting his fork down. We were halfway through dinner. I took a deep breath and held it. Papa had always kept the keys to our rooms.

'What?' Papa asked.

'The key to my room. I would like to have it. *Makana*, because I would like some privacy.'

Papa's pupils seemed to dart around in the whites of his eyes. 'What? What do you want privacy for? To commit a sin against your own body? Is that what you want to do, masturbate?'

'No,' Jaja said. He moved his hand and knocked his glass of water over.

'See what has happened to my children?' Papa asked the ceiling. 'See how being with a heathen has changed them, has taught them evil?'

We finished dinner in silence. Afterward, Jaja followed Papa upstairs. I sat with Mama in the living room, wondering why Jaja had asked for the key. Of course Papa would never give it to him, he knew that, knew that Papa would never let us lock our doors. For a moment, I wondered if Papa was right, if being with Papa-Nnukwu had made Jaja evil, had made us evil.

'It feels different to be back, *okwia*?' Mama asked. She was looking through samples of fabric, to pick out a shade for the new curtains. We replaced the curtains every year, toward the end of harmattan. Kevin brought samples for Mama to look at, and she picked some and showed Papa, so he could make the final decision. Papa usually chose her favorite. Dark beige last year. Sand beige the year before.

I wanted to tell Mama that it did feel different to be back, that our living room had too much empty space, too much wasted marble floor that gleamed from Sisi's polishing and housed nothing. Our ceilings were too high. Our furniture was lifeless: the glass tables did not shed twisted skin in the harmattan, the leather sofas' greeting was a clammy coldness, the Persian rugs were too lush to have any feeling. But I said, 'You polished the étagère.'

'Yes.'

'When?'

'Yesterday.'

I stared at her eye. It appeared to be opening now; it must have been swollen completely shut yesterday.

'Kambili!' Papa's voice carried clearly from upstairs. I held my breath and sat still. 'Kambili!'

'*Nne*, go,' Mama said.

I went upstairs slowly. Papa was in the bathroom, with the door ajar. I knocked on the open door and stood by, wondering why he had called me when he was in the bathroom. 'Come in,' he said. He was standing by the tub. 'Climb into the tub.'

I stared at Papa. Why was he asking me to climb into the tub? I looked around the bathroom floor; there was no stick anywhere. Maybe he would keep me in the bathroom and then go down-stairs, out through the kitchen, to break a stick off one of the trees in the backyard. When Jaja and I were younger, from elementary two until about elementary five, he asked us to get the stick ourselves. We always chose whistling pine because the branches were malleable, not as painful as the stiffer branches from the gmelina or the avocado. And Jaja soaked the sticks in cold water because he said that made them less painful when they landed on your body. The older we got, though, the smaller the branches we brought, until Papa started to go out himself to get the stick.

'Climb into the tub,' Papa said again.

I stepped into the tub and stood looking at him. It didn't seem that he was going to get a stick, and I felt fear, stinging and raw, fill my bladder and my ears. I did not know what he was going to do to me. It was easier when I saw a stick, because I could rub my palms together and tighten the muscles of my calves in preparation. He had never asked me to stand inside a tub. Then I noticed the kettle on the floor, close to Papa's feet, the green kettle Sisi used to boil hot water for tea and garri, the one that whistled when the water started to boil. Papa picked it up. 'You knew your grandfather was coming to Nsukka, did you not?' he asked in Igbo.

'Yes, Papa.'

'Did you pick up the phone and inform me of this, *gbo*?'

'No.'

'You knew you would be sleeping in the same house as a heathen?'

'Yes, Papa.'

'So you saw the sin clearly and you walked right into it?'

I nodded. 'Yes, Papa.'

'Kambili, you are precious.' His voice quavered now, like someone speaking at a funeral, choked with emotion. 'You should strive for perfection. You should not see sin and walk right into it.' He lowered the kettle into the tub, tilted it toward my feet. He poured the hot water on my feet, slowly, as if he were conducting an experiment and

226

wanted to see what would happen. He was crying now, tears streaming down his face. I saw the moist steam before I saw the water. I watched the water leave the kettle, flowing almost in slow motion in an arc to my feet. The pain of contact was so pure, so scalding, I felt nothing for a second. And then I screamed.

'That is what you do to yourself when you walk into sin. You burn your feet,' he said.

I wanted to say 'Yes, Papa,' because he was right, but the burning on my feet was climbing up, in swift courses of excruciating pain, to my head and lips and eyes. Papa was holding me with one wide hand, pouring the water carefully with the other. I did not know that the sobbing voice – 'I'm sorry! I'm sorry!' – was mine until the water stopped and I realized my mouth was moving and the words were still coming out. Papa put the kettle down, wiped at his eyes. I stood in the scalding tub; I was too scared to move – the skin of my feet would peel off if I tried to step out of the tub.

Papa put his hands under my arms to carry me out, but I heard Mama say, 'Let me, please.' I did not realize that Mama had come into the bathroom. Tears were running down her face. Her nose was running, too, and I wondered if she would wipe it before it got to her mouth, before she would have to taste it. She mixed salt with cold water and gently plastered the gritty mixture onto my feet. She helped me out of the tub, made to carry me on her back to my room, but I shook my head. She was too small. We might both fall. Mama did not speak until we were in my room. 'You should take Panadol,' she said.

I nodded and let her give me the tablets, although I knew they would do little for my feet, now throbbing to a steady, searing pulse. 'Did you go to Jaja's room?' I asked, and Mama nodded. She did not tell me about him, and I did not ask.

'The skin of my feet will be bloated tomorrow,' I said.

'Your feet will be healed in time for school,' Mama said.

After Mama left, I stared at the closed door, at the smooth surface, and thought about the doors in Nsukka and their peeling blue paint. I thought about Father Amadi's musical voice, about the wide gap that showed between Amaka's teeth when she laughed, about Aunty Ifeoma stirring stew at her kerosene stove. I thought about Obiora pushing his glasses up his nose and Chima curled up on the sofa, fast asleep. I got up and hobbled over to get the painting of Papa-Nnukwu from my bag. It was still in the black wrapping. Even though it was in an obscure side pocket of my bag, I was too scared to unwrap it. Papa would know, somehow. He would smell the painting in his house. I ran my finger along the plastic wrapping, over the slight ridges of paint that melded into the lean form of Papa-Nnukwu, the relaxed fold of arms, the long legs stretched out in front of him.

I had just hobbled back to my bed when Papa opened the door and came in. He knew. I wanted to shift and rearrange myself on the bed, as if that would hide what I had just done. I wanted to search his eyes to know what he knew, how he had found out about the painting. But I did not, could not. Fear. I was familiar with fear, yet each time I felt it, it was never the same as the other times, as though it came in different flavors and colors.

'Everything I do for you, I do for your own good,' Papa said. 'You know that?'

'Yes, Papa.' I still was not sure if he knew about the painting.

He sat on my bed and held my hand. 'I committed a sin against my own body once,' he said. 'And the good father, the one I lived with while I went to St Gregory's, came in and saw me. He asked me to boil water for tea. He poured the water in a bowl and soaked my hands in it.' Papa was looking right into my eyes. I did not know he had committed any sins, that he could commit any sins. 'I never sinned against my own body again. The good father did that for my own good.' he said.

After Papa left, I did not think about his hands soaked in hot water for tea, the skin peeling off, his face set in tight lines of pain. Instead I thought about the painting of Papa-Nnukwu in my bag.

★   ★   ★

I did not get a chance to tell Jaja about the painting until the next day, a Saturday, when he came into my room during study time. He wore thick socks and placed his feet gingerly one after the other, as I did. But we did not talk about our padded feet. After he felt the painting with his finger, he said he had something to show me, too. We went downstairs to the kitchen. It was wrapped in black cellophane paper, as well, and he had lodged it in the refrigerator, beneath bottles of Fanta. When he saw my puzzled look, he said they weren't just sticks; they were stalks of purple hibiscus. He would give them to the gardener. It was still harmattan and the earth was thirsty, but Aunty Ifeoma said the stalks might take root and grow if they were watered regularly, that hibiscuses didn't like too much water, but they didn't like to be too dry, either.

Jaja's eyes shone as he talked about the hibiscuses, as he held them out so I could touch the cold, moist sticks. He had told Papa about them, yet he quickly put them back into the fridge when we heard Papa coming.

Lunch was yam porridge, the smell wafting around the house even before we went to the dining table. It smelled good – pieces of dried fish drifting in yellow sauce alongside the greens and cubed yams. After prayers, as Mama dished out the food, Papa said, 'These pagan funerals are expensive. One fetish group will ask for a cow, then a witch doctor will demand a goat for some god of stone, then another cow for the hamlet and another for the *umuada*. Nobody ever asks why the so-called gods don't ever eat the animals and instead greedy men share the meat among themselves. The death of a person is just an excuse for heathens to feast.'

I wondered why Papa was saying this, what had prompted him. The rest of us remained silent while Mama finished dishing out the food.

'I sent Ifeoma money for the funeral. I gave her all she needed,' Papa said. After a pause, he added, 'For *nna anyi*'s funeral.'

'Thanks be to God,' Mama said, and Jaja and I repeated her.

Sisi came in before we finished lunch to tell Papa that Ade Coker was at the gate with another man. Adamu had asked them to wait at the gate; he always did that when people visited during weekend meal times. I expected Papa to ask them to wait on the patio until we finished lunch, but he told Sisi to have Adamu let them in and to open the front door. He said the prayer after meals while we still had food on our plates and then asked us to keep eating, he would be right back.

The guests came in and sat down in the living room. I could not see them from the dining table, but while I ate, I tried hard to make out what they were saying. I knew Jaja was listening, too. I saw the way his head was slightly tilted, his eyes focused on the empty space in front of him. They were talking in low tones, but it was easy to make out the name Nwankiti Ogechi, especially when Ade Coker spoke, because he did not lower his voice as much as Papa and the other man did.

He was saying that Big Oga's assistant – Ade Coker referred to the head of state as Big Oga even in his editorials – had called to say that Big Oga was willing to give him an exclusive interview. 'But they want me to cancel the Nwankiti Ogechi story. Imagine the stupid man, he said they knew some useless people had told me stories that I planned to use in my piece and that the stories were lies . . .'

I heard Papa interrupt in a low voice, and the other man added something afterward, something about the Big People in Abuja not wanting such a story out now that the Commonwealth Nations were meeting.

'You know what this means? My sources were right. They have really wasted Nwankiti Ogechi,' Ade Coker said. 'Why didn't they care when I did the last story about him? Why do they care now?'

I knew what story Ade was referring to, since it was in the *Standard* about six weeks ago, right around the time Nwankiti Ogechi first disappeared without a trace. I remembered the huge black question mark above the caption 'Where is Nwankiti?' And I remembered that the article was full of worried quotes from his family and colleagues. It was nothing like the first *Standard* feature I'd read about him, titled 'A Saint among Us,' which had focused on his activism, on his pro-democracy rallies that filled the stadium at Surulere.

'I am telling Ade we should wait, sir,' the other guest was saying. 'Let him do the interview with Big Oga. We can do the Nwankiti Ogechi story later.'

'No way!' Ade burst out, and if I had not known that slightly shrill voice, it would have been hard for me to imagine the round, laughing Ade sounding that way, so angry. 'They don't want Nwankiti Ogechi to become an issue now. Simple! And you know what it means, it means they have wasted him! Which one is for Big Oga to try and bribe me with an interview? I ask you, eh, which one is that?'

Papa cut him short then, but I could not hear much of what he said, because he spoke in low, soothing tones, as though he were calming Ade down. The next thing I heard him say was, 'Come, let us go to my study. My children are eating.'

They walked past us on their way upstairs. Ade smiled as he greeted us, but it was a strained smile. 'Can I come and finish the food for you?' he teased me, making a mock attempt to swoop down on my food.

After lunch, as I sat in my room, studying, I tried hard to hear what Papa and Ade Coker were saying in the study. But I couldn't. Jaja walked past the study a few times, but when I looked at him, he shook his head – he could hear nothing through the closed door, either.

It was that evening, before dinner, that the government agents came, the men in black who yanked hibiscuses off as they left, the men Jaja said had come to bribe Papa with a truckful of dollars, the men Papa asked to get out of our house.

When we got the next edition of the *Standard*, I knew it would have Nwankiti Ogechi on its cover. The story was detailed, angry, full of quotes from someone called The Source. Soldiers shot Nwankiti Ogechi in a bush in Minna. And then they poured acid on his body to melt his flesh off his bones, to kill him even when he was already dead.

During family time, while Papa and I played chess, Papa winning, we heard on the radio that Nigeria had been suspended from the Commonwealth because of the murder, that Canada and Holland were recalling their ambassadors in protest. The newscaster read a small portion of the press release from the Canadian government, which referred to Nwankiti Ogechi as 'a man of honor.'

Papa looked up from the board and said, 'It was coming to this. I knew it would come to this.'

Some men arrived just after we had dinner, and I heard Sisi tell Papa that they said they were from the Democratic Coalition. They stayed on the patio with Papa, and even though I tried to, I could not hear their conversation. The next day, more guests came during dinner. And even more the day after. They all told Papa to be careful.

Stop going to work in your official car. Don't go to public places. Remember the bomb blast at the airport when a civil rights lawyer was traveling. Remember the one at the stadium during the pro-democracy meeting. Lock your doors. Remember the man shot in his bedroom by men wearing black masks.

Mama told me and Jaja. She looked scared when she talked, and I wanted to pat her shoulder and tell her Papa would be fine. I knew he and Ade Coker worked with truth, and I knew he would be fine.

'Do you think Godless men have any sense?' Papa asked every night at dinner, often after a long stretch of silence. He seemed to drink a lot of water at dinner, and I would watch him, wondering if his hands were really shaking or if I was imagining it.

Jaja and I did not talk about the many people who came to the house. I wanted to talk about it, but Jaja looked away when I brought it up with my eyes, and he changed the subject when I spoke of it. The only time I heard him say anything about it was when Aunty Ifeoma called to find out how Papa was doing, because she had heard about the furor the *Standard* story had caused. Papa was not home, and so she spoke to Mama. Afterward, Mama gave the phone to Jaja.

'Aunty, they won't touch Papa,' I heard Jaja say. 'They know he has many foreign connections.'

As I listened to Jaja go on to tell Aunty Ifeoma

235

that the gardener had planted the hibiscus stalks, but that it was still too early to tell if they would live, I wondered why he had never said that to me about Papa.

When I took the phone, Aunty Ifeoma sounded close by and loud. After our greetings, I took a deep breath and said, 'Greet Father Amadi.'

'He asks about you and Jaja all the time,' Aunty Ifeoma said. 'Hold on, *nne*, Amaka is here.'

'Kambili, *ke kwanu?*' Amaka sounded different on the phone. Breezy. Less likely to start an argument. Less likely to sneer – or maybe that was simply because I would not see the sneer.

'I'm fine,' I said. 'Thank you. Thank you for the painting.'

'I thought you might want to keep it.' Amaka's voice was still hoarse when she spoke of Papa-Nnukwu.

'Thank you,' I whispered. I had not known that Amaka even thought of me, even knew what I wanted, even knew that I wanted.

'You know Papa-Nnukwu's *akwam ozu* is next week?'

'Yes.'

'We will wear white. Black is too depressing, especially that shade people wear to mourn, like burnt wood. I will lead the dance of the grandchildren.' She sounded proud.

'He will rest in peace,' I said. I wondered if she could tell that I, too, wanted to wear white, to join the funeral dance of the grandchildren.

'Yes, he will.' There was a pause. 'Thanks to Uncle Eugene.'

I didn't know what to say. I felt as if I were standing on a floor where a child had spilled talcum powder and I would have to walk carefully so as not to slip and fall.

'Papa-Nnukwu really worried about having a proper funeral,' Amaka said. 'Now I know he'll rest in peace. Uncle Eugene gave Mom so much money she's buying seven cows for the funeral!'

'That's nice.' A mumble.

'I hope you and Jaja can come for Easter. The apparitions are still going on, so maybe we can go on pilgrimage to Aokpe this time, if that will make Uncle Eugene say yes. And I am doing my confirmation on Easter Sunday and I want you and Jaja to be there.'

'I want to go, too,' I said, smiling, because the words I had just said, the whole conversation with Amaka, were dreamlike. I thought about my own confirmation, last year at St Agnes. Papa had bought my white lace dress and a soft, layered veil, which the women in Mama's prayer group touched, crowding around me after Mass. The bishop had trouble lifting the veil from my face to make the sign of the cross on my forehead and say, 'Ruth, be sealed with the gift of the Holy Spirit.' Ruth. Papa had chosen my confirmation name.

'Have you picked a confirmation name?' I asked.

'No,' Amaka said. '*Ngwanu*, Mom wants to remind Aunty Beatrice of something.'

'Greet Chima and Obiora,' I said, before I handed the phone to Mama.

Back in my room, I stared at my textbook and wondered if Father Amadi had really asked about us or if Aunty Ifeoma had said so out of courtesy, so it would be that he remembered us, just as we remembered him. But Aunty Ifeoma was not like that. She would not say it if he had not asked. I wondered if he had asked about us, Jaja and me at the same time, like asking about two things that went together. Corn and ube. Rice and stew. Yam and oil. Or if he had separated us, asked about me and then about Jaja. When I heard Papa come home from work, I roused myself and looked at my book. I had been doodling on a sheet of paper, stick figures, and 'Father Amadi' written over and over again. I tore up the piece of paper.

I tore up many more in the following weeks. They all had 'Father Amadi' written over and over again. On some I tried to capture his voice, using the symbols of music. On others I formed the letters of his name using Roman numerals. I did not need to write his name down to see him, though. I recognized a flash of his gait, that loping, confident stride, in the gardener's. I saw his lean, muscular build in Kevin and, when school resumed, even a flash of his smile in Mother Lucy. I joined the group of girls on the volleyball field on the second day of school. I did not hear the whispers of 'backyard snob' or the ridiculing laughter. I did not notice the amused pinches they gave one another. I stood waiting with my hands clasped until I was picked. I saw only Father Amadi's clay-colored face and heard only 'You have good legs for running.'

It rained heavily the day Ade Coker died, a strange, furious rain in the middle of the parched harmattan. Ade Coker was at breakfast with his family when a courier delivered a package to him. His daughter, in her primary school uniform, was sitting across the table from him. The baby was nearby, in a high chair. His wife was spooning Cerelac into the baby's mouth. Ade Coker was blown up when he opened the package – a package everybody would have known was from the Head of State even if his wife Yewande had not said that Ade Coker looked at the envelope and said 'It has the State House seal' before he opened it.

When Jaja and I came home from school, we were almost drenched by the walk from the car to the front door; the rain was so heavy it had formed a small pool beside the hibiscuses. My feet itched inside my wet leather sandals. Papa was crumpled on a sofa in the living room, sobbing. He seemed so small. Papa who was so tall that he sometimes lowered his head to get through doorways, that his tailor always used extra fabric to sew his trousers. Now he seemed small; he looked like a rumpled roll of fabric.

'I should have made Ade hold that story,' Papa was saying. 'I should have protected him. I should have made him stop that story.'

Mama held him close to her, cradling his face on her chest. 'No,' she said. '*O zugo*. Don't.'

Jaja and I stood watching. I thought about Ade Coker's glasses, I imagined the thick, bluish lenses shattering, the white frames melting into sticky goo. Later, after Mama told us what had happened, how it had happened, Jaja said, 'It was God's will, Papa,' and Papa smiled at Jaja and gently patted his back.

Papa organized Ade Coker's funeral; he set up a trust for Yewande Coker and the children, bought them a new house. He paid the *Standard* staff huge bonuses and asked them all to take a long leave. Hollows appeared under his eyes during those weeks, as if someone had suctioned the delicate flesh, leaving his eyes sunken in.

My nightmares started then, nightmares in which I saw Ade Coker's charred remains spattered on his dining table, on his daughter's school uniform, on his baby's cereal bowl, on his plate of eggs. In some of the nightmares, I was the daughter and the charred remains became Papa's.

Weeks after Ade Coker died, the hollows were still carved under Papa's eyes, and there was a slowness in his movements, as though his legs were too heavy to lift, his hands too heavy to swing. He took longer to reply when spoken to, to chew his food, even to find the right Bible passages to read. But he prayed a lot more, and some nights when I woke up to pee, I heard him shouting from the balcony overlooking the front yard. Even though I sat on the toilet seat and listened, I never could make sense of what he was saying. When I told Jaja about this, he shrugged and said that Papa must have been speaking in tongues, although we both knew that Papa did not approve of people speaking in tongues because it was what the fake pastors at those mushroom Pentecostal churches did.

Mama told Jaja and me often to remember to hug Papa tighter, to let him know we were there, because he was under so much pressure. Soldiers had gone to one of the factories, carrying dead rats in a carton, and then closed the factory down, saying the rats had been found there and could spread disease through the wafers and biscuits. Papa no longer went to the other factories as often as he used to. Some days, Father Benedict came before Jaja and I left for school, and was still in Papa's study when we came home. Mama said they were saying special novenas. Papa never came out to make sure Jaja and I were following our schedules on such days, and so Jaja came into my room to talk, or just to sit on my bed while I studied, before going to his room.

It was on one of those days that Jaja came into

my room, shut the door, and asked, 'Can I see the painting of Papa-Nnukwu?'

My eyes lingered on the door. I never looked at the painting when Papa was at home.

'He is with Father Benedict,' Jaja said. 'He will not come in.'

I took the painting out of the bag and unwrapped it. Jaja stared at it, running his deformed finger over the paint, the finger that had very little feeling.

'I have Papa-Nnukwu's arms,' Jaja said. 'Can you see? I have his arms.' He sounded like someone in a trance, as if he had forgotten where he was and who he was. As if he had forgotten that his finger had little feeling in it.

I did not tell Jaja to stop, or point out that it was his deformed finger that he was running over the painting. I did not put the painting right back. Instead I moved closer to Jaja and we stared at the painting, silently, for a very long time. A long enough time for Father Benedict to leave. I knew Papa would come in to say good night, to kiss my forehead. I knew he would be wearing his wine-red pajamas that lent a slightly red shimmer to his eyes. I knew Jaja would not have enough time to slip the painting back in the bag, and that Papa would take one look at it and his eyes would narrow, his cheeks would bulge out like unripe udala fruit, his mouth would spurt Igbo words.

And that was what happened. Perhaps it was what we wanted to happen, Jaja and I, without being aware of it. Perhaps we all changed after Nsukka – even Papa – and things were destined to not be the same, to not be in their original order.

'What is that? Have you all converted to heathen ways? What are you doing with that painting? Where did you get it?' Papa asked.

'*O nkem*. It's mine,' Jaja said. He wrapped the painting around his chest with his arms.

'It's mine,' I said.

Papa swayed slightly, from side to side, like a person about to fall at the feet of a charismatic pastor after the laying on of hands. Papa did not sway often. His swaying was like shaking a bottle of Coke that burst into violent foam when you opened it.

'Who brought that painting into this house?'

'Me,' I said.

'Me,' Jaja said.

If only Jaja would look at me, I would ask him not to blame himself. Papa snatched the painting from Jaja. His hands moved swiftly, working together. The painting was gone. It already represented something lost, something I had never had, would never have. Now even that reminder was gone, and at Papa's feet lay pieces of paper streaked with earth-tone colors. The pieces were very small, very precise. I suddenly and maniacally imagined Papa-Nnukwu's body being cut in pieces that small and stored in a fridge.

'No!' I shrieked. I dashed to the pieces on the floor as if to save them, as if saving them would mean saving Papa-Nnukwu. I sank to the floor, lay on the pieces of paper.

'What has gotten into you?' Papa asked. 'What is wrong with you?'

I lay on the floor, curled tight like the picture of a child in the uterus in my *Integrated Science for Junior Secondary Schools*.

'Get up! Get away from that painting!'

I lay there, did nothing.

'Get up!' Papa said again. I still did not move. He started to kick me. The metal buckles on his slippers stung like bites from giant mosquitoes. He talked nonstop, out of control, in a mix of Igbo and English, like soft meat and thorny bones. Godlessness. Heathen worship. Hellfire. The kicking increased in tempo, and I thought of Amaka's music, her culturally conscious music that sometimes started off with a calm saxophone and then whirled into lusty singing. I curled around myself tighter, around the pieces of the painting; they were soft, feathery. They still had the metallic smell of Amaka's paint palette. The stinging was raw now, even more like bites, because the metal landed on open skin on my side, my back, my legs. Kicking. Kicking. Kicking. Perhaps it was a belt now because the metal buckle seemed too heavy. Because I could hear a swoosh in the air. A low voice was saying, 'Please, *biko*, please.' More stings. More slaps. A salty wetness warmed my mouth. I closed my eyes and slipped away into quiet.

★   ★   ★

When I opened my eyes, I knew at once that I was not in my bed. The mattress was firmer than mine. I made to get up, but pain shot through my whole body in exquisite little packets. I collapsed back.

'*Nne*, Kambili. Thank God!' Mama stood up and pressed her hand to my forehead, then her face to mine. 'Thank God. Thank God you are awake.'

Her face felt clammy with tears. Her touch was light, yet it sent needles of pain all over me, starting from my head. It was like the hot water Papa had poured on my feet, except now it was my entire body that burned. Each movement was too painful to even think about.

'My whole body is on fire,' I said.

'Shhh,' she said. 'Just rest. Thank God you are awake.'

I did not want to be awake. I did not want to feel the breathing pain at my side. I did not want to feel the heavy hammer knocking in my head. Even taking a breath was agony. A doctor in white was in the room, at the foot of my bed. I knew that voice; he was a lector in church. He was speaking slowly and precisely, the way he did when he read the first and second readings, yet I could not hear it all. Broken rib. Heal nicely. Internal bleeding. He came close and slowly lifted my shirt-sleeve. Injections had always scared me – whenever I had malaria, I prayed I would need to take Novalgin tablets instead of chloroquine injections. But now the prick of a needle was nothing. I would take injections every day over the pain in my body. Papa's face was close to mine. It seemed so close that his nose almost brushed mine, and yet I could tell that his eyes were soft, that he was speaking and crying at the same time. 'My precious daughter. Nothing will happen to you. My precious daughter.' I was not sure if it was a dream. I closed my eyes.

When I opened them again, Father Benedict stood above me. He was making the sign of the cross on my feet with oil; the oil smelled like onions, and even his light touch hurt. Papa was nearby. He, too, was muttering prayers, his hands resting gently on my side. I closed my eyes.

'It does not mean anything. They give extreme unction to anyone who is seriously ill,' Mama whispered, when Papa and Father Benedict left.

I stared at the movement of her lips. I was not seriously ill. She knew that. Why was she saying I was seriously ill? Why was I here in St Agnes hospital?

'Mama, call Aunty Ifeoma,' I said.

Mama looked away. '*Nne*, you have to rest.'

'Call Aunty Ifeoma. Please.'

Mama reached out to hold my hand. Her face was puffy from crying, and her lips were cracked, with bits of discolored skin peeling off. I wished I could get up and hug her, and yet I wanted to push her away, to shove her so hard that she would topple over the chair.

★   ★   ★

Father Amadi's face was looking down at me when I opened my eyes. I was dreaming it, imagining it, and yet I wished that it did not hurt so much to smile, so that I could.

'At first they could not find a vein, and I was so scared.' It was Mama's voice, real and next to me. I was not dreaming.

'Kambili. Kambili. Are you awake?' Father Amadi's voice was deeper, less melodious than in my dreams.

'*Nne*, Kambili, *nne*.' It was Aunty Ifeoma's voice; her face appeared next to Father Amadi's. She had held her braided hair up, in a huge bun that looked like a raffia basket balanced on her head. I tried to smile. I felt woozy. Something was slipping out of me, slipping away, taking my strength and my sanity, and I could not stop it.

'The medication knocks her out,' Mama said.

'*Nne*, your cousins send greetings. They would have come, but they are in school. Father Amadi is here with me. *Nne*...' Aunty Ifeoma clutched my hand, and I winced, pulling it away. Even the effort to pull it away hurt. I wanted to keep my eyes open, wanted to see Father Amadi, to smell his cologne, to hear his voice, but my eyelids were slipping shut.

'This cannot go on, *nwunye m*,' Aunty Ifeoma said. 'When a house is on fire, you run out before the roof collapses on your head.'

'It has never happened like this before. He has never punished her like this before,' Mama said.

'Kambili will come to Nsukka when she leaves the hospital.'

'Eugene will not agree.'

'I will tell him. Our father is dead, so there is no threatening heathen in my house. I want Kambili and Jaja to stay with us, at least until Easter. Pack your own things and come to Nsukka. It will be easier for you to leave when they are not there.'

'It has never happened like this before.'

'Do you not hear what I have said, *gho*?' Aunty Ifeoma said, raising her voice.

'I hear you.'

The voices grew too distant, as if Mama and Aunty Ifeoma were on a boat moving quickly to sea and the waves had swallowed their voices. Before I lost their voices, I wondered where Father Amadi had gone. I opened my eyes hours later. It was dark, and the light bulbs were off. In the glimmer of light from the hallway that streamed underneath the closed door, I could see the crucifix on the wall and Mama's figure on a chair at the foot of my bed.

'*Kedu?* I will be here all night. Sleep. Rest,' Mama said. She got up and sat on my bed. She caressed my pillow; I knew she was afraid to touch me and cause me pain. 'Your father has been by your bedside every night these past three days. He has not slept a wink.'

It was hard to turn my head, but I did it and looked away.

★   ★   ★

My private tutor came the following week. Mama said Papa had interviewed ten people before he picked her. She was a young Reverend Sister and had not yet made her final profession. The beads of the rosary, which were twisted around the waist of her sky-colored habit, rustled as she moved. Her wispy blond hair peeked from beneath her scarf. When she held my hand and said, '*Kee ka ime?*' I was stunned. I had never heard a white person speak Igbo, and so well. She spoke softly in English when we had lessons and in Igbo, although not often, when we didn't. She created her own silence, sitting in it and fingering her rosary while I read comprehension passages. But she knew a lot of things; I saw it in the pools of her hazel eyes. She knew, for example, that I could move more body parts than I told the doctor, although she said nothing. Even the hot pain in my side had become lukewarm, the throbbing in my head had lessened. But I told the doctor it was as bad as before and I screamed when he tried to feel my side. I did not want to leave the hospital. I did not want to go home.

I took my exams on my hospital bed while Mother Lucy, who brought the papers herself, waited on a chair next to Mama. She gave me extra time for each exam, but I was finished long before the time was up. She brought my report card a few days later. I came first. Mama did not sing her Igbo praise songs; she only said, 'Thanks be to God.'

My class girls visited me that afternoon, their eyes wide with awed admiration. They had heard I had survived an accident. They hoped I would come back with a cast that they could all scribble their signatures on. Chinwe Jideze brought me a big card that read 'Get well soon to someone special,' and she sat by my bed and talked to me, in confidential whispers, as if we had always been friends. She even showed me her report card – she had come second. Before they left, Ezinne asked, 'You will stop running away after school, now, won't you?'

Mama told me that evening that I would be discharged in two days. But I would not be going home, I would be going to Nsukka for a week, and Jaja would go with me. She did not know how Aunty Ifeoma had convinced Papa, but he had agreed that Nsukka air would be good for me, for my recuperation.

Rain splashed across the floor of the verandah, even though the sun blazed and I had to narrow my eyes to look out the door of Aunty Ifeoma's living room. Mama used to tell Jaja and me that God was undecided about what to send, rain or sun. We would sit in our rooms and look out at the raindrops glinting with sunlight, waiting for God to decide.

'Kambili, do you want a mango?' Obiora asked from behind me.

He had wanted to help me into the flat when we arrived earlier in the afternoon, and Chima had insisted on carrying my bag. It was as if they feared my illness lingered somewhere within and would pounce out if I exerted myself. Aunty Ifeoma had told them mine was a serious illness, that I had nearly died.

'I will eat one later,' I said, turning.

Obiora was pounding a yellow mango against the living room wall. He would do that until the inside became a soft pulp. Then he would bite a tiny hole in one end of the fruit and suck it until the seed wobbled alone inside the skin, like a person in oversize clothing. Amaka and Aunty Ifeoma were eating mangoes too, but with knives, slicing the firm orange flesh off the seed.

I went out to the verandah and stood by the wet metal railings, watching the rain thin to a drizzle and then stop. God had decided on sunlight. There was the smell of freshness in the air, that edible scent the baked soil gave out at the first touch of rain. I imagined going into the garden, where Jaja was on his knees, digging out a clump of mud with my fingers and eating it.

'*Aku na-efe! Aku* is flying!' a child in the flat upstairs shouted.

The air was filling with flapping, water-colored wings. Children ran out of the flats with folded newspapers and empty Bournvita tins. They hit the flying aku down with the newspapers and then bent to pick them up and put them in the tins. Some children simply ran around, swiping at the aku just for the sake of it. Others squatted down to watch the ones that had lost wings crawl on the ground, to follow them as they held on to one another and moved like a black string, a mobile necklace.

'Interesting how people will eat *aku*. But ask them to eat the wingless termites and that's another thing. Yet the wingless ones are just a phase or two away from *aku*,' Obiora said.

Aunty Ifeoma laughed. 'Look at you, Obiora. A few years ago, you were always first to run after them.'

'Besides, you should not speak of children with such contempt,' Amaka teased. 'After all, they are your own kind.'

'I was never a child,' Obiora said, heading for the door.

'Where are you going?' Amaka asked. 'To chase *aku*?'

'I'm not going to run after those flying termites, I am just going to look,' Obiora said. 'To observe.'

Amaka laughed, and Aunty Ifeoma echoed her.

'Can I go, Mom?' Chima asked. He was already heading for the door.

'Yes. But you know we will not fry them.'

'I will give the ones I catch to Ugochukwu. They fry *aku* in their house,' Chima said.

'Watch that they do not fly into your ears, *inugo?* Or they will make you go deaf!' Aunty Ifeoma called as Chima dashed outside.

Aunty Ifeoma put on her slippers and went upstairs to talk to a neighbor. I was left alone with Amaka, standing side by side next to the railings. She moved forward to lean on the railings, her shoulder brushing mine. The old discomfort was gone.

'You have become Father Amadi's sweetheart,' she said. Her tone was the same light tone she had used with Obiora. She could not possibly know how painfully my heart lurched. 'He was really worried when you were sick. He talked about you so much. And, *amam*, it wasn't just priestly concern.'

'What did he say?'

Amaka turned to study my eager face. 'You have a crush on him, don't you?'

'Crush' was mild. It did not come close to what I felt, how I felt, but I said, 'Yes.'

'Like every other girl on campus.'

I tightened my grip on the railings. I knew Amaka would not tell me more unless I asked. She wanted me to speak out more, after all. 'What do you mean?' I asked.

'Oh, all the girls in church have crushes on him. Even some of the married women. People have crushes on priests all the time, you know. It's exciting to have to deal with God as a rival.' Amaka ran her hand over the railings, smearing the water droplets. 'You're different. I've never heard him talk about anyone like that. He said you never laugh. How shy you are although he knows there's a lot going on in your head. He insisted on driving Mom to Enugu to see you. I told him he sounded like a person whose wife was sick.'

'I was happy that he came to the hospital,' I said. It felt easy saying that, letting the words roll off my tongue. Amaka's eyes still bored into me.

'It was Uncle Eugene who did that to you, *okwia*?' she asked.

I let go of the railings, suddenly needing to ease myself. Nobody had asked, not even the doctor at the hospital or Father Benedict. I did not know what Papa had told them. Or if he had even told

255

them anything. 'Did Aunty Ifeoma tell you?' I asked.

'No, but I guessed so.'

'Yes. It was him,' I said, and then headed for the toilet. I did not turn to see Amaka's reaction.

The power went off that evening, just before the sun fell. The refrigerator shook and shivered and then fell silent. I did not notice how loud its nonstop hum was until it stopped. Obiora brought the kerosene lamps out to the verandah and we sat around them, swatting at the tiny insects that blindly followed the yellow light and bumped against the glass bulbs. Father Amadi came later in the evening, with roast corn and ube wrapped in old newspapers.

'Father, you are the best! Just what I was thinking about, corn and ube,' Amaka said.

'I brought this on the condition that you will not raise any arguments today,' Father Amadi said. 'I just want to see how Kambili is doing.'

Amaka laughed and took the package inside to get a plate.

'It's good to see you are yourself again,' Father Amadi said, looking me over, as if to see if I was all there. I smiled. He motioned for me to stand up for a hug. His body touching mine was tense and delicious. I backed away. I wished that Chima and Jaja and Obiora and Aunty Ifeoma and Amaka would all disappear for a while. I wished I were alone with him. I wished I could tell him how warm I felt that he was here, how my favorite color was now the same fired-clay shade of his skin.

A neighbor knocked on the door and came in with a plastic container of aku, anara leaves, and red peppers. Aunty Ifeoma said she did not think I should eat any because it might disturb my stomach. I watched Obiora flatten an anara leaf on his palm. He sprinkled the aku, fried to twisted crisps, and the peppers on the leaf and then rolled it up. Some of them slipped out as he stuffed the rolled leaf in his mouth.

'Our people say that after *aku* flies, it will still fall to the toad,' Father Amadi said. He dipped a hand into the bowl and threw a few into his mouth. 'When I was a child, I loved chasing *aku*. It was just play, though, because if you really wanted to catch them, you waited till evening, when they all lost their wings and fell down.' He sounded nostalgic.

I closed my eyes and let his voice caress me, let myself imagine him as a child, before his shoulders grew square, chasing aku outside, over soil softened by new rains.

Aunty Ifeoma said I would not help fetch water just yet, until she was sure I was strong enough. So I woke up after everyone else, when the sun's rays streamed steadily into the room, making the mirror glitter. Amaka was standing at the living room window when I came out. I went over and

257

stood by her. She was looking at the verandah, where Aunty Ifeoma sat on a stool, talking. The woman seated next to Aunty Ifeoma had piercing academic eyes and humorless lips and wore no makeup.

'We cannot sit back and let it happen, *mba*. Where else have you heard of such a thing as a sole administrator in a university?' Aunty Ifeoma said, leaning forward on the stool. Tiny cracks appeared in her bronze lipstick when she pursed her lips. 'A governing council votes for a vice chancellor. That is the way it has worked since this university was built, that is the way it is supposed to work, *oburia?*'

The woman looked off into the distance, nodding continuously in the way that people do when searching for the right words to use. When she finally spoke, she did so slowly, like someone addressing a stubborn child. 'They said there is a list circulating, Ifeoma, of lecturers who are disloyal to the university. They said they might be fired. They said your name is on it.'

'I am not paid to be loyal. When I speak the truth, it becomes disloyalty.'

'Ifeoma, do you think you are the only one who knows the truth? Do you think we do not all know the truth, eh? But, *gwakenem*, will the truth feed your children? Will the truth pay their school fees and buy their clothes?'

'When do we speak out, eh? When soldiers are appointed lecturers and students attend lectures with guns to their heads? When do we speak out?' Aunty Ifeoma's voice was raised. But the blaze in her eyes was not focused on the woman; she was angry at something that was bigger than the woman before her.

The woman got up. She smoothed her yellow-and-blue abada skirt that barely let her brown slippers show. 'We should go. What time is your lecture?'

'Two.'

'Do you have fuel?'

'*Ebekwanu?* No.'

'Let me drop you. I have a little fuel.'

I watched Aunty Ifeoma and the woman walk slowly to the door, as though weighed down by both what they had said and what they had not said. Amaka waited for Aunty Ifeoma to shut the door behind them before she left the window and sat down on a chair.

'Mom said you should remember to take your painkiller, Kambili,' she said.

'What was Aunty Ifeoma talking about with her friend?' I asked. I knew I would not have asked before. I would have wondered about it, but I would not have asked.

'The sole administrator,' Amaka said, shortly, as if I would immediately understand all that they had been talking about. She was running her hand down the length of the cane chair, over and over.

'The university's equivalent of a head of state,'

Obiora said. 'The university becomes a microcosm of the country.' I had not realized that he was there, reading a book on the living room floor. I had never heard anyone use the word *microcosm*.

'They are telling Mom to shut up,' Amaka said. 'Shut up if you do not want to lose your job because you can be fired *fiam*, just like that.' Amaka snapped her fingers to show how fast Aunty Ifeoma could be fired.

'They should fire her, eh, so we can go to America,' Obiora said.

'*Mechie onu*,' Amaka said. Shut up.

'America?' I looked from Amaka to Obiora.

'Aunty Phillipa is asking Mom to come over. At least people there get paid when they are supposed to,' Amaka said, bitterly, as though she were accusing someone of something.

'And Mom will have her work recognized in America, without any nonsense politics,' Obiora said, nodding, agreeing with himself in case nobody else did.

'Did Mom tell you she is going anywhere, *gbo*?' Amaka jabbed the chair now, with fast motions.

'Do you know how long they have been sitting on her file?' Obiora asked. 'She should have been senior lecturer years ago.'

'Aunty Ifeoma told you that?' I asked, stupidly, not even sure what I meant, because I could think of nothing else to say, because I could no longer imagine life without Aunty Ifeoma's family, without Nsukka.

Neither Obiora nor Amaka responded. They were glaring at each other silently, and I felt that they had not really been talking to me. I went outside and stood by the verandah railings. It had rained all night. Jaja was kneeling in the garden, weeding. He did not have to water anymore because the sky did it. Anthills had risen in the newly softened red soil in the yard, like miniature castles. I took a deep breath and held it, to savor the smell of green leaves washed clean by rain, the way I imagined a smoker would do to savor the last of a cigarette. The allamanda bushes bordering the garden bloomed heavily with yellow, cylindrical flowers. Chima was pulling the flowers down and sticking his fingers in them, one after the other. I watched as he examined flower after flower, looking for a suitable small bloom that would fit onto his pinky.

That evening, Father Amadi stopped by on his way to the stadium. He wanted us all to go with him. He was coaching some boys from Ugwu Agidi for the local government high-jump championships. Obiora had borrowed a video game from the flat upstairs, and the boys were clustered in front of the TV in the living room. They didn't want to go to the stadium because they would have to return the game soon.

Amaka laughed when Father Amadi asked her to come. 'Don't try to be nice, Father, you know you would rather be alone with your sweetheart,' she said. And Father Amadi smiled and said nothing.

I went alone with him. My mouth felt tight from embarrassment as he drove us to the stadium. I was grateful that he did not say anything about Amaka's statement, that he talked about the sweet-smelling rains instead and sang along with the robust Igbo choruses coming from his cassette player. The boys from Ugwu Agidi were already there when we got to the stadium. They were taller, older versions of the boys I had seen the last time; their hole-ridden shorts were just as worn and their faded shirts just as threadbare. Father Amadi raised his voice – it lost most of its music when he did – as he gave encouragement and pointed out the boys' weaknesses. When they were not looking, he took the rod up a notch, then yelled, 'One more time: set, go!' and they jumped over it, one after the other. He raised it a few more times before the boys caught on and said, '*Ah! Ah! Fada!*' He laughed and said he believed they could jump higher than they thought they could. And that they had just proved him right.

It was what Aunty Ifeoma did to my cousins, I realized then, setting higher and higher jumps for them in the way she talked to them, in what she expected of them. She did it all the time believing they would scale the rod. And they did. It was different for Jaja and me. We did not scale the rod because we believed we could, we scaled it because we were terrified that we couldn't.

'What clouds your face?' Father Amadi asked, sitting down beside me. His shoulder touched mine. The new smell of sweat and old smell of cologne filled my nostrils.

'Nothing.'

'Tell me about the nothing, then.'

'You believe in those boys,' I blurted out.

'Yes,' he said, watching me. 'And they don't need me to believe in them as much as I need it for myself.'

'Why?'

'Because I need to believe in something that I never question.' He picked up the water bottle, drank deeply from it. I watched the ripples in his throat as the water went down. I wished I were the water, going into him, to be with him, one with him. I had never envied water so much before. His eyes caught mine, and I looked away, wondering if he had seen the longing in my eyes.

'Your hair needs to be plaited,' he said.

'My hair?'

'Yes. I will take you to the woman who plaits your aunt's hair in the market.'

He reached out then and touched my hair. Mama had plaited it in the hospital, but because of my raging headaches, she did not make the braids tight. They were starting to slip out of the twists, and Father Amadi ran his hand over the loosening braids, in gentle, smoothing motions. He was looking right into my eyes. He was too close. His touch was so light I wanted to push my head toward him, to feel the pressure of his hand. I wanted to collapse against him. I wanted to press his hand to my head, my belly, so he could feel the warmth that coursed through me.

He let go of my hair, and I watched him get up and run back to the boys on the field.

It was too early when Amaka's movements woke me up the next morning; the room was not yet touched by the lavender rays of dawn. In the faint glow from the security lights outside, I saw her tying her wrapper round her chest. Something was wrong; she did not tie her wrapper just to go to the toilet.

'Amaka, *o gini?*'

'Listen,' she said.

I could make out Aunty Ifeoma's voice from the verandah, and I wondered what she was doing up so early. Then I heard the singing. It was the measured singing of a large group of people, and it came in through the window.

'Students are rioting,' Amaka said.

I got up and followed her into the living room. What did it mean, that students were rioting? Were we in danger? Jaja and Obiora were on the verandah with Aunty Ifeoma. The cool air felt heavy against my bare arms, as if it were holding on to raindrops that were reluctant to fall.

'Turn off the security lights,' Aunty Ifeoma said. 'If they pass and see the light, they might throw stones up here.'

Amaka turned off the lights. The singing was clearer now, loud and resonant. There had to be a least five hundred people. 'Sole administrator must go. He doesn't wear pant oh! Head of State must go. He doesn't wear pant oh! Where is running water? Where is light? Where is petrol?'

'The singing is so loud I thought they were right outside,' Aunty Ifeoma said.

'Will they come here?' I asked.

Aunty Ifeoma put an arm around me and drew me close. She smelled of talcum powder. 'No, *nne*, we are fine. The people who might worry are those that live near the vice chancellor. Last time, the students burned a senior professor's car.'

The singing was louder but not closer. The students were invigorated now. Smoke was rising in thick, blinding fumes that blended into the star-filled sky. Crashing sounds of breaking glass peppered the singing.

'All we are saying, sole administrator must go! All we are saying, he must go! No be so? Na so!'

Shouts and yells accompanied the singing. A solo voice rose, and the crowds cheered. The cool night wind, heavy with the smell of burning, brought clear snatches of the resonating voice speaking pidgin English from a street away.

'Great Lions and Lionesses! We wan people who dey wear clean underwear, no be so? Abi the Head of State dey wear common underwear, sef, talkless of clean one? No!'

'Look,' Obiora said, lowering his voice as if the

265

group of about forty students jogging past could possibly hear him. They looked like a fast-flowing dark stream, illuminated by the torches and burning sticks they held.

'Maybe they are catching up with the rest from down campus,' Amaka said, after the students had passed.

We stayed out to listen for a little while longer before Aunty Ifeoma said we had to go in and sleep.

Aunty Ifeoma came home that afternoon with the news of the riot. It was the worst one since they became commonplace some years ago. The students had set the sole administrator's house on fire; even the guest house behind it had burned to the ground. Six university cars had been burned down, as well. 'They say the sole administrator and his wife were smuggled out in the boot of an old Peugeot 404, *o di egwu*,' Aunty Ifeoma said, waving around a circular. When I read the circular, I felt a tight discomfort in my chest like the heartburn I got after eating greasy akara. It was signed by the registrar. The university was closed down until further notice as a result of the damage to university property and the atmosphere of unrest. I wondered what it meant, if it meant Aunty Ifeoma would leave soon, if it meant we would no longer come to Nsukka.

During my fitful siesta, I dreamed that the sole

administrator was pouring hot water on Aunty Ifeoma's feet in the bathtub of our home in Enugu. Then Aunty Ifeoma jumped out of the bathtub and, in the manner of dreams, jumped into America. She did not look back as I called to her to stop.

I was still thinking about the dream that evening as we all sat in the living room, watching TV. I heard a car drive in and park in front of the flat, and I clasped my shaky hands together, certain it was Father Amadi. But the banging on the door was unlike him; it was loud, rude, intrusive.

Aunty Ifeoma flew off her chair. '*Onyezi?* Who wants to break my door, eh?'

She opened the door only a crack, but two wide hands reached in and forced the door ajar. The heads of the four men who spilled into the flat grazed the door frame. Suddenly, the flat seemed cramped, too small for the blue uniforms and matching caps they wore, for the smell of stale cigarette smoke and sweat that came in with them, for the raw bulge of muscle under their sleeves.

'What is it? Who are you?' Aunty Ifeoma asked.

'We are here to search your house. We're looking for documents designed to sabotage the peace of the university. We have information that you have been in collaboration with the radical student groups that staged the riots . . .' The voice sounded mechanical, the voice of a person reciting something written. The man speaking had tribal marks all over his cheek; there seemed to be no area of skin free of the ingrained lines. The other three men walked briskly into the flat as he spoke. One opened the drawers of the sideboard, leaving each open. Two went into the bedrooms.

'Who sent you here?' Aunt Ifeoma asked.

'We are from the special security unit in Port Harcourt.'

'Do you have any papers to show me? You cannot just walk into my house.'

'Look at this *yeye* woman oh! I said we are from the special security unit!' The tribal marks curved even more on the man's face as he frowned and pushed Aunty Ifeoma aside.

'How you go just come enter like dis? Wetin be dis?' Obiora said, rising, the fear in his eyes not quite shielded by the brazen manliness in his pidgin English.

'Obiora, *nodu ani*,' Aunt Ifeoma quietly said, and Obiora sat down quickly. He looked relieved that he had been asked to. Aunty Ifeoma muttered to us all to remain seated, not to say a word, before she followed the men into the rooms. They did not look inside the drawers they flung open, they just threw the clothes and whatever else was inside on the floor. They overturned all the boxes and suitcases in Aunty Ifeoma's room, but they did not rummage through the contents. They scattered, but they did not search. As they left, the man with the tribal marks said to Aunty Ifeoma, waving a stubby finger with a curved nail in her face, 'Be careful, be very careful.'

We were silent until the sound of their car driving off faded.

'We have to go to the police station,' Obiora said.

Aunt Ifeoma smiled; the movement of her lips did not brighten her face. 'That is where they came from. They're all working together.'

'Why are they accusing you of encouraging the riot, Aunty?' Jaja asked.

'It's all rubbish. They want to scare me. Since when have students needed somebody to tell them when to riot?'

'I don't believe they just forced their way into our house and turned it upside down,' Amaka said. 'I don't believe it.'

'Thank God Chima is asleep,' Aunty Ifeoma said.

'We should leave,' Obiora said. 'Mom, we should leave. Have you talked to Aunty Phillipa since the last time?'

Aunty Ifeoma shook her head. She was putting back the books and table mats from the sideboard drawers. Jaja went over to help her.

'What do you mean, leave? Why do we have to run away from our own country? Why can't we fix it?' Amaka asked.

'Fix what?' Obiora had a deliberate sneer on his face.

'So we have to run away? That's the answer, running away?' Amaka asked, her voice shrill.

'It's not running away, it's being realistic. By the time we get into university, the good professors will be fed up with all this nonsense and they will go abroad.'

'Shut up, both of you, and come and clean up this place!' Aunty Ifeoma snapped. It was the first time she did not look on proudly and enjoy my cousins' arguments.

An earthworm was slithering in the bathtub, near the drain, when I went in to take a bath in the morning. The purplish-brown body contrasted with the whiteness of the tub. The pipes were old, Amaka had said, and every rainy season, earthworms made their way into the bathtub. Aunty Ifeoma had written the works department about the pipes, but, of course, it would take ages before anybody did anything about them. Obiora said he liked to study the worms; he'd discovered that they died only when you poured salt on them. If you cut them in two, each part simply grew back to form a whole earthworm.

Before I climbed into the tub, I picked the rope-like body out with a twig broken off a broom and threw it in the toilet. I could not flush because there was nothing to flush, it would be a waste of water. The boys would have to pee looking at a floating earthworm in the toilet bowl.

When I finished my bath, Aunty Ifeoma had

poured me a glass of milk. She had sliced my okpa, too, and red chunks of pepper gaped from the yellow slices. 'How do you feel, *nne*?' she asked.

'I'm fine, Aunty.' I did not even remember that I had once hoped never to open my eyes again, that fire had once dwelt in my body. I picked up my glass, stared at the curiously beige and grainy milk.

'Homemade soybean milk,' Aunty Ifeoma said. 'Very nutritious. One of our lecturers in agriculture sells it.'

'It tastes like chalk water,' Amaka said.

'How do you know, have you ever drunk chalk water?' Aunty Ifeoma asked. She laughed, but I saw the lines, thin as spiders' limbs, around her mouth and the faraway look in her eyes. 'I just can't afford milk anymore,' she added tiredly. 'You should see how the prices of dried milk rise every day, as if somebody is chasing them.'

The doorbell rang. My stomach heaved around itself whenever I heard it, although I knew Father Amadi usually knocked quietly on the door.

It was a student of Aunt Ifeoma's, in a tight pair of blue jeans. Her face was light-skinned, but her complexion was from bleaching creams – her hands were the dark brown color of Bournvita with no milk added. She held a huge gray chicken. It was a symbol of her formal announcement to Aunty Ifeoma that she was getting married, she said. When her fiancé learned of yet another university closure, he had told her he could no longer wait until she graduated, since nobody knew when the university would reopen. The wedding would be next month. She did not call him by his name, she called him 'dim,' 'my husband,' with the proud tone of someone who had won a prize, tossing her braided, reddish gold – dyed hair.

'I'm not sure I will come back to school when we reopen. I want to have a baby first. I don't want *dim* to think that he married me to have an empty home,' she said, with a high, girlish laugh. Before she left, she copied Aunty Ifeoma's address down, so she could send an invitation card.

Aunty Ifeoma stood looking at the door. 'She was never particularly bright, so I shouldn't be sad,' she said thoughtfully, and Amaka laughed and said, 'Mom!'

The chicken squawked. It was lying on its side because its legs were tied together.

'Obiora, please kill this chicken and put it in the freezer before it loses weight, since there's nothing to feed it,' Aunty Ifeoma said.

'They have been taking the light too often the past week. I say we eat the whole chicken today,' Obiora said.

'How about we eat half and put the other half in the freezer and pray NEPA brings back the light so it doesn't spoil,' Amaka said.

'Okay,' Aunty Ifeoma said.

'I'll kill it,' Jaja said, and we all turned to stare at him.

'*Nna m*, you have never killed a chicken, have you?' Aunty Ifeoma asked.

'No. But I can kill it.'

'Okay,' Aunty Ifeoma said, and I turned to stare, startled at how easily she had said that. Was she absentminded because she was thinking about her student? Did she really think Jaja could kill a chicken?

I followed Jaja out to the backyard, watched him hold the wings down under his foot. He bent the chicken's head back. The knife glinted, meeting with the sun rays to give off sparks. The chicken had stopped squawking; perhaps it had decided to accept the inevitable. I did not look as Jaja slit its feathery neck, but I watched the chicken dance to the frenzied tunes of death. It flapped its gray wings in the red mud, twisting and flailing. Finally, it lay in a puff of sullied feathers. Jaja picked it up and dunked it in the basin of hot water that Amaka brought. There was a precision in Jaja, a single-mindedness that was cold, clinical. He started to pluck the feathers off quickly, and he did not speak until the chicken had been reduced to a slim form covered with white-yellow skin. I did not realize how long a chicken's neck is until it was plucked.

'If Aunty Ifeoma leaves, then I want to leave with them, too,' he said.

I said nothing. There was so much I wanted to say and so much I did not want to say. Two vultures hovered overhead and then landed on the ground, close enough that I could have grabbed them if I had jumped fast. Their bald necks glistened in the early-morning sun.

'See how close the vultures come now?' Obiora asked. He and Amaka had come to stand by the back door. 'They are getting hungrier and hungrier. Nobody kills chickens these days, and so there are less entrails for them to eat.' He picked up a stone and threw it at the vultures. They flew up and perched on the branches of the mango tree only a little distance away.

'Papa-Nnukwu used to say that the vultures have lost their prestige,' Amaka said. 'In the old days, people liked them because when they came down to eat the entrails of animals used in sacrifice, it meant the gods were happy.'

'In these new days, they should have the good sense to wait for us to be done killing the chicken before they descend,' Obiora said.

Father Amadi came after Jaja had cut up the chicken and Amaka had put half of it in a plastic bag for the freezer. Aunty Ifeoma smiled when Father Amadi told her he was taking me to get my hair done. 'You are doing my job for me, Father, thank you,' she said. 'Greet Mama Joe. Tell her I will come soon to plait my hair for Easter.'

★   ★   ★

Mama Joe's shed in Ogige market just barely fit the high stool where she sat and the smaller stool in front of her. I sat on the smaller stool. Father Amadi stood outside, beside the wheelbarrows and pigs and people and chickens that went past, because his broad-shouldered form could not fit in the shed. Mama Joe wore a wool hat even though sweat had made yellow patches under the sleeves of her blouse. Women and children worked in the neighboring sheds, twisting hair, weaving hair, plaiting hair with thread. Wooden boards with lopsided print leaned on broken chairs in front of the sheds. The closest ones read MAMA CHINEDU SPECIAL HAIR STYLIST and MAMA BOMBOY INTERNATIONAL HAIR. The women and children called out to every female who walked past. 'Let us plait your hair!' 'Let us make you beautiful!' 'I will plait it well for you!' Mostly, the women shrugged off their pulling hands and walked on.

Mama Joe welcomed me as though she had been plaiting my hair all my life. If I was Aunty Ifeoma's niece, then I was special. She wanted to know how Aunty Ifeoma was doing. 'I have not seen that good woman in almost a month. I would be naked but for your aunty, who gives me her old clothes. I know she doesn't have that much, either. Trying so hard to raise those children well. *Kpau!* A strong woman,' Mama Joe said. Her Igbo dialect came out sounding strange, with words dropped; it was difficult to understand. She told Father Amadi that she would be done in an hour. He bought a bottle of Coke and placed it at the foot of my stool before he left.

'Is he your brother?' Mama Joe asked, looking after him.

'No. He's a priest.' I wanted to add that he was the one whose voice dictated my dreams.

'Did you say he is a *fada*?'

'Yes.'

'A real Catholic *fada*?'

'Yes.' I wondered if there were any unreal Catholic priests.

'All that maleness wasted,' she said, combing my thick hair gently. She put the comb down and untangled some ends with her fingers. It felt strange, because Mama had always plaited my hair. 'Do you see the way he looks at you? It means something, I tell you.'

'Oh,' I said, because I did not know what Mama Joe expected me to say. But she was already shouting something to Mama Bomboy across the aisle. While she turned my hair into tight corn-rows, she chattered nonstop to Mama Bomboy and to Mama Caro, whose voice I heard but whom I could not see because she was a few sheds away. The covered basket at the entrance of Mama Joe's shed moved. A brown spiraled shell crawled out from underneath. I nearly jumped – I did not know the basket was full of live snails that Mama Joe sold. She stood up and retrieved the snail and put it back in. 'God take

276

power from the devil,' she muttered. She was on the last corn row when a woman walked up to her shed and asked to see the snails. Mama Joe took the covering basket off.

'They are big,' she said. 'My sister's children picked them today at dawn near Adada lake.'

The woman picked up the basket and shook it, searching for tiny shells hidden among the big ones. Finally, she said they were not that big anyway and left. Mama Joe shouted after the woman, 'People who have bad stomachs should not spread their bad will to others! You will not find snails this size anywhere else in the market!'

She picked up an enterprising snail that was crawling out of the open basket. She threw it back in and muttered, 'God take power from the devil.' I wondered if it was the same snail, crawling out, being thrown back in, and then crawling out again. Determined. I wanted to buy the whole basket and set that one snail free.

Mama Joe finished my hair before Father Amadi came back. She gave me a red mirror, neatly broken in half, so that I saw my new hairstyle in fractions.

'Thank you. It's nice,' I said.

She reached out to straighten a cornrow that did not need to be straightened. 'A man does not bring a young girl to dress her hair unless he loves that young girl, I am telling you. It does not happen,' she said. And I nodded because again I did not know what to say.

'It doesn't happen,' Mama Joe repeated, as if I had disagreed. A cockroach ran out from behind her stool, and she stepped on it with her bare foot. 'God take power from the devil.'

She spit into her palm, rubbed her hands together, drew the basket closer, and started to rearrange the snails. I wondered if she had spit in her hand before she started on my hair. A woman in a blue wrapper with a bag tucked under her armpit bought the whole basketful of snails just before Father Amadi came to pick me up. Mama Joe called her 'nwanyi oma,' although she was not pretty at all, and I imagined the snails fried to a crisp, warped corpses floating in the woman's soup pot.

'Thank you,' I said to Father Amadi, as we walked to the car. He had paid Mama Joe so well that she protested, weakly, and said she should not take so much for plaiting the hair of Aunty Ifeoma's niece.

Father Amadi brushed my gratitude aside in the good-natured way of someone who had done what was his duty. 'O maka, it brings out your face,' he said, looking at me. 'You know, we still don't have anybody playing Our Lady in our play. You should try out. When I was in the juniorate, the prettiest girl in the junior convent always played Our Lady.'

I took a deep breath and prayed I would not stutter. 'I can't act. I've never acted.'

'You can try,' he said. He turned the key in the

ignition, and the car started with a squeaky shudder. Before he eased it onto the crowded market road, he looked at me and said, 'You can do anything you want, Kambili.'

As he drove, we sang Igbo choruses. I lifted my voice until it was smooth and melodious like his.

The green sign outside the church was lit with white lights. The words ST PETER'S CATHOLIC CHAPLAINCY, UNIVERSITY OF NIGERIA seemed to twinkle as Amaka and I walked into the incense-scented church. I sat with her in the front pew, our thighs touching. We had come alone; Aunty Ifeoma had gone to the morning service with the others.

St Peter's did not have the huge candles or the ornate marble altar of St Agnes. The women did not tie their scarves properly around their heads, to cover as much hair as possible. I watched them as they came up for offertory. Some just draped see-through black veils over their hair; others wore trousers, even jeans. Papa would be scandalized. A woman's hair must be covered in the house of God, and a woman must not wear a man's clothes, especially in the house of God, he would say.

I imagined the plain wooden crucifix above the altar swinging back and forth as Father Amadi raised the host at consecration. His eyes were shut, and I knew that he was no longer behind the altar draped in white cotton, that he was somewhere else that only he and God knew about. He gave me communion and when his finger grazed my tongue, I wanted to fall at his feet. But the thunderous singing from the choir propped me up and strengthened me to walk back to my seat.

After we said the Lord's Prayer, Father Amadi did not say, 'Offer to each other the sign of peace.' He broke into an Igbo song instead.

*'Ekene nke udo – ezigbo nwanne m nye m aka gi.'* 'The greeting of peace – my dear sister, dear brother, give me your hand.'

People clasped hands and hugged. Amaka hugged me, then turned to exchange brief hugs with the family seated behind. Father Amadi smiled right at me from the altar, his lips moving. I was not sure what he said, but I knew I would think about it over and over. I was still thinking about it, wondering what it was he had said, as he drove Amaka and me home after Mass.

He told Amaka that he still had not received her confirmation name. He needed to get all the names together and have the chaplain look at them by the next day, Saturday. Amaka said she was not interested in choosing an English name, and Father Amadi laughed and said he would help her choose a name if she wanted. I looked out the window as we drove. There was no power, and so the campus looked as though a giant blue-black blanket had covered it. The streets we drove past were like tunnels darkened by the hedges on each side. Gold-yellow lights of kerosene lamps flickered from behind windows and on verandahs of homes, like the eyes of hundreds of wild cats.

Aunty Ifeoma was sitting on a stool on the verandah, across from a friend of hers. Obiora was on the mat, seated between the two kerosene lamps. Both were turned low, filling the verandah with shadows. Amaka and I greeted Aunty Ifeoma's friend, who wore a bright tie-dye boubou and her short hair natural. She smiled and said, *'Kedu?'*

'Father Amadi said to greet you, Mom. He couldn't stay, he has people coming to see him at the chaplaincy house,' Amaka said. She made to take one kerosene lamp.

'Keep the lamp. Jaja and Chima have a lit candle inside. Close the door so the insects don't follow you in,' Aunty Ifeoma said.

I pulled my scarf off and sat down next to Aunty Ifeoma, watching the insects crowd around the lamps. There were many tiny beetles with something sticking out at their backs, as if they had forgotten to tuck in their wings properly. They were not as active as the small yellow flies that sometimes flew away from the lamp and too close to my eyes. Aunty Ifeoma was recounting how the security agents had come to the flat. The dim light blurred her features. She paused often, to add dramatic urgency to her story, and even though her friend kept saying *'Gini mezia?'* – What happened next? – Aunty Ifeoma said *'Chelu nu'* – wait – and took her time.

Her friend was silent a long time after Aunty

Ifeoma finished her story. The crickets seemed to take up the conversation then; their loud shrilling seemed so close, although they well might have been miles away.

'Did you hear what happened to Professor Okafor's son?' Aunty Ifeoma's friend finally asked. She spoke more Igbo than English, but all her English words came out with a consistent British accent, not like Papa's, which came on only when he was with white people and sometimes skipped a few words so that half a sentence sounded Nigerian and the other half British.

'Which Okafor?' Aunty Ifeoma asked.

'Okafor who lives on Fulton Avenue. His son, Chidifu.'

'The one who is Obiora's friend?'

'Yes, that one. He stole his father's exam papers and sold them to his father's students.'

'*Ekwuzina!* That small boy?'

'Yes. Now that the university is closed, the students came to the house, to harass the boy for the money. Of course he had spent it. Okafor beat his son's front tooth out yesterday. Yet this is the same Okafor who will not speak out about what is going wrong in this university, who will do anything to win favor with the Big Men in Abuja. He is the one who makes the list of lecturers who are disloyal. I hear he included my name and yours.'

'I heard that, too. *Mana*, what does it have to do with Chidifu?'

'Do you try to treat cancer sores or the cancer

283

itself? We cannot afford to give pocket money to our children. We cannot afford to eat meat. We cannot afford bread. So your child steals and you turn to him in surprise? You must try to heal the cancer because the sores will keep coming back.'

'*Mba*, Chiaku. You cannot justify theft.'

'I do not justify it. What I am saying is that Okafor should not be surprised and should not waste his energy breaking a stick on his poor son's body. It is what happens when you sit back and do nothing about tyranny. Your child becomes what you cannot recognize.'

Aunty Ifeoma sighed heavily and looked at Obiora, perhaps wondering if he, too, could turn into something she would not recognize. 'I talked to Phillipa the other day,' she said.

'Oh? How is she, how is *oyinbo* land treating her?'

'She is well.'

'And life as a second-class citizen in America?'

'Chiaku, your sarcasm is unbecoming.'

'But it is true. All my years in Cambridge, I was a monkey who had developed the ability to reason.'

'It is not that bad now.'

'That is what they tell you. Every day our doctors go there and end up washing plates for *oyinbo* because *oyinbo* does not think we study medicine right. Our lawyers go and drive taxis because *oyinbo* does not trust how we train them in law.'

Aunty Ifeoma cut in, quickly, interrupting her friend. 'I sent my CV to Phillipa.'

Her friend brought the ends of her boubou together and tucked them in, between her stretched-out legs. She looked out into the dark night, her eyes narrowed, either in thought or maybe in an attempt to figure exactly how far away the crickets were. 'So you, too, Ifeoma,' she finally said.

'It is not about me, Chiaku.' Aunty Ifeoma paused. 'Who will teach Amaka and Obiora in university?'

'The educated ones leave, the ones with the potential to right the wrongs. They leave the weak behind. The tyrants continue to reign because the weak cannot resist. Do you not see that it is a cycle? Who will break that cycle?'

'That is simply unrealistic pep-rally nonsense, Aunty Chiaku,' Obiora said.

I saw the tension fall from the sky and envelop us all. A child's crying upstairs interrupted the silence.

'Go into my room and wait for me, Obiora,' Aunty Ifeoma said.

Obiora stood up and left. He looked grave, as if he had only just realized what he had done. Aunty Ifeoma apologized to her friend. But it was different after that. The insult of a child – a fourteen year old – hung between them, made their tongues heavy so that speech became a labor. Her friend left soon afterward, and Aunty Ifeoma stormed inside, nearly knocking a lamp over. I heard the thud of a slap and then her raised voice.

'I do not quarrel with your disagreeing with my friend. I quarrel with how you have disagreed. I do not raise disrespectful children in this house, do you hear me? You are not the only child who has skipped a class in school. I will not tolerate this rubbish from you! *I na-anu?*' She lowered her voice then. I heard the click of her bedroom door closing.

'I always got the stick on my palm,' Amaka said, joining me on the verandah. 'And Obiora got his on his buttocks. I think Mom felt giving it to me on my buttocks would somehow affect me and maybe I would end up not growing breasts or something. I preferred the stick to her slaps, though, because her hand is made of metal, *ezi okwum.*' Amaka laughed. 'Afterward we would talk about it for hours. I hated that. Just give me the lashes and let me out. But no, she explained why you had been flogged, what she expected you to do not to get flogged again. That's what she's doing with Obiora.'

I looked away. Amaka took my hand in hers. It felt warm, like the hand of someone just recovering from malaria. She did not speak, but I felt as though we were thinking the same thing – how different it was for Jaja and me.

I cleared my throat. 'Obiora must really want to leave Nigeria.'

'He's stupid,' Amaka said. She squeezed my hand tight before letting go.

★    ★    ★

286

Aunty Ifeoma was cleaning out the freezer, which had started to smell because of the incessant power outages. She wiped up the puddle of wine-colored foul water that had leaked to the floor and then brought out the bags of meat and laid them in a bowl. The tiny beef pieces had turned a mottled brown. The pieces of the chicken Jaja had killed had turned a deep yellow.

'So much wasted meat,' I said.

Aunty Ifeoma laughed. 'Wasted, *kwa?* I will boil it well with spices and cook away the spoilage.'

'Mom, she is talking like a Big Man's daughter,' Amaka said, and I was grateful that she did not sneer at me, that she echoed her mother's laughter instead.

We were on the verandah, picking the stones out of rice. We sat on mats on the floor, beyond the shade so we could feel the mild morning sun emerging after the rain. The dirty and clean rice were in two careful mounds on the enamel trays before us, with the stones placed on the mat. Amaka would divide the rice into smaller portions to blow the chaff out afterward.

'The problem with this kind of cheap rice is that it cooks into a pudding, no matter how little water you put in. You start to wonder if it is *garri* or rice that you are eating,' Amaka muttered, when Aunty Ifeoma left. I smiled. I had never felt the companionship I felt sitting next to her, listening to her Fela and Onyeka cassettes on the tiny tape-player-radio, which she had put batteries into. I had never felt the comfortable silence we shared as we cleaned the rice, carefully, because the grains were stunted and sometimes looked like the glassy stones. Even the air seemed still, slowly rousing itself after the rain. The clouds were just starting to clear, like cotton-wool tufts reluctantly letting go of one another.

The sound of a car driving toward the flat disrupted our peace. I knew Father Amadi had office hours that morning at the chaplaincy, yet I still hoped it was him. I imagined him walking up to the verandah, holding his soutane in one hand so he could run up the short stairs, smiling.

Amaka turned to look. 'Aunty Beatrice!'

I whipped around. Mama was climbing out of a yellow unsteady-looking taxi. What was she doing here? What had happened? Why was she wearing her rubber slippers all the way from Enugu? She walked slowly, holding on to her wrapper that seemed so loose it would slip off her waist any minute. Her blouse did not look ironed.

'Mama, *o gini?* Did something happen?' I asked, hugging her quickly so I could stand back and examine her face. Her hand was cold.

Amaka hugged her and took her handbag. 'Aunty Beatrice, *nno*.'

Aunty Ifeoma came hurrying out to the verandah, drying her hands in front of her shorts. She hugged Mama and then led her into the living room, supporting her as one would support a cripple.

'Where is Jaja?' Mama asked.

'He is out with Obiora,' Aunty Ifeoma said. 'Sit down, *nwunye m*. Amaka, get money from my purse and go and buy a soft drink for your Aunty.'

'Don't worry, I will drink water,' Mama said.

'We have not had light, the water will not be cold.'

'It does not matter. I will drink it.'

Mama sat carefully at the edge of a cane chair. Her eyes were glazed over as she looked around. I knew she could not see the picture with the cracked frame or the fresh African lilies in the oriental vase.

'I do not know if my head is correct,' she said, and pressed the back of her hand to her forehead, in the way that one checks the degree of a fever. 'I got back from the hospital today. The doctor told me to rest, but I took Eugene's money and asked Kevin to take me to the park. I hired a taxi and came here.'

'You were in hospital? What happened?' Aunty Ifeoma asked quietly.

Mama looked around the room. She stared at the wall clock for a while, the one with the broken second hand, before she turned to me. 'You know that small table where we keep the family Bible, *nne*? Your father broke it on my belly.' She sounded as if she were talking about someone else, as if the table were not made of sturdy wood. 'My blood finished on that floor even before he took me to St Agnes. My doctor said there was nothing he could do to save it.' Mama shook her head slowly.

289

A thin line of tears crawled down her cheeks as though it had been a struggle for them to get out of her eyes.

'To save it?' Aunty Ifeoma whispered. 'What do you mean?'

'I was six weeks gone.'

'*Ekwuzina!* Don't say that again!' Aunty Ifeoma's eyes widened.

'It is true. Eugene did not know, I had not yet told him, but it is true.' Mama slid down to the floor. She sat with her legs stretched out in front of her. It was so undignified, but I lowered myself and sat next to her, our shoulders touching.

She cried for a long time. She cried until my hand, clasped in hers, felt stiff. She cried until Aunty Ifeoma finished cooking the rotting meat in a spicy stew. She cried until she fell asleep, her head against the seat of the chair. Jaja laid her on a mattress on the living room floor.

Papa called that evening, as we sat around the kerosene lamp on the verandah. Aunty Ifeoma answered the phone and came out to tell Mama who it was. 'I hung up. I told him I would not let you come to the phone.'

Mama flew up from her stool. 'Why? Why?'

'*Nwunye m*, sit down right now!' Aunty Ifeoma snapped.

But Mama did not sit down. She went into Aunty Ifeoma's room and called Papa. The phone rang shortly afterward, and I knew he had called back. She emerged from the room after about a quarter of an hour.

'We are leaving tomorrow. The children and I,' she said, staring straight ahead, above everyone's eye level.

'Leaving for where?' Aunty Ifeoma asked.

'Enugu. We're going back home.'

'Has a nut come loose in your head, *gbo*? You are not going anywhere.'

'Eugene is coming himself to pick us up.'

'Listen to me.' Aunty Ifeoma softened her voice; she must have known the firm voice would not penetrate the fixed smile on Mama's face. Mama's eyes were still glazed, but she looked like a different woman from the one who had come out of the taxi that morning. She looked possessed by a different demon. 'At least stay a few days, *nwunye m*, don't go back so soon.'

Mama shook her head. Except for the stiff stretch of her lips, she was expressionless. 'Eugene has not been well. He has been having migraines and fever,' she said. 'He is carrying more than any man should carry. Do you know what Ade's death did to him? It is too much for one person.'

'*Ginidi*, what are you saying?' Aunty Ifeoma swiped impatiently at an insect that flew close to her ears. 'When Ifediora was alive, there were times, *nwunye m*, when the university did not pay salaries for months. Ifediora and I had nothing, eh, yet he never raised a hand to me.'

'Do you know that Eugene pays the school fees

of up to a hundred of our people? Do you know how many people are alive because of your brother?'

'That is not the point and you know it.'

'Where would I go if I leave Eugene's house? Tell me, where would I go?' She did not wait for Aunty Ifeoma to respond. 'Do you know how many mothers pushed their daughters at him? Do you know how many asked him to impregnate them, even, and not to bother paying a bride price?'

'And so? I ask you – and so?' Aunty Ifeoma was shouting now.

Mama lowered herself to the floor. Obiora had spread a mat and there was room on it, but she sat on the bare cement, resting her head against the railings. 'You have come again with your university talk, Ifeoma,' she said, mildly, and then looked away to signal that the conversation was over.

I had never seen Mama like that, never seen that look in her eyes, never heard her say so much in such a short time.

Long after she and Aunty Ifeoma had gone to bed, I sat on the verandah with Amaka and Obiora, playing whot – Obiora had taught me to play all the card games.

'Last card!' Amaka announced, smug, placing down a card.

'I hope Aunty Beatrice sleeps well,' Obiora said, picking up a card. 'She should have taken a mattress. The mat is hard.'

'She'll be fine,' Amaka said. She looked at me and repeated, 'She'll be fine.'

Obiora reached out and patted my shoulder. I did not know what to do, so I asked 'It's my turn?' even though I knew it was.

'Uncle Eugene is not a bad man, really,' Amaka said. 'People have problems, people make mistakes.'

'*Mh,*' Obiora said, pushing his glasses up.

'I mean, some people can't deal with stress,' Amaka said, looking at Obiora as though she expected him to say something. He remained silent, examining the card he held up to his face.

Amaka picked up an extra card. 'He paid for Papa-Nnukwu's funeral, after all.' She was still watching Obiora. But he made no response to her; instead, he placed his card down and said, 'Check up!' He had won again.

As I lay in bed, I did not think about going back to Enugu; I thought about how many card games I had lost.

When Papa arrived in the Mercedes, Mama packed our bags herself and put them in the car. Papa hugged Mama, holding her close, and she rested her head on his chest. Papa had lost weight; usually, Mama's small hands barely went round to his back, but this time her hands rested on the small of his back. I did not notice the rashes on his face until I came close to hug him. They were like tiny pimples, each with whitish pus at the tips, and they covered the whole of his face, even his eyelids. His face looked swollen, oily, discolored. I had intended to hug him and have him kiss my forehead, but instead I stood there and stared at his face.

'I have a little allergy,' he said. 'Nothing serious.'

When he took me in his arms, I closed my eyes as he kissed my forehead.

'We will see you soon,' Amaka whispered before we hugged good-bye. She called me nwanne m nwanyi – my sister. She stood outside the flat, waving, until I could no longer see her through the rear windscreen.

When Papa started the rosary as we drove out of the compound, his voice was different, tired. I stared at the back of his neck, which was not covered by the pimples, and it looked different, too – smaller, with thinner folds of skin.

I turned to look at Jaja. I wanted our eyes to meet, so I could tell him how much I had wanted to spend Easter in Nsukka, how much I had wanted to attend Amaka's confirmation and Father Amadi's Pascal Mass, how I had planned to sing with my voice raised. But Jaja glued his eyes to the window, and except for muttering the prayers, he was silent until we got to Enugu.

The scent of fruits filled my nose when Adamu opened our compound gates. It was as if the high walls locked in the scent of the ripening cashews and mangoes and avocados. It nauseated me.

'See, the purple hibiscuses are about to bloom,' Jaja said, as we got out of the car. He was pointing, although I did not need him to. I could see the sleepy, oval-shape buds in the front yard as they swayed in the evening breeze.

The next day was Palm Sunday, the day Jaja did not go to communion, the day Papa threw his heavy missal across the room and broke the figurines.

# THE PIECES OF GODS

## After Palm Sunday

Everything came tumbling down after Palm Sunday. Howling winds came with an angry rain, uprooting frangipani trees in the front yard. They lay on the lawn, their pink and white flowers grazing the grass, their roots waving lumpy soil in the air. The satellite dish on top of the garage came crashing down, and lounged on the driveway like a visiting alien spaceship. The door of my wardrobe dislodged completely. Sisi broke a full set of Mama's china.

Even the silence that descended on the house was sudden, as though the old silence had broken and left us with the sharp pieces. When Mama asked Sisi to wipe the floor of the living room, to make sure no dangerous pieces of figurines were left lying somewhere, she did not lower her voice to a whisper. She did not hide the tiny smile that drew lines at the edge of her mouth. She did not sneak Jaja's food to his room, wrapped in cloth so it would appear that she had simply brought his laundry in. She took him his food on a white tray, with a matching plate.

There was something hanging over all of us.

Sometimes I wanted it all to be a dream – the missal flung at the étagère, the shattered figurines, the brittle air. It was too new, too foreign, and I did not know what to be or how to be. I walked to the bathroom and kitchen and dining room on tiptoe. At dinner, I kept my gaze fixed on the photo of Grandfather, the one where he looked like a squat superhero in his Knights of St Mulumba cape and hood, until it was time to pray and I closed my eyes. Jaja did not come out of his room even though Papa asked him to. The first time Papa asked him, the day after Palm Sunday, Papa could not open his door because he had pushed his study desk in front of it.

'Jaja, Jaja,' Papa said, pushing the door. 'You must eat with us this evening, do you hear me?'

But Jaja did not come out of his room, and Papa said nothing about it while we ate; he ate very little of his food but drank a lot of water, telling Mama to ask 'that girl' to bring more bottles of water. The rashes on his face seemed to have become bigger and flatter, less defined, so that they made his face look even puffier.

Yewande Coker came with her little daughter while we were at dinner. As I greeted her and shook her hand, I examined her face, her body, looking for signs of how different life was now that Ade Coker had died. But she looked the same, except for her attire – a black wrapper, black blouse, and a black scarf covering all of her hair and most of her forehead. Her daughter sat stiffly on the sofa, tugging at the red ribbon that held her braided hair up in a ponytail. When Mama asked if she would drink Fanta, she shook her head, still tugging at the ribbon.

'She has finally spoken, sir,' Yewande said, her eyes on her daughter. 'She said "mommy" this morning. I came to let you know that she has finally spoken.'

'Praise God!' Papa said, so loudly that I jumped.

'Thanks be to God,' Mama said.

Yewande stood up and knelt before Papa. 'Thank you, sir,' she said. 'Thank you for everything. If we had not gone to the hospital abroad, what would have become of my daughter?'

'Get up, Yewande,' Papa said. 'It is God. It is all from God.'

That evening, when Papa was in the study praying – I could hear him reading aloud a psalm – I went to Jaja's door, pushed it and heard the scraping sound of the study desk lodged against it as it opened. I told Jaja about Yewande's visit, and he nodded and said Mama had told him about it. Ade Coker's daughter had not spoken since her father died. Papa had paid to have her see the best doctors and therapists in Nigeria and abroad.

'I didn't know she hadn't talked since he died,' I said. 'It is almost four months now. Thanks be to God.'

Jaja looked at me silently for a while. His expression reminded me of the old looks Amaka used to give me, that made me feel sorry for what I was not sure of.

'She will never heal,' Jaja said. 'She may have started talking now, but she will never heal.'

As I left Jaja's room, I pushed the study desk a little way aside. And I wondered why Papa could not open Jaja's door when he tried earlier; the desk was not that heavy.

I dreaded Easter Sunday. I dreaded what would happen when Jaja did not go to communion again. And I knew that he would not go; I saw it in his long silences, in the set of his lips, in his eyes that seemed focused on invisible objects for a long time.

On Good Friday, Aunty Ifeoma called. She might have missed us if we had gone to the morning prayers, as Papa had planned. But during breakfast, Papa's hands kept shaking, so much that he spilled his tea; I watched the liquid creep across the glass table. Afterward, he said he needed to rest and we would go to the Celebration of the Passion of Christ in the evening, the one Father Benedict usually led before the kissing of the cross. We had gone to the evening celebration on Good Friday of last year, because Papa had been busy with something at the *Standard* in the morning. Jaja and I walked side by side to the altar to kiss the cross, and Jaja pressed his lips to the wooden crucifix first, before the Mass server wiped the cross and held it out to me. It felt cool to my lips.

A shiver ran across me and I felt goose bumps appear on my arms. I cried afterward, when we were seated, silent crying with tears running down my cheeks. Many people around me cried, too, the way they did during the Stations of the Cross when they moaned and said, 'Oh, what the Lord did for me' or 'He died for a common me!' Papa was pleased with my tears; I still remembered clearly how he leaned toward me and caressed my cheek. And although I was not sure why I was crying, or if I was crying for the same reasons as those other people kneeling in front of the pews, I felt proud to have Papa do that.

I was thinking about this when Aunty Ifeoma called. The phone rang for too long, and I thought Mama would pick it up, since Papa was asleep. But she didn't, so I went to the study and answered it.

Aunty Ifeoma's voice was many notches lower than usual. 'They have given me notice of termin- ation,' she said, without even waiting for me to reply to her 'How are you?' 'For what they call illegal activity. I have one month. I have applied for a visa at the American Embassy. And Father Amadi has been notified. He is leaving for missionary work in Germany at the end of the month.'

It was a double blow. I staggered. It was as if my calves had sacks of dried beans tied to them. Aunty Ifeoma asked for Jaja, and I nearly tripped, nearly fell to the floor, as I went to his room to call him. After Jaja talked to Aunty Ifeoma, he put the phone down and said, 'We are going to Nsukka today. We will spend Easter in Nsukka.'

I did not ask him what he meant, or how he would convince Papa to let us go. I watched him knock on Papa's door and go in.

'We are going to Nsukka. Kambili and I,' I heard him say.

I did not hear what Papa said, then I heard Jaja say, 'We are going to Nsukka today, not tomorrow. If Kevin will not take us, we will still go. We will walk if we have to.'

I stood still in front of the staircase, my hands trembling violently. Yet I did not think to close my ears; I did not think to count to twenty. Instead, I went into my room and sat by the window, looking out at the cashew tree. Jaja came in to say that Papa had agreed that Kevin could take us. He held a bag so hastily packed he had not even done up the zipper, and he watched me throw some things into a bag, saying nothing. He was moving his weight from one leg to the other impatiently.

'Is Papa still in bed?' I asked, but Jaja did not answer as he turned to go downstairs.

I knocked on Papa's door and opened it. He was sitting up in bed; his red silk pajamas looked disheveled. Mama was pouring water into a glass for him.

'Bye, Papa,' I said.

He got up to hug me. His face looked much

brighter than in the morning, and the rashes seemed to be clearing.

'We will see you soon,' he said, kissing my forehead.

I hugged Mama before I left the room. The stairs seemed delicate all of a sudden, as if they would crumble and a huge hole would appear and prevent me from leaving. I walked slowly until I got downstairs. Jaja was waiting for me at the bottom of the stairs, and he reached out to take my bag.

Kevin stood by the car when we came outside. 'Who will take your father to church, now?' he asked, looking at us suspiciously. 'Your father is not well enough to drive himself.'

Jaja remained silent for so long that I realized he was not going to give Kevin an answer, and I said, 'He said you should take us to Nsukka.'

Kevin shrugged, and muttered, 'This kind of trip, can't you go tomorrow?' before starting the car. He remained silent throughout the drive, and I saw his eyes often dart to us, mostly to Jaja, in the rearview mirror.

A film of sweat coated my entire body like a transparent second skin. It gave way to a dripping wetness on my neck, my forehead, underneath my breasts. We had left the back door of Aunty Ifeoma's kitchen wide open although flies buzzed in, circling over a pot of old soup. It was a choice between flies and even more heat, Amaka had said, swiping at them.

Obiora was wearing a pair of khaki shorts and nothing else. He was bent over the kerosene stove, trying to get the fire to spread across the wick. His eyes were blotchy from the fumes.

'This wick has thinned so much there's nothing left to hold the fire,' he said, when he finally got the fire to spread around. 'We should use the gas cooker for everything now, anyway. There's no point saving the gas, since we won't be needing it for much longer.' He stretched, the sweat clinging to the outline of his ribs. He picked up an old newspaper and fanned himself for a while, then swatted at some flies.

'*Nekwa!* Don't knock them into my pot,' Amaka said. She was pouring bright reddish-orange palm oil into a pot.

'We shouldn't be bleaching any more palm oil. We should splurge on vegetable oil for these last few weeks,' Obiora said, still swatting at the flies.

'You sound like Mom has already gotten the visa,' Amaka snapped. She placed the pot on the kerosene burner. The fire snaked around to the side of the pot, still a wild orange, spewing fumes; it had not yet stabilized to a clean blue.

'She will get the visa. We should be positive.'

'Haven't you heard how those American embassy people treat Nigerians? They insult you and call you a liar and on top of it, eh, refuse to give you a visa,' Amaka said.

'Mom will get the visa. A university is sponsoring her,' Obiora said.

'So? Universities sponsor many people who still don't get visas.'

I started to cough. Thick white smoke from the bleaching palm oil filled the kitchen, and in the stuffy mix of the fumes and heat and flies, I felt faint.

'Kambili,' Amaka said. 'Go to the verandah until the smoke blows out.'

'No, it's nothing,' I said.

'Go, *biko*.'

I went to the verandah, still coughing. It was clear that I was unused to bleaching palm oil, that I was used to vegetable oil, which did not need bleaching. But there had been no resentment in Amaka's eyes, no sneer, no turndown of her lips. I was grateful when she called me back later to ask that I help her cut the ugu for the soup. I did not just cut the ugu, I made the garri also. Without her still eyes bearing down on me, I did not pour in too much hot water, and the garri turned out firm and smooth. I ladled my garri onto a flat plate, pushed it to the side, and then spooned my soup beside it. I watched the soup spreading, seeping in underneath the garri. I had never done this before; at home, Jaja and I always used separate dishes for garri and soup.

We ate on the verandah, although it was almost as hot as the kitchen. The railings felt like the metal handles of a boiling pot.

'Papa-Nnukwu used to say that an angry sun like this in rainy season means that a swift rain will come. The sun is warning us of the rain,' Amaka said, as we settled down on the mat with our food.

We ate quickly because of the heat, because even the soup tasted like sweat. Afterward, we trooped to the neighbors' flat on the topmost floor and stood on their verandah, to see if we could catch a breeze. Amaka and I stood by the railings, looking down. Obiora and Chima squatted to watch the children playing on the floor, clustered around the plastic Ludo board and rolling dice. Somebody poured a bucket of water on the verandah and the boys lay down, with their backs on the wet floor.

I looked out at Marguerite Cartwright Avenue below, at a red Volkswagen driving past. It revved loudly as it went over the speed bump, and even from the verandah, I could see where the color had faded to a rusty orange. I felt nostalgic as I watched the Volkswagen disappear down the street, and I was not sure why. Maybe it was because it revved like Aunty Ifeoma's car sometimes did, and it reminded me that very soon, I would not see her or her car anymore. She had gone to the police station to get a statement, which she would take to her visa interview at the American embassy to prove that she had never been convicted of a crime. Jaja had gone with her.

'I suppose we won't need to protect our doors with metal in America,' Amaka said, as if she knew what I was thinking about. She was fanning herself briskly with a folded newspaper.

'What?'

'Mom's students broke into her office once and stole exam questions. She told the works department that she wanted metal bars on her office doors and windows, and they said there was no money. You know what she did?'

Amaka turned to look at me; a small smile at the edges of her lips. I shook my head.

'She went to a construction site, and they gave her metal rods for free. Then she asked Obiora and me to help her install them. We drilled holes and fit the rods in with cement, across her windows and doors.'

'Oh,' I said. I wanted to reach out and touch Amaka.

'And then she put up a sign at her door that said EXAM QUESTIONS ARE IN THE BANK.' Amaka smiled and then started to fold and refold the newspaper. 'I won't be happy in America. It won't be the same.'

'You will drink fresh milk from a bottle. No more stunted tins of condensed milk, no more homemade soybean milk,' I said.

Amaka laughed, a hearty laugh that showed her gap. 'You're funny.'

I had never heard that before. I saved it for later, to ruminate over and over that I had made her laugh, that I could make her laugh.

The rains came then, pouring down in strong

sheets that made it impossible to see the garages across the yard. The sky and rain and ground merged into one silver-colored film that seemed to go on and on. We dashed back to the flat and placed buckets on the verandah to catch the rainwater and watched them fill rapidly. All the children ran out to the yard in their shorts, twirling and dancing, because this was clean rain, the kind that did not come with dust, that did not leave brown stains on clothes. It stopped as quickly as it had started, and the sun came out again, mildly, as if yawning after a nap. The buckets were full; we fished out floating leaves and twigs and took the buckets in.

I saw Father Amadi's car turning into the compound when we went back out to the verandah. Obiora saw it, too, and asked, laughing, 'Is it me or does Father visit more often whenever Kambili is here?'

He and Amaka were still laughing when Father Amadi came up the short flight of stairs. 'I know Amaka just said something about me,' he said, sweeping Chima into his arms. He stood backing the setting sun. The sun was red, as if it were blushing, and it made his skin look radiant.

I watched how Chima clung to him, how Amaka's and Obiora's eyes shone as they looked up at him. Amaka was asking him about his missionary work in Germany, but I did not hear much of what she said. I was not listening. I felt so many things churning inside me, emotions that made my stomach growl and swirl.

'Do you see Kambili bothering me like this?' Father Amadi asked Amaka. He was looking at me, and I knew he had said that to include me, to get my attention.

'The white missionaries brought us their god,' Amaka was saying. 'Which was the same color as them, worshiped in their language and packaged in the boxes they made. Now that we take their god back to them, shouldn't we at least repackage it?'

Father Amadi smirked and said, 'We go mostly to Europe and America, where they are losing priests. So there is really no indigenous culture to pacify, unfortunately.'

'Father, be serious!' Amaka was laughing.

'Only if you will try to be more like Kambili and not bother me so much.'

The phone started to ring, and Amaka made a face at him before walking into the flat.

Father Amadi sat down next to me. 'You look worried,' he said. Before I could think of what to say, he reached out and slapped my lower leg. He opened his palm to show me the bloody, squashed mosquito. He had cupped his palm so that it would not hurt too much and yet would kill the mosquito. 'It looked so happy feeding on you,' he said, watching me.

'Thank you,' I said.

He reached out and wiped the spot on my leg with a finger. His finger felt warm and alive. I did not realize that my cousins had left; now the verandah was so silent I could hear the sound of the raindrops sliding off the leaves.

'So tell me what you're thinking about,' he said.

'It doesn't matter.'

'What you think will always matter to me, Kambili.'

I stood up and walked to the garden. I plucked off yellow allamanda flowers, still wet, and slid them over my fingers, as I had seen Chima do. It was like wearing a scented glove. 'I was thinking about my father. I don't know what will happen when we go back.'

'Has he called?'

'Yes. Jaja refused to go to the phone, and I did not go, either.'

'Did you want to?' He asked gently. It was not what I expected him to ask.

'Yes,' I whispered, so Jaja wouldn't hear, although he was not even in the area. I did want to talk to Papa, to hear his voice, to tell him what I had eaten and what I had prayed about so that he would approve, so that he would smile so much his eyes would crinkle at the edges. And yet, I did not want to talk to him; I wanted to leave with Father Amadi, or with Aunty Ifeoma, and never come back. 'School starts in two weeks, and Aunty Ifeoma might be gone then,' I said. 'I don't know what we will do. Jaja does not talk about tomorrow or next week.'

Father Amadi walked over to me, standing so close that I if I puffed out my belly, it would touch his body. He took my hand in his, carefully slid one flower off my finger and slid it onto his. 'Your aunt thinks you and Jaja should go to boarding school. I am going to Enugu next week to talk to Father Benedict; I know your father listens to him. I will ask him to convince your father about boarding school so you and Jaja can start next term. It will be fine, *inugo?*'

I nodded and looked away. I believed him, that it would be fine, because he said so. I thought then of catechism classes, about chanting the answer to a question, an answer that was 'because he has said it and his word is true.' I could not remember the question.

'Look at me, Kambili.'

I was afraid to look into the warm brownness of his eyes, I was afraid I would swoon, that I would throw my hands around him and lace my fingers together behind his neck and refuse to let go. I turned.

'Is this the flower you can suck? The one with the sweet juices?' he asked. He had slid the alla-manda off his finger and was examining its yellow petals.

I smiled. 'No. It's ixora you suck.'

He threw the flower away and made a wry face. 'Oh.'

I laughed. I laughed because the allamanda flowers were so yellow. I laughed imagining how bitter their white juices would taste if Father Amadi had really sucked them. I laughed because

Father Amadi's eyes were so brown I could see my reflection in them.

That night when I bathed, with a bucket half full of rainwater, I did not scrub my left hand, the hand that Father Amadi had held gently to slide the flower off my finger. I did not heat the water, either, because I was afraid that the heating coil would make the rainwater lose the scent of the sky. I sang as I bathed. There were more earthworms in the bathtub, and I left them alone, watching the water carry them and send them down the drain.

The breeze following the rain was so cool
that I wore a sweater and Aunty Ifeoma
wore a long-sleeved shirt, although she
usually walked around the house in only a wrapper.
We were all sitting on the verandah, talking, when
Father Amadi's car nosed its way to the front of
the flat.

'You said you would be very busy today, Father,'
Obiora said.

'I say these things to justify being fed by the
church,' Father Amadi said. He looked tired. He
handed Amaka a piece of paper and told her he had
written some suitably boring names on it, that she
had only to choose one and he would leave. After
the bishop used it in confirming her, she need
never even mention the name again. Father Amadi
rolled his eyes, speaking with a painstaking slowness, and although Amaka laughed, she did not
take the paper.

'I told you I am not taking an English name,
Father,' she said.

'And have I asked you why?'

'Why do I have to?'

'Because it is the way it's done. Let's forget if it's right or wrong for now,' Father Amadi said, and I noticed the shadows under his eyes.

'When the missionaries first came, they didn't think Igbo names were good enough. They insisted that people take English names to be baptized. Shouldn't we be moving ahead?'

'It's different now, Amaka, don't make this what it's not,' Father Amadi said, calmly. 'Nobody has to use the name. Look at me. I've always used my Igbo name, but I was baptized Michael and confirmed Victor.'

Aunty Ifeoma looked up from the forms she was going through. 'Amaka, *ngwa*, pick a name and let Father Amadi go and do his work.'

'But what's the point, then?' Amaka said to Father Amadi, as if she had not heard her mother. 'What the church is saying is that only an English name will make your confirmation valid. "Chiamaka" says God is beautiful. "Chima" says God knows best, "Chiebuka" says God is the greatest. Don't they all glorify God as much as "Paul" and "Peter" and "Simon"?'

Aunty Ifeoma was getting annoyed; I knew by her raised voice, by her snappy tone. '*O gini!* You don't have to prove a senseless point here! Just do it and get confirmed, nobody says you have to use the name!'

But Amaka refused. '*Ekwerom*,' she said to Aunty Ifeoma – I do not agree. Then she walked into her room and turned her music on very loud until

316

Aunty Ifeoma knocked on the door and shouted that Amaka was asking for a slap if she did not turn it down right away. Amaka turned the music down. Father Amadi left, with a bemused sort of smile on his face.

That evening, tempers cooled and we had dinner together, but there was not much laughter. And the next day, Easter Sunday, Amaka did not join the rest of the young people who wore all white and carried lit candles, with folded newspapers to trap the melting wax. They all had pieces of paper pinned to their clothes, with names written on them. Paul. Mary. James. Veronica. Some of the girls looked like brides, and I remembered my own confirmation, how Papa had said I was a bride, Christ's bride, and I had been surprised because I thought the Church was Christ's bride.

Aunty Ifeoma wanted to go on pilgrimage to Aokpe. She was not sure why she suddenly wanted to go, she told us, probably the thought that she might be gone for a long time. Amaka and I said we would go with her. But Jaja said he would not go, then was stonily silent as if he dared anyone to ask him why. Obiora said he would stay back, too, with Chima. Aunty Ifeoma did not seem to mind. She smiled and said that since we didn't have a male, she would ask Father Amadi if he wanted to accompany us.

'I will turn into a bat if Father Amadi says yes,' Amaka said.

But he did say yes. When Aunty Ifeoma hung up the phone after talking to him and said he would be coming with us, Amaka said, 'It's because of Kambili. He would never have come if not for Kambili.'

Aunty Ifeoma drove us to the dusty village about two hours away. I sat in the back with Father Amadi, separated from him by the space in the middle. He and Amaka sang as we drove; the undulating road made the car sway from side to side, and I imagined that it was dancing. Sometimes I joined in the singing, and other times I remained quiet and listened, wondering what it would feel like if I moved closer, if I covered the space between us and rested my head on his shoulder.

When we finally turned into the dirt road with the hand-painted sign that read WELCOME TO AOKPE APPARITION GROUND, all I saw at first was chaos. Hundreds of cars, many bearing scrawled signs that read CATHOLICS ON PILGRIMAGE, jostled to fit into a tiny village that Aunty Ifeoma said had not known as many as ten cars until a local girl started to see the vision of the Beautiful Woman. People were packed so close that the smell of other people became as familiar as their own. Women crashed to their knees. Men shouted prayers. Rosaries rustled. People pointed and shouted, 'See, there, on the tree, that's Our Lady!' Others pointed at the glowing sun. 'There she is!'

We stood underneath a huge flame-of-the-forest

tree. It was in bloom, its flowers fanning out on wide branches and the ground underneath covered with petals the color of fire. When the young girl was led out, the flame-of-the-forest swayed and flowers rained down. The girl was slight and solemn, dressed in white, and strong-looking men stood around her so she would not be trampled. She had hardly passed us when other trees nearby started to quiver with a frightening vigor, as if someone were shaking them. The ribbons that cordoned off the apparition area shook, too. Yet there was no wind. The sun turned white, the color and shape of the host. And then I saw her, the Blessed Virgin: an image in the pale sun, a red glow on the back of my hand, a smile on the face of the rosary-bedecked man whose arm rubbed against mine. She was everywhere.

I wanted to stay longer, but Aunty Ifeoma said we had to leave, because it would be impossible to drive out if we waited until most people were leaving. She bought rosaries and scapulars and little vials of holy water from the vendors as we walked to the car.

'It doesn't matter if Our Lady appeared or not,' Amaka said, when we got to the car. 'Aokpe will always be special because it was the reason Kambili and Jaja first came to Nsukka.'

'Does that mean you don't believe in the apparition?' Father Amadi asked, a teasing lilt in his voice.

'No, I didn't say that,' Amaka said. 'What about you? Do you believe it?'

Father Amadi said nothing; he seemed to be focused on rolling the window down to get a buzzing fly out of the car.

'I felt the Blessed Virgin there. I felt her,' I blurted out. How could anyone not believe after what we had seen? Or hadn't they seen it and felt it, too?

Father Amadi turned to study me; I saw him from the corner of my eye. There was a gentle smile on his face. Aunty Ifeoma glanced at me, then turned back and faced the road.

'Kambili is right,' she said. 'Something from God was happening there.'

I went with Father Amadi to say his good-byes to the families on campus. Many of the lecturers' children clung tightly to him, as if the tighter they held him, the less likely he could break free and leave Nsukka. We did not say much to each other. We sang Igbo chorus songs from his cassette player. It was one of those songs – '*Abum onye n'uwa, onye ka m bu n'uwa*' – that eased the dryness in my throat as we got into his car, and I said, 'I love you.'

He turned to me with an expression that I had never seen, his eyes almost sad. He leaned over the gear and pressed his face to mine. I wanted our lips to meet and hold, but he moved his face away. 'You are almost sixteen, Kambili. You are beautiful. You will find more love than you will need in a life-time,' he said. And I did not know whether to laugh or cry. He was wrong. He was so wrong.

As he drove me home, I looked out of the open window at the compounds we drove past. The gaping holes in the hedges had closed up, and green branches snaked across to meet each other. I wished that I could see the backyards so I could occupy myself with imagining the lives behind the hanging clothes and fruit trees and swings. I wished I could think about something, anything, so that I would no longer feel. I wished I could blink away the liquid in my eyes.

When I got back, Aunty Ifeoma asked if I was all right, if something was wrong.

'I'm fine, Aunty,' I said.

She was looking at me as though she knew I was not fine. 'Are you sure, *nne*?'

'Yes, Aunty.'

'Brighten up, *inugo*? And please pray for my visa interview. I will leave for Lagos tomorrow.'

'Oh,' I said, and I felt a new, numbing rush of sadness. 'I will, Aunty,' Yet I knew that I would not, could not, pray that she get the visa. I knew it was what she wanted, that she did not have many other choices. Or any other choices. Still, I would not pray that she get the visa. I could not pray for what I did not want.

Amaka was in the bedroom, lying in bed, listening to music with the cassette player next to her ear. I sat on the bed and hoped she would not ask me how my day with Father Amadi had gone. She didn't say anything, just kept nodding to the music.

'You are singing along,' she said after a while.

'What?'

'You were just singing along with Fela.'

'I was?' I looked at Amaka and wondered if she was imagining things.

'How will I get Fela tapes in America, eh? Just how will I get them?'

I wanted to tell Amaka that I was sure she would find Fela tapes in America, and any other tapes that she wanted, but I didn't. It would mean I assumed that Aunty Ifeoma would get the visa – and besides, I was not sure Amaka wanted to hear that.

My stomach was unsteady until Aunty Ifeoma came back from Lagos. We had been waiting for her on the verandah, although there was power and we could have been inside, watching TV. The insects did not buzz around us, perhaps because the kerosene lamp was not on or perhaps because they sensed the tension. Instead, they flitted around the electric bulb above the door, making surprised *thuds* when they bumped against it. Amaka had brought the fan out, and its whir created music with the hum of the refrigerator inside. When a car stopped in front of the flat, Obiora jumped up and ran out.

'Mom, how did it go? Did you get it?'

'I got it,' Aunty Ifeoma said, coming onto the verandah.

'You got the visa!' Obiora screamed, and Chima promptly repeated him, rushing over to hug his mother. Amaka and Jaja and I did not stand; we said welcome to Aunty Ifeoma and watched her go inside to change. She came out soon, with a wrapper tied casually around her chest. The wrapper that stopped above her calves would stop above the ankles of an average-size woman. She sat down and asked Obiora to get her a glass of water.

'You do not look happy, Aunty,' Jaja said.

'Oh, *nna m*, I am. Do you know how many people they refuse? A woman next to me cried until I thought that blood would run down her cheeks. She asked them, "How can you refuse me a visa? I have shown you that I have money in the bank. How can you say I will not come back? I have property here, I have property." She kept saying that over and over: "I have property." I think she had wanted to attend her sister's wedding in America.'

'Why did they refuse her?' Obiora asked.

'I don't know. If they are in a good mood, they will give you a visa, if not, they will refuse you. It is what happens when you are worthless in somebody's eyes. We are like footballs that they can kick in any direction they want to.'

'When are we leaving?' Amaka asked, tiredly, and I could tell that right now she did not care about the woman who had nearly cried blood or about Nigerians being kicked around or about anything at all.

Aunty Ifeoma drank the whole glass of water before speaking. 'We have to move out of this flat in two weeks. I know they are waiting to see that I don't, so they can send security men to throw my things out on the street.'

'You mean we leave Nigeria in two weeks?' Amaka asked, shrilly.

'Am I a magician, eh?' Aunty Ifeoma retorted. The humor was lacking in her tone. There was nothing in her tone to speak of, really, except for fatigue. 'I have to get the money for our tickets first. They are not cheap. I will have to ask your Uncle Eugene to help, so I think we will go to Enugu with Kambili and Jaja, perhaps next week. We will stay in Enugu until we are ready to leave, that will also give me an opportunity to talk to your Uncle Eugene about Kambili and Jaja going to boarding school.' Aunty Ifeoma turned to Jaja and me. 'I will convince your father in any way I can. Father Amadi has offered to ask Father Benedict to talk to your father, too. I think it is the best thing for you both now, to go to school away from home.'

I nodded. Jaja got up and walked into the flat. Finality hung in the air, heavy and hollow.

Father Amadi's last day sneaked up on me. He came in the morning, smelling of that masculine cologne I had come to smell even when he was not there, wearing the same boyish smile, wearing the same soutane.

Obiora looked up at him and intoned, 'From darkest Africa now come missionaries who will reconvert the West.'

Father Amadi started to laugh. 'Obiora, whoever gives you those heretical books should stop.'

His laugh was the same, too. Nothing seemed to have changed about him, yet my new, fragile life was about to break into pieces. Anger suddenly filled me, constricting my air passages, pressing my nostrils shut. Anger was alien and refreshing. With my eyes, I traced the lines of his lips, the flare of his nose, as he spoke to Aunty Ifeoma and my cousins, all the while nursing my anger. Finally, he asked me to walk him to the car.

'I have to join the chaplaincy council members for lunch; they are cooking for me. But come and spend an hour or two with me, while I do the final cleaning up at the chaplaincy office,' he said.

'No.'

He stopped to stare at me. 'Why?'

'No. I don't want to.'

I was standing with my back to his car. He moved toward me and stood in front of me. 'Kambili,' he said.

I wanted to ask him to say my name in a different way because he did not have the right to say it the old way. Nothing should be the same, was the same anymore. He was leaving. I breathed through my mouth now. 'The first day you took me to the stadium, did Aunty Ifeoma ask you to?' I asked.

'She was worried about you, that you could not

hold a conversation with even the children upstairs. But she didn't ask me to take you.' He reached out to straighten the sleeve of my shirt. 'I wanted to take you. And after that first day, I wanted to take you with me every day.'

I bent down to pick up a grass stalk, narrow like a green needle.

'Kambili,' he said. 'Look at me.'

But I did not look at him. I kept my eyes on the grass in my hand as if it held a code I could decipher by concentrated staring, as if it could explain to me why I wished he had said he didn't want to take me even that first time so that I would have a reason to be angrier, so that I would not have this urge to cry and cry.

He climbed into his car and started it. 'I will come back and see you this evening.'

I stared at his car until it disappeared down the slope that led to Ikejiani Avenue. I was still staring when Amaka walked over to me. She placed her arm lightly on my shoulder.

'Obiora says you must be having sex, or something close to sex, with Father Amadi. We have never seen Father Amadi look so bright-eyed.' Amaka was laughing.

I did not know whether or not she was serious. I did not want to dwell on how strange it felt discussing whether or not I had had sex with Father Amadi.

'Maybe when we are in the university you will join me in agitating for optional celibacy in the priesthood?' Amaka asked. 'Or maybe fornication should be permitted all priests once in a while. Say, once a month?'

'Amaka, please stop it.' I turned and walked to the verandah.

'Do you want him to leave the priesthood?' Amaka sounded more serious now.

'He will never leave.'

Amaka tilted her head thoughtfully, and then smiled. 'You never know,' she said, before walking into the living room.

I copied Father Amadi's German address over and over in my notebook. I was copying it again, trying at different writing styles, when he came back. He took the notebook from me and closed it. I wanted to say, 'I will miss you' but instead I said, 'I will write you.'

'I will write you first,' he said.

I did not know that tears slipped down my cheeks until Father Amadi reached out and wiped them away, running his open palm over my face. Then he enclosed me in his arms and held me.

Aunty Ifeoma cooked dinner for Father Amadi, and we all ate the rice and beans at the dining table. I knew that there was much laughter, much talk about the stadium and about remembering, but I did not feel that I was involved. I was busy locking little parts of me up, because I would not need them if Father Amadi was not here.

I did not sleep well that night; I tossed around

so often that I woke Amaka up. I wanted to tell her about my dream where a man chased me down a rocky path littered with bruised allamanda leaves. First the man was Father Amadi, his soutane flying behind him, then it was Papa, in the floor-length gray sack he wore when he distributed ash on Ash Wednesday. But I didn't tell her. I let her hold and soothe me like a little child, until I fell asleep. I was glad to wake up, glad to see morning stream in through the window in shimmering strips the color of a ripe orange.

The packing was done; the hallway looked oddly big now that the bookshelves were gone. In Aunty Ifeoma's room, only a few things remained on the floor, the things we would use until we all left for Enugu: a bag of rice, a tin of milk, a tin of Bournvita. The other cartons and boxes and books had been cleared up or given away. When Aunty Ifeoma gave some clothes to the neighbors, the woman from the flat upstairs told her, '*Mh*, why won't you give me that blue dress you wear to church? After all, you will get more in America!'

Aunty Ifeoma had narrowed her eyes, annoyed. I was not sure if it was because the woman was asking for the dress or because she had brought up America. But she did not give her the blue dress.

There was restlessness in the air now, as if we had all packed everything too quickly and too well and we needed something else to do.

'We have fuel, let's go for a drive,' Aunty Ifeoma suggested.

'A good-bye tour of Nsukka,' Amaka said, with a wry smile.

We piled into the car. It swerved as Aunty Ifeoma turned onto the stretch of road bordered by the faculty of engineering, and I wondered if it would crash into the gutter and then Aunty Ifeoma would not get the fair rate she said a man in town had offered for it. She had also said that the money she would get for the car would pay only for Chima's ticket, which was half the full price of a ticket.

Since my dream, the night before, I had had a feeling that something big would happen. Father Amadi would come back; it had to be what would happen. Maybe there was a mistake in his departure date; maybe he had postponed his trip. So as Aunty Ifeoma drove, I looked at the cars on the road, seeking Father Amadi, looking for that pastel-colored small Toyota.

Aunty Ifeoma stopped at the foot of Odim hill and said, 'Let's climb to the top.'

I was surprised. I was not sure Aunty Ifeoma had planned to have us climb up the hill; it sounded like something she had said on impulse. Obiora suggested we have a picnic up the hill, and Aunty Ifeoma said it was a good idea. We drove to town and bought moi-moi and bottles of Ribena from Eastern Shop and then came back to the hill. The climb was easy because there were many zigzagging paths. There was a fresh smell in the air and, once in a while, a crackling in the long grass that bordered the paths.

'The grasshoppers make that sound with their wings,' Obiora said. He stopped by a mighty anthill, with ridges running across the red mud as if they were deliberate designs. 'Amaka, you should paint something like this,' he said. But Amaka did not respond; instead, she started to run up the hill. Chima ran after her. Jaja joined them. Aunty Ifeoma looked at me. 'What are you waiting for?' she asked, and she raised her wrapper, almost above her knees, and ran after Jaja. I took off, too, feeling the wind rush past my ears. Running made me think of Father Amadi, made me remember the way his eyes had lingered on my bare legs. I ran past Aunty Ifeoma, past Jaja and Chima, and I got to the top of the hill at about the same time as Amaka.

'Hei!' Amaka said, looking at me. 'You should be a sprinter.' She flopped down on the grass, breathing hard. I sat next to her and brushed away a tiny spider on my leg. Aunty Ifeoma had stopped running before she got to the top of the hill. '*Nne*,' she said to me. 'I will find you a trainer, eh, there is big money in athletics.'

I laughed. It seemed so easy now, laughter. So many things seemed easy now. Jaja was laughing, too, as was Amaka, and we were all sitting on the grass, waiting for Obiora to come up to the top. He walked up slowly, holding something that turned out to be a grasshopper. 'It's so strong,' he said. 'I can feel the pressure of its wings.' He spread his palm and watched the grasshopper fly off.

We took our food into the damaged building tucked into the other side of the hill. It may have once been a storeroom, but its roof and doors had been blown off during the civil war years ago, and it had remained that way. It looked ghostly, and I did not want to eat there, although Obiora said people spread mats on the charred floors to have picnics all the time. He was examining the writings on the walls of the building, and he read some of them aloud. 'Obinna loves Nnenna forever.' 'Emeka and Unoma did it here.' 'One love Chimsimdi and Obi.'

I was relieved when Aunty Ifeoma said we would eat outside on the grass, since we did not have a mat. As we ate the moi-moi and drank the Ribena, I watched a small car crawl around the base of the hill. I tried to focus, to see who was inside, even though it was too far away. The shape of the head looked very much like Father Amadi's. I ate quickly and wiped my mouth with the back of my hand, smoothed my hair. I didn't want to look untidy when he appeared.

Chima wanted to race down the other side of the hill, the side that didn't have many paths, but Aunty Ifeoma said it was too steep. So he sat down and slithered on his behind down the hill. Aunty Ifeoma called out, 'You will use your own hands to wash your shorts, do you hear me?'

I knew that, before, she would have scolded him some more and probably made him stop. We all sat and watched him slide down the hill, the brisk wind making our eyes water.

The sun had turned red and was about to fall when Aunty Ifeoma said we had to leave. As we trudged down the hill, I stopped hoping that Father Amadi would appear.

We were all in the living room, playing cards, when the phone rang that evening.

'Amaka, please answer it,' Aunty Ifeoma said, even though she was closest to the door.

'I can bet it's for you, Mom,' Amaka said, focused on her cards. 'It's one of those people who want you to dash them our plates and our pots and even the underwear we have on.'

Aunty Ifeoma got up laughing and hurried to the phone. The TV was off and we were all silently absorbed in our cards, so I heard Aunty Ifeoma's scream clearly. A short, strangled scream. For a short moment, I prayed that the American embassy had revoked the visa, before I rebuked myself and asked God to disregard my prayers. We all rushed to the room.

'Hei, Chi m o! nwunye m! Hei!' Aunty Ifeoma was standing by the table, her free hand placed on her head in the way that people do when they are in shock. What had happened to Mama? She was holding the phone out; I knew she wanted to give it to Jaja, but I was closer and I grasped it.

My hand shook so much the earpiece slid away from my ear to my temple.

Mama's low voice floated across the phone line and quickly quelled my shaking hand. 'Kambili, it's your father. They called me from the factory, they found him lying dead on his desk.'

I pressed the phone tighter to my ear. 'Eh?'

'It's your father. They called me from the factory, they found him lying dead on his desk.' Mama sounded like a recording. I imagined her saying the same thing to Jaja, in the same exact tone. My ears filled with liquid. Although I had heard her right, heard her say he was found dead on his office desk, I asked, 'Did he get a letter bomb? Was it a letter bomb?'

Jaja grabbed the phone. Aunty Ifeoma led me to the bed. I sat down and stared at the bag of rice that leaned against the bedroom wall, and I knew that I would always remember that bag of rice, the brown interweaving of jute, the words ADADA LONG GRAIN on it, the way it slumped against the wall, near the table. I had never considered the possibility that Papa would die, that Papa could die. He was different from Ade Coker, from all the other people they had killed. He had seemed immortal.

I sat with Jaja in our living room, staring at the space where the étagère had been, where the ballet-dancing figurines had been. Mama was upstairs, packing Papa's things. I had gone up to help and saw her kneeling on the plush rug, holding his red pajamas pressed to her face. She did not look up when I came in; she said, 'Go, *nne*, go and stay with Jaja,' the silk muffling her voice.

Outside, the rain came down in slants, hitting the closed windows with a furious rhythm. It would hurl down cashews and mangoes from the trees and they would start to rot in the humid earth, giving out that sweet-and-sour scent.

The compound gates were locked. Mama had told Adamu not to open the gates to all the people who wanted to throng in for mgbalu, to commiserate with us. Even members of our umunna who had come from Abba were turned away. Adamu said it was unheard of, to turn sympathizers away. But Mama told him we wished to mourn privately, that they could go to offer Masses for the repose of Papa's soul. I had never heard Mama talk to

Adamu that way; I had never even heard Mama talk to Adamu at all.

'Madam said you should drink some Bournvita,' Sisi said, coming into the living room. She was carrying a tray that held the same cups Papa had always used to drink his tea. I could smell the thyme and curry that clung to her. Even after she had a bath, she still smelled like that. It was only Sisi who had cried in the household, loud sobs that had quickly quieted in the face of our bewildered silence.

I turned to Jaja after she left and tried speaking with my eyes. But Jaja's eyes were blank, like a window with its shutter drawn across.

'Won't you drink some Bournvita?' I asked, finally.

He shook his head. 'Not with those cups.' He shifted on his seat and added, 'I should have taken care of Mama. Look how Obiora balances Aunty Ifeoma's family on his head, and I am older than he is. I should have taken care of Mama.'

'God knows best,' I said. 'God works in mysterious ways.' And I thought how Papa would be proud that I had said that, how he would approve of my saying that.

Jaja laughed. It sounded like a series of snorts strung together. 'Of course God does. Look what He did to his faithful servant Job, even to His own son. But have you ever wondered why? Why did He have to murder his own son so we would be saved? Why didn't He just go ahead and save us?'

I took off my slippers. The cold marble floor

drew the heat from my feet. I wanted to tell Jaja that my eyes tingled with unshed tears, that I still listened for, wanted to hear, Papa's footsteps on the stairs. That there were painfully scattered bits inside me that I could never put back because the places they fit into were gone. Instead, I said, 'St Agnes will be full for Papa's funeral Mass.'

Jaja did not respond.

The phone started to ring. It rang for a long time; the caller must have dialed a few times before Mama finally answered it. She came into the living room a short while later. The wrapper casually tied across her chest hung low, exposing the birthmark, a little black bulb, above her left breast.

'They did an autopsy,' she said. 'They have found the poison in your father's body.' She sounded as though the poison in Papa's body was something we all had known about, something we had put in there to be found, the way it was done in the books I read where white people hid Easter eggs for their children to find.

'Poison?' I said.

Mama tightened her wrapper, then went to the windows; she pushed the drapes aside, checking that the louvers were shut to keep the rain from splashing into the house. Her movements were calm and slow. When she spoke, her voice was just as calm and slow. 'I started putting the poison in his tea before I came to Nsukka. Sisi got it for me; her uncle is a powerful witch doctor.'

For a long, silent moment I could think of

nothing. My mind was blank, I was blank. Then I thought of taking sips of Papa's tea, love sips, the scalding liquid that burned his love onto my tongue. 'Why did you put it in his tea?' I asked Mama, rising. My voice was loud. I was almost screaming. 'Why in his tea?'

But Mama did not answer. Not even when I stood up and shook her until Jaja yanked me away. Not even when Jaja wrapped his arms around me and turned to include her but she moved away.

The policemen came a few hours later. They said they wanted to ask some questions. Somebody at St Agnes Hospital had contacted them, and they had a copy of the autopsy report with them. Jaja did not wait for their questions; he told them he had used rat poison, that he put it in Papa's tea. They allowed him to change his shirt before they took him away.

# A DIFFERENT SILENCE

## The Present

The roads to the prison are familiar. I know the houses and shops, I know the faces of the women who sell oranges and bananas just before you turn into the pot-hole-filled road that leads to the prison yard.

'You want to buy oranges, Kambili?' Celestine asks, slowing the car to a crawl, as the hawkers start to wave and call out to us. His voice is gentle; Mama says it is the reason she hired him after she asked Kevin to leave. That and also that he does not have a dagger-shape scar on his neck.

'What we have in the boot should do,' I say. I turn to Mama. 'Do you want us to buy anything here?'

Mama shakes her head, and her scarf starts to slip off. She reaches out to knot it again as loosely as before. Her wrapper is just as loose around her waist, and she ties and reties it often, giving her the air of the unkempt women in Ogbete market, who let their wrappers unravel so that everyone sees the hole-riddled slips they have on underneath.

She does not seem to mind that she looks this

way; she doesn't even seem to know. She has been different ever since Jaja was locked up, since she went about telling people that she killed Papa, that she put the poison in his tea. She even wrote letters to newspapers. But nobody listened to her; they still don't. They think grief and denial – that her husband is dead and that her son is in prison – have turned her into this vision of a painfully bony body, of skin speckled with blackheads the size of watermelon seeds. Perhaps it is why they forgive her for not wearing all black or all white for a year. Perhaps it is why nobody criticized her for not attending the first- and second-year memorial Masses, for not cutting her hair.

'Try and make your scarf tighter, Mama,' I say, reaching out to touch her shoulder.

Mama shrugs, still looking out of the window. 'It is tight enough.'

Celestine is looking at us in the rearview mirror. His eyes are gentle. He once suggested to me that we take Mama to a dibia in his hometown, a man who is an expert in 'these things.' I was not sure what Celestine meant by 'these things,' if he was suggesting that Mama was mad, but I thanked him and told him she would not want to go. He means well, Celestine. I have seen the way he looks at Mama sometimes, the way he helps her get out of the car, and I know he wishes he could make her whole.

Mama and I hardly ever come to the prison together. Usually Celestine takes me a day or two before he takes her, every week. She prefers it, I think. But today is different, special – we have finally been told, for certain, that Jaja will get out.

After the Head of State died months ago – they say he died atop a prostitute, foaming at the mouth and jerking – we thought Jaja's release would be immediate, that our lawyers would quickly work something out. Especially with the prodemocracy groups demonstrating, calling for a government investigation into Papa's death, insisting that the old regime killed him. But it took a few weeks before the interim civilian government announced that it would release all prisoners of conscience, and weeks more for our lawyers to get Jaja on the list. His name is number four on the list of more than two hundred. He will be out next week.

They told us yesterday, two of our most recent lawyers; both of them have the prestigious *SAN*, for senior advocate of Nigeria, after their names. They came to our house with the news and with a bottle of champagne tied with a pink ribbon. After they left, Mama and I did not talk about it. We went about carrying, but not sharing, the same new peace, the same hope, concrete for the first time.

There is so much more that Mama and I do not talk about. We do not talk about the huge checks we have written, for bribes to judges and policemen and prison guards. We do not talk about how much money we have, even after half of Papa's estate went to St Agnes and to the fostering of missions in the church. And we have never talked about finding out that Papa had anonymously donated to the children's hospitals and motherless babies' homes and disabled veterans from the civil war. There is still so much that we do not say with our voices, that we do not turn into words.

'Please put in the Fela tape, Celestine,' I say, leaning back on the seat. The brash voice soon fills the car. I turn to see if Mama minds, but she is looking straight ahead at the front seat; I doubt that she can hear anything. Most times, her answers are nods and shakes of the head, and I wonder if she really heard. I used to ask Sisi to talk to her, because she would sit with Sisi in the living room for long hours, but she said Mama would not reply to her, that Mama simply sat and stared. When Sisi got married last year, Mama gave her cartons and cartons of china and Sisi sat on the floor of the kitchen, crying loudly, while Mama watched her. Sisi comes in now, once in a while, to instruct our new steward, Okon, and to ask if Mama needs anything. Mama usually says nothing, just shakes her head while rocking herself.

Last month, when I told her I was going to Nsukka, she did not say anything, either, did not ask me why, though I don't know anybody in Nsukka anymore. She simply nodded. Celestine drove me, and we arrived around noon, just about when the sun was changing to the searing sun I have long imagined can suck the moisture from bone marrow. Most of the lawns on the university grounds are overgrown now; the long grasses stick up like green arrows. The statue of the preening lion no longer gleams.

I asked the new family in Aunty Ifeoma's flat if I could come in, and although they looked at me strangely, they asked me in and offered me a glass of water. It would be warm, they said, because there was no power. The blades of the ceiling fan were encrusted with woolly dust, so I knew there had been no power in a while or the dust would have flown away as the fan turned. I drank all the water, sitting on a sofa with uneven holes at the sides. I gave them the fruits I bought at Ninth Mile and apologized because the heat in the boot had blackened the bananas.

As we drove back to Enugu, I laughed loudly, above Fela's stringent singing. I laughed because Nsukka's untarred roads coat cars with dust in the harmattan and with sticky mud in the rainy season. Because the tarred roads spring potholes like surprise presents and the air smells of hills and history and the sunlight scatters the sand and turns it into gold dust. Because Nsukka could free something deep inside your belly that would rise up to your throat and come out as a freedom song. As laughter.

'We are here,' Celestine says.

We are at the prison compound. The bleak walls have unsightly patches of blue-green mold. Jaja is back in his old cell, so crowded that some people have to stand so that others can lie down. Their toilet is one black plastic bag, and they struggle over who will take it out each afternoon, because that person gets to see sunlight for a brief time. Jaja told me once that the men do not always bother to use the bag, especially the angry men. He does not mind sleeping with mice and cockroaches, but he does mind having another man's feces in his face. He was in a better cell until last month, with books and a mattress all to himself, because our lawyers knew the right people to bribe. But the wardens moved him here after he spat in a guard's face for no reason at all, after they stripped him and flogged him with koboko. Although I do not believe Jaja would do something like that unprovoked, I have no other version of the story because Jaja will not talk to me about it. He did not even show me the welts on his back, the ones the doctor we bribed in told me were puffy and swollen like long sausages. But I see other parts of Jaja, the parts I do not need to be shown, like his shoulders.

Those shoulders that bloomed in Nsukka, that grew wide and capable, have sagged in the thirty-one months that he has been here. Almost three years. If somebody gave birth when Jaja first came here, the child would be talking now, would be in nursery school. Sometimes, I look at him and cry, and he shrugs and tells me that Oladipupo, the chief of his cell – they have a system of hierarchy

346

in the cells – has been awaiting trial for eight years. Jaja's official status, all this time, has been Awaiting Trial.

Amaka used to write the office of the Head of State, even the Nigerian Ambassador in America, to complain about the poor state of Nigeria's justice system. She said nobody acknowledged the letters but still it was important to her that she do *something*. She does not tell Jaja any of this in her letters to him. I read them – they are chatty and matter-of-fact. They do not mention Papa and they hardly mention prison. In her last letter, she told him how Aokpe had been covered in a secular American magazine; the writer had sounded pessimistic that the Blessed Virgin Mary could be appearing at all, especially in Nigeria: all that corruption and all that heat. Amaka said she had written the magazine to tell them what she thought. I expected no less, of course.

She says she understands why Jaja does not write. What will he say? Aunty Ifeoma doesn't write Jaja, she sends him cassette tape recordings of their voices, instead. Sometimes, he lets me play them on my cassette player when I visit, and other times, he asks me not to. Aunty Ifeoma writes to Mama and me, though. She writes about her two jobs, one at a community college and one at a pharmacy, or drugstore, as they call it. She writes about the huge tomatoes and the cheap bread. Mostly, though, she writes about things that she misses and things she longs for, as if she ignores the present to dwell on the past and future. Sometimes, her letters go on and on until the ink gets smudgy and I am not always sure what she is talking about. There are people, she once wrote, who think that we cannot rule ourselves because the few times we tried, we failed, as if all the others who rule themselves today got it right the first time. It is like telling a crawling baby who tries to walk, and then falls back on his buttocks, to stay there. As if the adults walking past him did not all crawl, once.

Although I was interested in what she wrote, so much that I memorized most of it, I still do not know why she wrote it to me.

Amaka's letters are often quite as long, and she never fails to write, in every single one, how everybody is growing fat, how Chima 'outfats' his clothes in a month. Sure, there has never been a power outage and hot water runs from the tap, but we don't laugh anymore, she writes, because we don't have the time to laugh, because we don't even see one another. Obiora's letters are the cheeriest and the most irregular. He has a scholarship to a private school where, he says, he is praised and not punished for challenging his teachers.

'Let me do it,' Celestine says. He has opened the boot, and I am about to bring out the plastic bag of fruits and the cloth bag with the food and plates.

'Thank you,' I say, moving aside.

Celestine carries the bags and leads the way into the prison building. Mama trails behind. The policeman at the front desk has a toothpick stuck in his mouth. His eyes are jaundiced, so yellow they look dyed. The desk is bare except for a black phone, a fat, tattered logbook, and a pile of watches and hand-kerchiefs and necklaces crumpled down on one corner.

'How are you, sister?' he says when he sees me, beaming, although his eyes are focused on the bag in Celestine's hand. 'Ah! You come with madam today? Good afternoon, madam.'

I smile, and Mama nods vacuously. Celestine places the bag of fruit on the counter in front of the guard. Inside is a magazine with an envelope stuffed full of crisp naira notes, fresh from the bank.

The man puts his toothpick down and grabs the bag. It disappears behind the desk. Then he leads Mama and me to an airless room with benches on both sides of a low table. 'One hour,' he mutters before leaving.

We sit on the same side of the table, not close enough to touch. I know that Jaja will appear soon, and I try to prepare myself. It has not become any easier for me, seeing him here, even after so long. It will be even harder with Mama sitting next to me. It will be hardest because we finally have good news, because the emotions we used to hold back are dissolving and new ones are forming. I take a deep breath and hold it.

Jaja will come home soon, Father Amadi wrote in his last letter, which is tucked in my bag. You must believe this. And I believed it, I believed him, even though we had not heard from the lawyers and were not sure. I believe what Father Amadi says; I believe the firm slant of his handwriting. *Because he has said it and his word is true.*

I always carry his latest letter with me until a new one comes. When I told Amaka that I do this, she teased me in her reply about being lovey-dovey with Father Amadi and then drew a smiling face. But I don't carry his letters around because of anything lovey-dovey; there is very little lovey-dovey, anyway. He signs off with nothing more than 'as always.' He never responds with a yes or a no when I ask if he is happy. His answer is that he will go where the Lord sends him. He hardly even writes about his new life, except for brief anecdotes, such as the old German lady who refuses to shake his hand because she does not think a black man should be her priest, or the wealthy widow who insists he have dinner with her every night.

His letters dwell on me. I carry them around because they are long and detailed, because they remind me of my worthiness, because they tug at my feelings. Some months ago, he wrote that he did not want me to seek the whys, because there are some things that happen for which we can formulate no whys, for which whys simply do not exist and, perhaps, are not necessary. He did not mention Papa – he hardly mentions Papa in his letters – but I knew what he meant, I understood that he was stirring what I was afraid to stir myself.

And I carry them with me, also, because they give me grace. Amaka says people love priests because they want to compete with God, they want God as a rival. But we are not rivals, God and I, we are simply sharing. I no longer wonder if I have a right to love Father Amadi; I simply go ahead and love him. I no longer wonder if the checks I have been writing to the Missionary Fathers of the Blessed Way are bribes to God; I just go ahead and write them. I no longer wonder if I chose St Andrew's church in Enugu as my new church because the priest there is a Blessed Way Missionary Father as Father Amadi is; I just go.

'Did we bring the knives?' Mama asks. Her voice is loud. She is setting out the cylindrical food flask full of jollof rice and chicken. She places a pretty china plate down, as if she were setting a fancy table, the kind Sisi used to set.

'Mama, Jaja doesn't need knives,' I say. She knows Jaja always eats right from the flask, yet she takes a dinner plate with her every time, changes the colors and patterns weekly.

'We should have brought them, so he can cut the meat.'

'He doesn't cut the meat, he just eats it.' I smile at Mama and reach out to touch her arm, to calm her. She places a gleaming silver spoon and fork on the dirt-encrusted table and leans back to survey it. The door opens, and Jaja comes in. I brought his T-shirt, new, only two weeks ago, but already it has brown patches like stains from cashew juice, which never come off. As children, we ate cashews bent over so that the gushing sweet juices did not get on our clothes. His shorts end a long way above his knees, and I look away from the scabs on his thighs. We do not rise to hug him, because he does not like us to.

'Mama, good afternoon. Kambili, *ke kwanu*?' he says. He opens the food flask and starts to eat. I feel Mama trembling next to me, and because I don't want her to break down, I speak quickly. The sound of my voice may stop her tears. 'The lawyers will get you out next week.'

Jaja shrugs. Even the skin of his neck is covered with scabs that look dry until he scratches them and the yellowish pus underneath seeps out. Mama has bribed all kinds of ointments in and none seem to work.

'This cell has many interesting characters,' Jaja says. He spoons the rice into his mouth as quickly as he can. His cheeks bulge as though he has stuffed them with whole, unripe guavas.

'I mean out of prison, Jaja. Not to a different cell,' I say.

He stops chewing and stares at me silently with those eyes that have hardened a little every month he has spent here; now they look like the bark of a palm tree, unyielding. I even wonder if we ever really had an *asusu anya*, a language of the eyes, or if I imagined it all.

'You'll be out of here next week,' I say. 'You're coming home next week.'

I want to hold his hand, but I know he will shake it free. His eyes are too full of guilt to really see me, to see his reflection in my eyes, the reflection of my hero, the brother who tried always to protect me the best he could. He will never think that he did enough, and he will never understand that I do not think he should have done more.

'You are not eating,' Mama says. Jaja picks up the spoon and starts to wolf the rice down again. Silence hangs over us, but it is a different kind of silence, one that lets me breathe. I have nightmares about the other kind, the silence of when Papa was alive. In my nightmares, it mixes with shame and grief and so many other things that I cannot name, and forms blue tongues of fire that rest above my head, like Pentecost, until I wake up screaming and sweating. I have not told Jaja that I offer Masses for Papa every Sunday, that I want to see him in my dreams, that I want it so much I sometimes make my own dreams, when I am neither asleep nor awake: I see Papa, he reaches out to hug me, I reach out, too, but our bodies never touch before something jerks me up and I realize that I cannot control even the dreams that I have made. There is so much that is still silent between Jaja and me. Perhaps we will talk more with time, or perhaps we never will be able to say it all, to clothe things in words, things that have long been naked.

'You did not tie your scarf well,' Jaja says to Mama.

I stare in amazement. Jaja has never noticed what anybody wears. Mama hastily unties and reties her scarf – and this time, she knots it twice and tight at the back of her head.

'Time is up!' The guard comes in the room. Jaja says a brief, distant '*Ka o di,*' not making eye contact with either of us, before he lets the guard lead him away.

'We should go to Nsukka when Jaja comes out,' I say to Mama as we walk out of the room. I can talk about the future now.

Mama shrugs and says nothing. She is walking slowly; her limp has become more noticeable, her body moving sideways with each step. We are close to the car when she turns to me and says, 'Thank you, *nne.*' It is one of the few times in the past three years that she has spoken without being first spoken to. I do not want to think about why she is thanking me or what it means. I only know that, all of a sudden, I no longer smell the damp and urine of the prison yard.

'We will take Jaja to Nsukka first, and then we'll go to America to visit Aunty Ifeoma,' I say. 'We'll plant new orange trees in Abba when we come back, and Jaja will plant purple hibiscus, too, and I'll plant ixora so we can suck the juices of the flowers.' I am laughing. I reach out and place my arm around Mama's shoulder and she leans toward me and smiles.

Above, clouds like dyed cotton wool hang low, so low I feel I can reach out and squeeze the moisture from them. The new rains will come down soon.

# ACKNOWLEDGMENTS

Kenechukwu Adichie, 'baby' brother and best friend, draft reader and story mailer – for sharing each early 'no,' for making me laugh.

Tokunbo Oremule, Chisom and Amaka Sony-Afoekelu, Chinedum Adichie, Kamsiyonna Adichie, Arinze Maduka, Ijeoma and Obinna Maduka, Uche and Sony Afoekelu, Chukwunwike and Tinuke Adichie, Okechukwu Adichie, Nneka Adichie Okeke, Bee and Wasp, all the Odigwes, all the Adichies – for being my pillars, for propping me up. Uju Egonu and Urenna Egonu, sisters more than friends – for proving that water can be just as thick as blood; for getting it, always.

Charles Methot – for being so solidly there.

Ada Echetebu, Binyavanga Wainaina, Arinze Ufoeze, Austin Nwosu, Ikechukwu Okorie, Carolyn DeChristopher, Nnake Nweke, Amaechi Awurum, Ebele Nwala – for beating my drums.

Antonia Fusco – for editing so wisely and so warmly, for that phone call that nearly had me doing cartwheels.

Djana Pearson Morris, my agent – for believing.

The people and spirit of Stonecoast Writers' Conference, Summer 2001 – for that loud ovation, complete with whistles.

Friends all – for pretending to understand when I did not return phone calls.

Thank you. *Dalu nu.*